Farid Hotaki is an Afghan American U.S. Combat Marine. Farid has served behind enemy lines during the Afghan War Operation Enduring Freedom for seven years in a row with boots on ground. His unique background and language specialty has taken this Marine to a world of unimaginable war stories and military life.

Farid Hotaki

TORN IN TWO:
VALOR OF A U.S. MARINE

AUSTIN MACAULEY PUBLISHERS™

LONDON • CAMBRIDGE • NEW YORK • SHARJAH

Copyright © Farid Hotaki (2018)

Ordering Information:
Quantity sales: special discounts are available on quantity purchases by corporations, associations, and others. For details, contact the publisher at the address below.

Publisher's Cataloging-in-Publication data
Hotaki, Farid
Torn in Two: Valor of a U.S. Marine

ISBN 9781641826389 (Paperback)
ISBN 9781641826396 (Hardback)
ISBN 9781641826402 (E-Book)

The main category of the book — Fiction / Thrillers / Espionage

www.austinmacauley.com/us

First Published (2018)
Austin Macauley Publishers LLC
40 Wall Street, 28th Floor
New York, NY 10005
USA

mail-usa@austinmacauley.com
+1 (646) 5125767

In the name of God, the most merciful and gracious, first and foremost I would like to thank God for giving me life, courage, hope, and the will to live life to the fullest. God has blessed me in every way possible, and is my reason for writing and doing anything I've done up to this point in my life. I hope we all have faith and live to respect each other's faith to live a more fulfilling life together as one human kind.

Secondly, I would like to thank my family, friends, and fans for believing in me and in this book. The list is long and would go on for hours, but everyone knows his or her place in my heart. Without their help and motivation, *Torn in Two* would be nothing. All those who know me either for a lifetime or just for a little while also know that I will never forget those who've crossed my path in this long journey. I thank all of you once again for helping me make my dreams true.

Table of Contents

Introduction
Letter from a Traitor

What is a traitor, and what makes him a hero? Can someone who turns his back on his country, though once its native son, later on be seen as its champion? Or is he permanently, silently relegated to the pits of Hell, never able to see the light of day again, imprisoned more by his own actions than by any containing walls?

In the Oval Office, bright morning sunbeams reflect off the Resolute Desk, with somber noises from the morning news broadcasting from a portable radio in the background. Doing business as usual, the President of the United States heavily pores over his daily paperwork, dealing with the latest words on terror threats at home and abroad. What appears to be most prominent are recent tales of espionage concerning a U.S. Marine corporal, who has significantly morphed into a Taliban terrorist.

His motives unknown, he poses a major threat; America will surely demand an answer. Amid the terror plots and attacks of the last many years, this was turning into another stereotypical situation of a Muslim becoming an extremist. Over the radio, the President hears a media correspondent exploiting for show all the salient facts, attempting to instill morbid fear into his audience – mentioning the precautionary measures that would have to be taken into consideration by the government. This includes a map of many vital areas vulnerable to attack in the United States. Homeland Security analysts are brought into the discussion, and psychologists from prestigious colleges pose their points, thoughts, and ideas about this serious issue.

HS's biggest fear is that the terrorist is a member of a much broader network, with terror cells located in the major cities. Statistical data shows that Muslims are located almost everywhere, with the presence of a mosque available in all major areas. HS touches on how these mosques could be planning centers for the terrorists, while the psychologists are asked why someone would go this route after having been raised as a loyal American. One famous psychologist responds by telling the media that a traumatic experience might lead to a citizen taking the needed steps, and that no one knows at what particular stage of development the young U.S. Marine turncoat experienced the occurrence of becoming a devout terrorist protégé.

"Something emotionally suppressed for a long time," states the psychologist, "Important life events could trigger the involvement of joining the enemy; they might play a major factor. Mental pictures, words, conversations, and images from the past often flow through a highly motivated brain without anyone outside, the person noticing any dramatic changes in someone they may have known for years."

The media discusses the multiple deployments, harsh areas, and conditions the Marine had gone through while remaining in active military service. He'd become deeply involved with other government agencies over time, probably only in order to collect information for the terrorists, to further their horrifying actions.

"Are there many more Muslims within these agencies," asks a journalist, "or within the Department of Defense, with security clearance like this Marine – who are still active?" Clamoring with questions, the media makes the President wince deep inside. The Marine terrorist had held top security clearance for several years, with friends, family, and military members failing to see this type of personality displayed by him.

Special guests join the show on the phone, sharing their thoughts. A conservative 'anti-hero' broadcasts that all military and government personnel should swiftly be pulled from their current positions, asked questions about their loyalty, and polygraphed. People reply that this measure would be far too extreme, and also un-American.

"Measures have to be taken, before it's too late!" cries the radio pundit.

The HS analyst agrees, stating, "We didn't act on the intelligence we received before September 11th, and we saw the grisly outcome of that."

Lashing back, the news anchor retaliates. "So…what do we do now…throw all Muslims in America into a concentration camp, or something? Is this the route we want to go, when we've only caught one U.S. Marine at being a terrorist?"

Stopping for a moment in confusion, aghast at this sobering fact, the President considers what the media is covering; his thoughts reflect the political turmoil coming his way, presently and in the immediate future. Frowning darkly, he knows that the last thing his country or its military needs, during the longest-lasting war since Vietnam, is a hidden 'mole' or traitor to his country.

Renewed thoughts of different nations abroad and the threats they've been making lately lead to even more concern on the President's part. The controversy of the war has proceeded for many years, with American families wanting only to have the troops come home safely, and in one piece. Death tolls are still being calculated, stats of soldiers and others killed or wounded in action.

What has Afghanistan produced *now?* What horribly depraved plans has one of its native-born sons brought to America? After going through wretched, genocidal major wars with Great Britain, Russia, and recently the United States, the split-up country still has phony aces up its sleeves – even though they are torn in two.

With a sigh longer than his tie, the President tensed up, releasing a prolonged cough from his diaphragm. What will he tell a certain three-letter agency to do next, pertaining to a potential spy? He knows that both the conservative and the liberal media will slice him and his policies to ribbons, once the full story on this matter leaks out. As he ponders his fate, his morning coffee is carried into the room by an advisor – who also clutches a stuffed envelope, obviously of great importance.

The advisor's drawn, wan face and timid appearance signal something amiss, and the President assumes his most aggressive posture to confront the man. Normal morning routines fly out the window; the President and Commander in Chief's deep stare demonstrates how focused he is, his eyes pointing upward as he attempts to pry into the envelope before it reaches him. The advisor pushes the coffee cup forward, but the seated President thrusts out his opposite hand, blocking him.

"Give me the envelope!" he sternly commands.

Stuttering, the advisor simply states, "Mr. President...it's from him."

"John, before I open this, is there anything I need to be briefed on?"

Groping for words, the advisor finally says, "Sir, I was only told it was urgent, and nothing more – and of course, that it's straight from the traitor..."

Yanking the envelope out of John's hand, the President slams it down on his thick, chunky, wooden desk, gracing the White House since the 19th century. Grabbing up his precisely hand-crafted, gold-plated letter opener, he rips the top of the envelope, dust rising in clots from the far corner of the Resolute Desk as he leans on it.

Telling the advisor to leave, the President reduces the volume on his portable radio. Pausing, he tensely waits for a few seconds before pulling the letter out, reflecting on his time in office and everything else he's gone through. This is the sort of thing that could bring down his presidency, but he feels selfish for thinking only of himself and his own family. This is an important matter for his entire beloved country; he must address it without any further hesitation.

Flapping the letter's first page flat in his extended, shaking hand, he hunkers down responsibly at his desk. Slanting sunlight illuminates his view of the paper, making it gleam and shimmer. Looking over the entire letter, it seems quite long, much longer than he had expected. *"Dear Mr. President,"* reads the message, *"I have a great deal of information to give you. By now, I am surely receiving a lot of negative attention. It will take you some time to fully attend to this matter. But my complete story stretches far beyond the mere physical boundaries of space and time. As God is my witness, you will now learn the whole and utmost truth, so help me God.*

"Semper fi..."

Chapter One
Coming to America

"In Afghanistan, the Mi-24 Russian helicopter known as 'the Crocodile' for its rugged camouflage colors, soared like a demonic dragon over mountain tops and desert flatlands. The pilots renamed it the 'Flying Tank' due to its impressive size, and this massive machine shadowed many different provinces and states in Afghanistan, destroying anything in the air or below that crossed its path. It was not widely used for transport of soldiers, as it could only carry eight at a time, but was dreaded for its casualty count," my father righteously told me, stirring up my early fascination with the military and the high-tech instruments they used to kill soldiers and civilians.

As a child, I was highly fascinated by every old memory Dad shared; he was detailed about the death scenes, but even more scrupulous about the weapons. I peppered and interrupted his many stories with frequent questions, but he always elaborated his stories vividly, painting starkly dramatic mental pictures for me. So, I grew up hearing these highly evocative military service tales, interspersed with TV cartoon characters and elementary school fables. As I grew older, I realized that Dad's stories were more than just graphic; the main difference here was that death itself was discussed at an early, tender age in our Afghan-American culture.

It took me many years to understand the norms of 'regular' Americans versus the ones of fresh refugees like us. The Russians, being the other superpower, fell unexpectedly to their knees fighting the unruly country of

Afghanistan – known to be one of the most stubborn nations in the world. I soon learned that Afghans could be found anywhere, all across the globe, and the main reason they were highlighted as a people was that their history is far more devastating than that of most other countries. Sir Arthur Conan Doyle, creator of Sherlock Holmes, had Dr. Watson coming back from the Afghan War around 1880 – my country of origin has been a battleground forever, it seems.

My father called Afghanistan's Mujahideen the 'Holy Warriors', painting them in my mind as the heroes of those times. Strong words like 'hero' were a big issue for me as a kid, as I contrasted real-life heroes with cartoon characters, how they fought and were recognized. I greatly liked the word 'warrior', as it outranked or trumped any normal fighters, and from the start, I was impressed mostly by bravery and strong-willed people. And like most boys, I dreamed about someday having huge muscles and intimidating folks just by staring them down. But Dad told me most of his compatriots in the services were not terribly big or muscular, not like Superman; the reason they fought as well as they did was their 'heart' – because they lacked any fear.

"When outnumbered or outgunned, the only thing left is heart," he'd explain to me, and I later understood much more about this. Also, Dad said the fight in Afghanistan during the Russian crisis was called the 'Jihad'. I had no idea what that meant, so Dad said it translated directly to 'Struggle'. This confused me; Dad explained it thus: "Son, it was a religious parallel of how the struggle comes with war as you fight for your own land, country and people, as the heroes fighting the invaders." The word 'jihad' is used out of context a lot these days, but the meaning is actually quite deep and can be researched from many different angles.

Dad would continue, "The Russians wanted to invade us, son, and our people fought for what they believed to be a struggle to keep their land and never give in." Russians were known to Afghans as 'Godless soldiers', and my father depicted his scenarios of fighting them as hugely gruesome and heart-wrenching, involving the killing of men, women and children. People were left limbless and crippled by the military aircrafts, destructive missiles, and continuous rounds of heavy gunfire.

This left the Mujahideen with nothing but limited weapons and their own courageous determination to fight till death. Their faith fostered the sheer guts that made them fearless in battle, Dad said, as they'd already experienced many previous wars and invasions from other countries. But the genocidal bloodshed throughout the entire 1980s left millions to become wandering refugees, dispersing from their homeland, mostly fleeing to Pakistan, like our family. In the South, the usual escape route led to a major city called Karachi. The Southern border of Afghanistan was the easiest access point to leave from, and it was popular for those fleeing the invasions.

I didn't know the exact reason Dad fled, but it ensured the safety of my mother and their children. He swallowed his Afghan pride, and his large family of eight was the most important influence on his final decision to leave Afghanistan. Coming to America, he learned English, gaining proficiency at it through his college years. Writing the U.S. wasn't an issue for him; he knew America was the place to go, as in the early 1980s, the U.S. was accepting refugees from various war-torn countries. The journey didn't happen overnight, but Dad knew he couldn't stay in Pakistan for long, as he truly despised it there, almost hating their people. Afghans and Pakistanis are not close, and most of the neighboring nations didn't get along either, while in other parts of the world, nobody could so much as tell us apart.

For example, if I saw any Puerto Ricans and thought they might be from the Dominican Republic, this was a common American mistake. Still, folks were often highly offended by such errors. As an American, in my perspective, it all seemed the same to me, as I mostly grew up in this country. When I saw a Japanese and a Chinese person standing side by side, I couldn't tell the difference. I wasn't being racist, but found that to them, the differences are immeasurable. This sort of thing led to my conclusion that most people fall vulnerable to stereotypical patterns of behavior, and become incensed over small matters far too easily.

I really think that the differences between international races are in the breakdowns of their cultures. Sociological studies show that the norms and deviances are subject to variants that accompany the nurture factors, religious beliefs, and the various cultural upbringings. Though many find it simple to categorize human beings by color, saying 'black people, brown people and white people', it's much more complex than that, varying widely from country to country.

Anyway, we left Pakistan with my father for multiple reasons, moving further on in our journey to Deutschland, or Germany. This was during the Reagan Era, and the Great Wall was still standing, but I recall the open lands and farms spreading out far and wide throughout the country. The emerald green fields glowed with life, and the infrastructure of the buildings was incredible. I was two years old, but the little memories I have remain those of great beauty and peacefulness; things that spark visions in my mind, certain scenes like the smell of the air and the grass. When I visited Germany later on in life, memories of those times tumbled back into my brain.

I remember our neighbors owned a black Labrador, taller than me, a nice dog trained to protect kids, though I didn't know that at the time. Having a dog later on, I observed its demeanor and the way it walked with young children. But back then, I only remember slapping the Labrador on his side repeatedly, to make him go away – he just kept his distance, following me obediently through the open fields.

Seeing people today, I notice how when their kids stray for only a moment, they go insane, yelling and screaming for them to come back. But we Afghans tend to let our children venture out and explore, learning things for themselves. It's a cultural norm for us. Many people confuse 'culture' with 'religion', thinking they are one and the same thing; people who don't know about this blame differences on the religious variations. From my perspective, Afghans have a sense of comfort when a solid answer is right there in front of our faces, instead of trying to figure out the verbal answers to our questions. Information gets passed on this way; but I've also noticed that other types of people assume whatever they heard in a conversation or elsewhere is really true. Just because someone stated or wrote something, that doesn't make it accurate; only concrete evidence makes something absolutely real and valid. The funny thing is, often it's all about the delivery and presentation of the message or information.

In a sales pitch, delivery is vital in order to enhance the prospect's thoughts, getting them to the point where they really believe in it. My favorite word for this is one Dad used a lot: 'swindle'. Most know it nowadays as a 'hustle' instead, slang or jargon used to define creating misconception in order to make your point get across whatever you intend to convey to the other person. To me, the somewhat unsung gift of speech and communication is wonderful, truly making this world go around.

My dear old grandmother used to complain, saying she was having a heart attack once every couple of days; realistically, all she experienced was bad gas. So my father swindled her – he said he knew this new miracle pill that'd cure her heart disease. Buying Pez candy from the grocery store, he gave it to her, making his delivery and terminology sound intellectual and medical, promoting this new 'wonder drug'; she totally believed him. Also, Dad said the pill's one side effect was the buildup of intestinal gas, so she should make sure she relieved herself properly in the bathroom. Never complaining again, Grandma thought herself completely cured!

Using similar strategies while growing up, whenever I felt pushed to the corner on topics that overwhelmed me, seemed to work just fine. While living in Germany, my father had to use his 'techniques', as he didn't speak German well; but he was great at using non-verbal gestures in order to communicate. We were barely getting by, and so Dad focused on coming to America as soon as humanly possible. First, he decided to go there by himself, getting the basic necessities met before preparing the rest of the family to travel out of the country. America, the welcoming nation that it is, accepted him due to his refugee status – he left quickly upon receiving his acceptance letter. Oddly enough, my Mom's whole family arrived in Germany shortly after his departure.

We weren't left sitting and waiting for my father, as my mother's family loved Germany, making the decision to stay there forever. They mostly didn't have anyone to stay with in America, and it would've been difficult for them to find a home together there during those refugee times. They didn't stress the issue, but Mom wouldn't have any of that, wanting to stay closer to her nuclear family. This is understandable, due to Afghan culture often forcing women to leave their new family and accept living with their in-laws instead. I thought leaving your folks behind was really hard, but apparently, some things needed to be done; the immigration paperwork was finalized by 1983, and we shortly left for the United States of America.

I don't remember the trip, how we traveled, what happened, or anything else. My first memories are of our new neighborhood, located in the gorgeous town of Arlington, Virginia. We lived in a Section Eight apartment, commonly given to refugees like us, public housing where a lot of Cambodian and Vietnamese families lived. We called them, as Afghans do, 'Hazara'. This was a native tribe in Afghanistan, descending from the era of Genghis Khan, looking almost identical to these people – with the same facial features but a lighter, more coffee-colored skin tone. Sticking like glue close to each other, the Southeast Asians didn't mix with other races and ethnicities like we did.

One remarkable thing about Afghans is that we adapt to any culture immediately, and mimic it remarkably fast. Our desire to fit in is critical, while pleasing others is a common characteristic shared by Afghans. Our skin tone was similar to the Vietnamese, having an olive or light brown tone, while our dominant features were thick eyebrows, long eyelashes, and slightly bigger noses. You could tell us by these, real quick, but the thing that made us similar was our cultures. Respect for elders mattered a great deal – if you were so much as five minutes younger than your twin brother, you had to show him vast lifelong respect. Of course, this didn't mean you couldn't argue or fight with him, but your age, among other attributes, would be noticed.

The Asians we lived among, kept to the same ethics and morals as ours, but were a lot craftier in many ways than us. They could make perfect, working bows and arrows from tree limbs and twigs, and there was one particular Vietnamese boy named Boone, a master at making stuff out of almost anything. He too was a refugee, and he always went outside to play with only shorts on during every season but winter. Being highly unorthodox with his attire, he was all about living as he used to in his original homeland, and I respected that about him. Tons of people come to America every day, thinking they have to change themselves markedly in order to become part of our society. Boone lived a simple, tropical lifestyle, totally proud of who he was and where he came from. And I believe he truly missed his life back in Vietnam. The culture shock he underwent as a kid hit him in the stomach, being a refugee like us from a foreign land.

Boone was frustrated, had his dander up most of the time, spoiling for a fight with anyone who crossed his path. I was much younger than him, and extremely intimidated by his sudden fits of anger and frustration. But my older brother Sal and Boone were the same age, so the two of them used to 'get it on' all the time, arguing and fighting. This didn't matter much to Sal, a known warrior from day one, born with the heart and soul of a roaring, courageous lion. It made him the very type of heroic person I looked up to; but he was also hugely mischievous, catching lots of grief from Dad, though I dearly loved watching him fight. He'd take on boys twice his age and size, laying them straight down with a single punch to the jaw!

Boone intimidated me daily. But my hero, Sal, constantly found new ways to have fun, or make money by having fun too. When you live in America, you absolutely require money, in order to maintain a healthy, entertaining lifestyle. Sal, forever on the hunt for cash, would observe Boone as he made those bows and arrows, mimicking him in order to sell the implements to other kids in our neighborhood. I was his trusty, faithful sidekick, getting a piece of the action every day. In mornings, I waited in the house for Sal to wake up, so we could go right out and locate new methods for amusing ourselves.

I never went out by myself. Boone despised me for being Sal's little brother – that alone made him more of an enemy than a friend. Sal was the one person locally who could beat up Boone, whom everyone saw as only a skinny little kid; but he had heart, and at that age it was all you needed, back in those days. And Boone was incredibly smart, in so many ways. He had enough potential to be main on a Special Operations Team, or to join a Scout Sniper Unit, considering the things he appeared to know about. He could even make spears and slingshots, maybe other fantastic weapons, all entirely by hand. In the services, his survival techniques could've been honed to razor perfection, and he would've been a real, talented asset to his special team members.

But his precise aim was what I dreaded the most. I understood later on why snipers play such a psychological threat role in war. When you walk out of your house, knowing your enemy is somewhere near but you can't see him, the fear builds up in keen intensity, crippling you inwardly. Boone, unfortunately, had a tendency to hunt a person for sheer laughs, and he could strike from a position of utmost surprise. This was his drug, and he needed his 'fix' often; normal folks may think it crazy, but those who're snipers for a living learn to show great respect for it. The sad part is when someone like Boone initiates a strike on a totally innocent person.

Sometimes, though, the tide can turn. The innocent becomes the hunter, and that feeling is overwhelmingly sweet. It only took Sal and I to come up with a great idea, using Boone's own medicine against him. In a precise plan, Sal broke the 'y' shaped portion off a thick tree branch, cutting it from all three ends and skinning the bark completely off. Running to the corner store, we bought a pack of rubber bands, crafting our own extra-large slingshot, one that could hit its target from a huge distance. The sling's cloth was cut from a sturdy old leather jacket – perfect for the weapon – gleaned from a basement trash dumpster. We practiced using our deadly device on glass bottles, and it worked fantastically well, shattering them into chunky fragments.

Being more experienced than me, Sal had discovered that if you break a spark plug and remove the porcelain, this piece is useful to break and shatter glass, and most anything else it contacts, at least thoroughly piercing it. We took such a porcelain piece, breaking it up and using it against a car, fortunately, one left behind in an abandoned vehicle lot. With the size of a marble, this piece broke the driver's side window with a simple flick of the wrist; I begged Sal to let me use it to break another window, and he gave me a piece. I smiled, now having a unique 'super-power' that no one else knew anything about. These spark plugs were scattered everywhere around the mechanic shops, as nobody disposed of hazardous materials in those days. So, tons of marble-sized porcelain pieces were available, cheap and deadly, easy to use for target practice.

Rocks later replaced the pieces, having to be round like marbles. Sal ordered me to save all our 'shots' up in a little bag, for future use. He was deeply compelled to 'get a hit' on Boone, as after the first time, the two of them had fought, Sal was attacked numerous times – caught by surprise from afar. He never knew where the ambush point was, and couldn't do anything back the right way until now. This was Sal's personal vendetta, but I was extremely fearful that if Boone found out about our plans, he'd be coming for me.

Lacking the courage and skills to take him on alone, I wanted him to feel fear, pain, or something equally awful, and really learn his lesson.

Warning me direly that we'd have to get up early on weekends and sit totally still in hidden locations for a couple hours, Sal proudly coached me; but I had no problems with any of this, I was so excited those first couple days of waiting. It eventually grew incredibly boring, waiting around in the thick bushes for Boone to waltz by. The bushes were loaded with plenty of biting mosquitoes; I whined, and Sal, glaring harshly, told me to shut my damn mouth!

We could also see into Boone's apartment from below, with his window staying open and no screen in the sill. Sal pretended to follow their conversations, and I found this deeply humorous, as one term we learned from Boone's family was 'Do Ma Mai'. Sal swore that it meant 'motherfucker'. But how could he be sure of this?

"Just listen...he uses the word every time his kids act stupid. Try to hear the way they talk, and what they say when they're angry. Their voices raise up high, and most of the time, the stupidity stops, moments later."

Sal also swore that he used the word at school, and that a kid almost fought with him over it. I was convinced this was true, while Sal brought my attention to some pigeons above, telling me to watch as they grabbed up their dinner.

Confused as I was frequently, I asked him, "What?"

"Those people eat pigeons!"

"How the heck are they going to eat those birds when they're fluttering on the roof, way out of reach?"

But I watched, and minutes later, Boone's father marched to the windowsill, spreading a handful of raw rice along the ledge as he kept an eye on the pigeons. Seconds later, a string was attached to the window's latch. Before I could ask Sal another dumb question, the birds flew down, eating the raw rice, communicating with each other to inform them all of the feast. The trail of rice apparently led into the apartment, and Boone's dad waited for about five minutes, letting several of them strut right in. Pulling the string, the window slammed shut, and I could see the pigeons flapping around inside, slapping the window in bewilderment. Boone's dad, jumping up and down, snagged each plump bird by the talons.

"Dinner is *served*!" Sal chuckled. We laughed until our tummies ached; we had yet to see anything like this in America.

The window opened back up, and no squawking birds flew out. About an hour later, thick bluish smoke poured forth, smelling exactly like fried food. I thought this was hilarious, making fun of it until Sal sighed, "Yeah, it's funny, but don't you wish you were smart enough to think of that? Free, good, juicy bird meat, man."

I concurred, telling Sal that Boone should be coming out after dinner. He agreed, because in our neighborhood, kids left the house right after supper in the summertime, as the sun was only up for a few more hours. Sal told me to grab a couple of our round rocks, holding them cupped in my hand until given the signal to pass them on to him. Finding the roundest, best ones, we waited until Boone walked out the main lobby door of his apartment building. Sal cocked his enormous slingshot so far back that his elbow began to shake as he aimed it.

I stopped him briefly, whispering "Wait; not now...you might miss...and break the lobby window."

He didn't want to spoil his aim, so he said, "Come on, and let's move in much closer." We bent over so as not to be conspicuous, still hunched down in the bushes, as Sal kneeled saying, "I'm going for it!"

Popping out like a caveman, no shirt, dirty and ugly as ever, Boone was right beside us, exiting the door. We had to grab the moment! Sal cocked his slingshot, took a deep breath, and let it fly. It moved stupendously fast, making a whizzing noise as it shot from the leather sling; the trajectory was perfect – it penetrated Boone's upper back, dangerously near his spine. I figured he was thinking, *What's that bee sting*? We ducked deeper into the bush, hiding fast, having decent concealment, situated nicely.

Although we weren't seen, my heart beat rapidly, genuinely scared; my breathing grew labored as I heard Boone yell about the awful pain he so righteously experienced.

Sal said, "Look!" and opened up some of the bush branches. Boone furiously scrabbled at his back with his long, slinky fingers, reminding me of an alien movie character, due to his skinny body and oversized head. Our victory was glorious; a stream of blood flowed down Boone's filthy spine, and I insanely hugged Sal from behind. It was a moment in time I'll never forget, and I almost peed my pants from fear, laughter, and excitement, while Sal bragged himself up about his perfect 'one shot' hit.

Glancing around frantically, Boone was obviously thinking about whom it was that had planned this studious attack, breaking it up mentally into possibilities. But Sal ordered me not to move, to keep completely calm. We finished our silent laughter as he dug a hole, hiding the slingshot like a squirrel does with an acorn.

"We got his ass...finally!" Sal exulted. I thought about it, realizing that Sal could beat on Boone with his fists, but due to Boone being sneaky, this meant a whole lot more to us. We were the 'good guys' getting at the 'bad guy', changing his ignorant perception by battering him mentally and physically from afar. It was much more satisfying than punching that skinny, sneaky kid in the face!

Boone went immediately home and I'm sure he thought about the incident all night long: who could it have been...how come he didn't see it coming? Trying to put myself in his shoes, I guess I may have thought about it more than he did; but it was a fun learning experience for me. Sal and I shared a room, and I remember him laughing that night, loudly and gratefully. I joined in, and it was a choice moment for two brothers to bond together forever as heroes from their great success!

Chapter Two
My Electrocution

Time passed swiftly during my days in Arlington, Virginia –
living the city life was all I ever wanted as a kid. But I didn't
grow up the way kids do nowadays, faces glued to a TV set
and game controls. Our entertainment came straight from
our limitless imaginations. Although I learned to love some
of the new, high-graphics games eventually, I was glad back
then just to enter real-life situations, because they made me
into much more of a social being.

Talking and joking around to pass the time helped me
grow up; now people freely accept my social skills, and the
reflective image I've gotten from them has been quite
remarkable. I think I owe this to my childhood upbringing,
and my good fortune to not have all the luxuries kids possess
these days. Video games that arrest children's attention at an
early age turn out to be a crutch over time. But my childhood
was blessed with the gift and the art of communication with
other people.

To be honest, it was completely not having access to
video games that made me better at communicating. I have
to break down and thank God for all the life experiences I
went through; I believe God touches everyone and my best
experiences with Him came when I was very young. Dear
God, I deeply thank you, knowing that my life would've
been a total disaster without God's blessings!

I was a mischievous, curious kid, but always kind at
heart. My mother told me that if children weren't bad
sometimes when they were young, it meant something was
wrong; kids are curious by nature, and that leads to trouble

for most of them. They learn primarily through trial and error, and those who don't head outside on their own tend not to get the better life experiences, falling behind their peers. Going out every day to mess around, tamper with things, and explore gave me wonderful thrills, especially since I faced a serious issue with my speech, leading to a host of related problems.

I had a really, really bad stutter. Wondering what caused stuttering, I learned that sometimes children coming from multilingual families end up as stutterers. We spoke Pashto at home, but I was hearing nothing but English everywhere else, although I also heard some of the language of Dari. So I figured that might be the problem, mixing up the languages in my brain. It may have led to a slight neurological problem as well. I researched this when I got older, making my own self-assessment by approaching this matter on the neurological side.

Basically, I was terrified to speak until the age of ten. I was embarrassed, insecure, and Mom and the rest of my family felt for me. Being one of my parents' favorite children, due to being their last son, I was always trying to impress them. I wouldn't talk very much, but if I did it tended to be with my big brother, Sal. Other times, I would sit around and keep quiet, just to observe things. Often, I'd follow conversations and try to 'read' the talkers, not merely listen to them, to pick up the dynamics of their vocal tones and decibel levels. This got me fascinated with verbal gestures, watching them closely in order to mimic them.

I needed to do this, as I couldn't get my own words out fast enough. Like everyone else's, my inner dialogue and ego flowed naturally, but mine was sped-up for some unknown reason, and it drove me silently crazy. It's a gift and a curse; being naturally sped-up has saved my life countless times, but it also has given me lots of sleepless nights. I just wanted to be normal, to be able to convey my thoughts and ideas properly, like the other people around me did.

But language difficulties weren't actually my real problem. I wasn't confused with differentiating between languages; I was getting stuck in between ideas, not being able to properly deliver my thoughts through my speech. As an adult, I eventually learned to greet different people in many languages, so accepting the theory it had to do with being exposed to multiple languages isn't really an option. There was something else hanging up my tongue, something mysterious, but what was it?

One normal summer day, hanging around the local swimming pool with my cousin brought me around to stray onto a vastly new path. Life and death met as a thunderclap in the middle, coming to me with all the latent power of one hugely traumatic experience – making me intact, more whole, and transforming me into an entirely different person. That day, my cousin Habib and I discovered a long, white pole sticking out of the ground within a small construction site near the swimming pool. It thrust skyward from the ground at an angle, about eight feet tall. It hadn't been there the day before, so we were wondering why it showed up out of nowhere. Asking Habib if he saw someone sticking it into the ground, he laughed and said, "Hell, *no!*"

He was from Dad's side of the family, and we were the same age, except that I was three months older than him – and therefore should've gotten more respect. He was smart, so he didn't take too many treacherous risks. More a friend than a relative, he and I spent lots of time together on a daily basis. Habib lived on the other side of our neighborhood, coming to America around the same time we did. He'd challenge me frequently, which kept me close to him; the competition was something I craved, and that day, he went right ahead and double-dared me.

"I bet you're too chicken to climb up that weird pole," he crowed.

"Ahh, you're a *monkey*! Show me your skills first…and step up to the plate. The minute you…climb down that pole, I'll climb up it…twice as fast as *you*!" I should mention that this didn't come out as straightforwardly as I'm wording it here.

Anyway, with Habib accepting my challenge, it was on. Shrugging, he yanked off his old, beat-up sneakers, realizing that the sweat from his feet was useful for traction purposes. Like a trained squirrel, he shimmied up the pole, using hands, forearms, the inside of his feet and all his heartfelt little-kid will. He made it to the top pretty fast, taking some extra time to climb up further and peek inside the hollow white pole.

His eyes opening wide with a surprised look, he stopped. I yelled up at him, begging for what he'd found. But he didn't reply, on purpose, to heighten my anticipation, and it frustrated me. I was the type to get impatient quickly, as I felt that when someone had information and didn't share it with me, it was like being slapped in the face. Whenever I had any info, I'd share it as fast as my stuttering would let me. Finally, Habib spoke – but all he said was that something weird was inside the pole.

"What is it...you...you idiot?" I yelled in a stern voice.

"I don't know, man, crazy wires and something else with real cool colors."

Advising him to come back down, I considered degrading his ability to observe an object correctly. One of Habib's strongest traits was that he wasn't thin-skinned, and he could absorb harsh criticism without getting sensitive or misty-eyed. So I cursed him out on a regular basis, but he never took any offense at me.

Once he was down, I said, "Watch...and see how a pro climbs, loser."

Chuckling, he cried, "Okay, Mr. Perfect, let's see it!"

I left my shoes on, stating, "Real athletes...don't need to use their feet."

He only smirked back, stating that I was stupid. I began climbing, using just my hands, swinging my weight and shifting my body by slapping one hand across from the other on the way up. Getting Habib to be a little jealous was my main intent. But I tired quickly, as I used most of my energy purposefully to show off at him.

When I reached the top of the strange white pole, Habib shouted, "You ready to fall off yet?"

"Whatever…is in this damn…pole, I'm gonna get it!"

Gripping the pole as tightly as I could with my left hand, I swung my right hand around and landed it inside the top of the hollow area. I wasn't able to peer in, but bravely thrust in my hand for a blind sweep. I could feel the wires Habib had mentioned, digging in deeper to see what else I could discover. My right palm was deeply burrowed in when suddenly my index finger contacted something. Instantly, it felt like a sharp knife stabbed my fingertip, a feeling like no other. It yanked me around, whipping my body back and forth, almost making me fall off the pole!

Fear helped me take my left arm away, hoping my bodyweight would drop me down to the ground. But I didn't fall, and the sharp feeling was now piercing me throughout my entire torso. Screaming louder, I saw Habib staring upward and laughing his lungs out; I can vividly recall how uncaring he seemed. He really had no idea how much heavy, potentially fatal voltage was electrocuting me.

Everything moved in liquid slow motion, like I was floating around in a tub of melted butter. Something painfully pinched my index finger, tugging, jerking and pulling my whole body to thrash back and forth, up and down, in and out of consciousness. My arm was being wrenched from my shoulder socket; strangely enough, this only lasted for a few seconds, though it felt like an eternity to me.

Finally, it stopped. I dropped like a rag doll all the way down to the ground, and the moment I impacted, my toe folded under, hurting me even more. My head fell back, and I entered a hazy, lingering daze, while Habib finally realized this was something serious and I wasn't joking around anymore. Rushing to me to check, he said things I couldn't hear or understand, and I couldn't even respond. I was in deep shock and trauma, not knowing if I'd died or was still alive. Habib grabbed up my right hand; it was coated with black burns on the palm area. He was horrified, afraid I would tell on him – he didn't know me well enough about this. Meanwhile, my heart was in my mouth, racing like an engine, but I was coming to my senses.

Looking at Habib, I yelled a fervent, "Shut your face, already!" That kid had definite 'female' tendencies, and I hated him for that. Here I was the one getting electrocuted, and it seemed like it was all about him again. So I punched him hard in the chest, yelling, "Why the hell didn't you help me? What was so funny about me dying, with you smiling, pointing and laughing at me?" At the time, I had no knowledge that if Habib had climbed up and tried to help me, he would've also been electrocuted. But I was incensed, needing someone on which to take out my frustration.

Habib laughed again, probably in relief, saying, "Man, that's some burn. Does it hurt?"

"Yeah, idiot, what do you think?" My foot was burning, and I didn't know why, so I told him to remove my left shoe. He only gave me that infamous surprised stare of his, and so I said to him, clearly without any stuttering, "See? It's because of that stupid look on your face that I'm in this damn situation!"

Tucking my left foot inward, I noticed that it had the same black, burned flesh on its sole. Amazed, Habib stammered, "Wow…dude…maybe it was some kind of magic trick…" Glowering in a hate-ridden way at him, I put my sock back on, slowly working my aching foot into my shoe, and told Habib to help me get up. We prepared to go home, as I was quit for the day when it came to adventures. I figured if Habib couldn't help me while I was getting electrocuted, the least he could do was not laugh at me. Limping away toward home, my heart was still racing. What a day! I'd gone through something most people couldn't walk away from without an emergency team assisting them.

We were inside a building that was partly functional, partly under construction. I entered the elevator to go to the fifth floor, and a drunk was loitering inside – I smelled alcohol on his breath, and by the way he leaned over and mumbled to himself, he obviously had significant other problems. I'd seen plenty of drunks in our neighborhood, so I wasn't impressed. He assumed I was Hispanic from my looks, and started speaking Spanish to me.

Usually, I wasn't much of a talker due to my stutter. I kept it down to one-sentence phrases, so as not to embarrass myself. But I could reply to him in Spanish, having picked it up over time in America. Strangely, this was the first time it came out as fast as I was thinking the words and phrases. "No hablo Español, Señor. Soy de Afghanistan," I replied trippingly, the words rolling for a change right off my tongue: I don't speak Spanish, I am from Afghanistan.

Guffawing in an awful way, the drunk turned around, urinating right there in the elevator, with me standing behind him. Streaming down, steaming in the elevator's coolness, his puddle reached my sneakers. Once the door opened, I bounded out, screaming 'Bendejo!' at him – it means 'Idiot'! But he only laughed some more at me as the doors closed. Standing there, I took stock. Somehow, I had gotten out two short sentences in a row without *any* stuttering. Whatever had happened downstairs in the building's yard was changing my destiny.

At home, I began talking again, and everyone realized something sensational had occurred. I ran straight to the bathtub, leaving the door cracked open, laughing and singing nonsensical songs perfectly well – no stuttering! I was young, and thought I could rub the burn marks away with soap. But my twin sister snuck in.

"What the hell is so funny that you're all happy?" she said in a wondering tone.

Still in shock, I was experiencing a natural high. My stuttering was completely gone, like a real miracle from God transpired that day. My poor sister thought I was crazy, because no one had ever heard me singing before. She left to tell my other sisters, and they came back wanting to know what happened to my burnt hand. Lying, I just told them it got dirty when I fell down, skidding on the ground when I tried to brace myself against falling. However, my older sister guessed that something had changed; she was the one who tended to help me, trying to teach me to speak more normally. She began talking, but backed up fast when I replied to her just as quickly.

Screaming her little lungs out, she exited the bathroom. I began laughing loudly, appreciatively, going, "Yeah, my time has come – I'm alive!"

My older sister called Mom at work; she was doing a double shift at a fast-food restaurant. My mother couldn't believe it, but was too busy and couldn't talk, so my sister returned to investigate things further. One thing I knew for sure was not to incriminate myself, so I told her the 'whole' story but left a lot of facts out, filling in the gaps with little white lies. It came down to me having tripped over a wire in the backyard, which I followed up by showing off my burnt toe as proof. My sister was shocked that matching points of my body had similar burn marks.

Years later, she told me the current must've traveled through my entire body – I was hugely lucky, and probably should've died. It wasn't my time; the event had happened to suit a far bigger purpose than just killing me. Death wasn't on the list that day. God gave me life, and I was thankful for it. Now, I could ramble all my fast-moving thoughts and ideas, conveying everything smoothly. There were a few glitches at the beginning, as I was going a little too fast at first, stumbling again on my words as they came out of my mouth. But I was mostly, definitely *cured!*

Mom found out about this later on that night, when she finally came home, spent and exhausted from a long day at work. She wasn't ready to deal with my problems, or the new lack of them, until the next day. This puzzled me; I thought she simply didn't care about my miracle cure. I had no idea what it was like, working five double shifts in a row at a fast-food restaurant. Mom was striving like a maniac to make enough to feed all of us, on a $3.25 minimum wage job. Dad was suffering under some very similar circumstances. I was more ungrateful than I knew.

That night, I awakened to see blood seeping from my nose into my ear. Alarmed, I sprinted to the bathroom, noticing a lot of blood, and grew hugely scared. I had only given up one problem to gain a worse one! Washing my face, I pinched and held my nose up high, and thank God, it stopped flowing. I whispered to myself rapidly, to see if I'd lost my new gift, but I was talking quite normally now.

The next morning, when I entered our dining nook, Mom clasped some money in her open hand, extending it toward me. I got excited, thinking I was going to be paid for my lucky freak accident. But when I reached out for the cash, she smacked me hard, right in the face! The money was a decoy, not a reward, it seemed.

"Didn't I tell you not to play in that construction yard? Didn't I tell you not to go far away without your siblings?"

My eyes watered up; I wasn't sure why she was so angry with me. I sat down on a chair, gazing deeply into a vast nothingness, starting to daydream as my sisters piped up on my behalf. This only sent Mom into a further, more dramatic speech.

"This boy is *insane,* thinking he should get paid for what God gave him. Now is the time, boy, to pay your thanks and dues! You owe God now for the rest of your life; you owe Him, the poor, and the less fortunate ones than you. God has blessed you, and I am very happy for you and our family; but you cannot turn your face away, since you have gotten something out of being such an evil, little monster."

I really didn't comprehend any of this until I was somewhat older. Mom was simply noticing that I owed something in return as a fortunate human being to all the people less fortunate than myself. Touched by the miracle of what God gave me, a final end to my endless stuttering, I had to pay homage, or what we called 'Zakat', to God. From then on, I had to live my life for others, and truly serve people.

Chapter Three
Jimmy and I

Moving to North Arlington, Virginia was a step up from our old neighborhood, which was really something of a ghetto. Our new home was fashionable, up-to-date, and contained plenty of amenities. Still an apartment, it held three large bedrooms, which meant we could separate our siblings into the three boys in one room, the three sisters in another one. It gave us more privacy and less stress, as my sisters grew older and needed to be away from us boys.

Landing a much better job, my mother was deservedly getting more pay, working hard at a fancy hotel in our nation's capital. She had easy access to the Metro, which was great for her, although what she really wanted was to get her driver's license. She didn't want to have to depend on Dad taking time out from his busy schedule. But he was stubborn, not wanting her to drive for some reason. They argued about it for weeks; Mom finally gave up, and that was the end of it.

Dad's caveman mentality carried over into our lives, which meant a kind of sexist cultural shock to me, as I had already been going to school locally and felt like I was part of American culture now. I remember having to tell people where I was from, but back in those days, nobody could even pronounce Afghanistan. They all just figured I was from India, the Middle East, South America, or something.

Our elementary school was named after Francis Scott Key, author of 'The Star-Spangled Banner', and it was a five-minute walk from where I lived. So, this worked out great for me, as I could sleep in later than the rest of the kids, waking up at the very last minute to get ready for school. And our apartment complex was bigger here, but it didn't have lots of fun things to do in the rear of the building, like our old one did; no boys were running around back there. It seemed like there was nothing but African-American families, except for one Hispanic family. This didn't matter much, as Dad was getting stricter, not letting us play out of doors. But I didn't care about pleasing him, even if he insisted we had to play indoors. I would find a way to go outside.

One fine weekend, I saw some kids playing football – finally something great was going on in the back of our building. It was time to head out and make some new friends. There was a nice, grassy field back there, perfect for football. Poking my way out, I approached the other kids who came right up to me. Happy as a lark, I knew I wasn't going to stutter my words now, so I gamely asked, "Can I play with you?"

Immediately, one of the boys leaned over, sniffing at me. "This guy smells really, really bad," he crooned, and everybody but me laughed their heads off.

This made me feel like crap, and I pulled my shirt up to take a whiff, wondering why he said that – I'd taken a shower that very morning. The boy turned out to be Howard, the youngest kid in his family, always raising his voice to get attention. This was just another example of his regular antics.

After I carefully checked myself over, I cried out, "No, I *don't* smell!"

The other kid with Howard was Chris, who stayed strangely silent. I already knew he was friendlier than Howard, that he didn't want to fight or put me down. But he was more of a follower than a leader type. Unsure of what to do, I stood my ground, while Howard seemed upset that I had denied his curt remark. Looming closer, he shoved up to my face, trying to intimidate me; I was ready for anything, as I'd gained experience in a couple of fights due to Sal's useful coaching. Seriously, I wasn't going to get beat up by a shorter, smaller dude than me, regardless that I was the new guy here. I smelled that Howard was pulling a 'scare tactic' on me from the first.

Balling his fists up tight, he stood right in my face, putting his forehead against mine; but I merely flared my nostrils, balled my own fists, and thought that this was going to be yet another bad day. Both boys stepped back for a minute, and I felt like I had won, successfully scaring them away. However, I wasn't the reason for their hesitation; another kid instantly ran by us, screaming like a maniac.

Turning around, I saw an unusual boy, full of life and excitement – scraping Cloud Nine, happy as he could be! Not daring to speak, I only stared at him, unknowing what to do next as he leapt down some concrete steps, landing lightly on his feet like it was nothing. He wore really cool clothes, and was bigger than all of us combined; pretty soon, he sprinted up to Howard, pushing him out of the way like he was a rag doll. Then, without a care in the world, he got in my face, too.

"Who's this?" he demanded, looking like he was in charge of things.

I couldn't do anything but stare, and try to keep calm. In spite of his large size, I wanted to show these boys that I was completely fearless. But gaining in confidence, Howard started up with me again, going on about how I stunk.

Chris called the new kid Jimmy, so after another long stare, I asked Jimmy, "Did you come to fight, or did you come to play football?"

He laughed again, backing off a few steps, and said, "That's what I like to do, so let's do this!" Looking at both of the other boys, he told them I didn't stink any more than they did, and then he said to Chris, "Last week you smelled like piss, remember?"

Chris had a bed-wetting problem. I couldn't help but laugh, and Jimmy asked for my name. I replied, "I'm Farid," and he asked where I was from. "Afghanistan," I breathed with a sigh, expecting more torment. But he blithely ignored it. I knew why; he simply had no idea where Afghanistan was. I left the matter alone, wanting only to show off my skills on the football field, so I could gain some respect.

Jimmy told Howard to shut up and grab the nearby football, because they were on the same team. Chris asked me, "Do you even know how to play ball?" Pausing, I told him to let me be quarterback, and he would find out. He appreciated the offer, because he wanted to play running back and wide receiver.

Our two-man teams were formed, and the competition began. We kicked off to them first. Jimmy wanted to play wide receiver, as he thought he could catch the ball pretty well. Howard was shorter and smaller than all three of us, so that gave our team the advantage. Back then, we used the old rule to count to ten seconds, better known as 'ten Mississippi', in order to rush in and tackle the quarterback. This time increment allowed the opposing team to create a play and have the opportunity to make a first down. After the count finished, it was legal to rush in and try to tackle the quarterback. Or he could run, try not to get tackled, and pass the ball instead.

Howard launched the ball short of Jimmy twice, soon wasting two downs. Feeling thwarted, Jimmy told him, "You suck at this position." Meanwhile, I was seriously motivated, needing to tackle Howard and make him feel my strength, without having to fight him. At this point, their team made it to our forty-yard line and we got possession, due to them not being able to handle our defense.

I whispered to Chris to run way out there, far and deep. He wanted to manage the play his way, but I insisted it wouldn't work; he got mad, but decided to listen. I told him to run, stop, and turn toward me after three seconds, so I could yell really loud and pump-fake the ball. After the false throw, he would turn around to the front and not stop running, waiting for my real throw.

He didn't believe I could hurl it far enough. I told him not to worry, and I hiked the ball. Chris took off like a beautiful bird in flight, doing exactly as I said. Jimmy played defense on him, but Howard made the expected mistake, backing up, thinking it was a short play as I'd anticipated. This gave me the room to yell out Chris's name and pretend I was going to throw the ball to him; instead, I pump-faked it. The other boys bit, pressing close to Chris, expecting the ball to land soon. Being pretty smart, Chris played it nice and dramatic; I gripped that leather pigskin tight by its seams, yanking back and throwing it down the sideline as far as I could.

Breaking free from the other team's tight press, Chris had them confused. They looked at me, thinking that I was going to run. Then they both realized the ball was in the air, and they took off wildly after it. Jimmy caught on quick about the faked pass, so he sprinted fast, not wanting Chris to catch that ball, dying with embarrassment. Picking up speed, Jimmy watched the ball float in the air like slow motion. Chris was also picking up speed, but Howard could do nothing but uselessly watch.

The ball went as far as planned, and the only way to get it was to run faster. Chris was about two feet in front of Jimmy, and wasn't slowing down. We weren't playing on a real football field, after all, but our childhood play was glorious as it came to fruition. Chris made it to the ball just in time for its descent, but it tipped on his fingers as he juggled it around – purchasing a good enough grip to hug it to his ribcage. Jimmy was fearless, not scared of damaging any body parts for the sake of a well-placed tackle, and so he took a splayed-out dive after Chris's legs. One hard foot conked Jimmy's chin, while he managed to grab an open ankle.

Stumbling, Chris flew into the air, something like a beautiful bird, falling a couple feet short of the touchdown zone. He fell flat, screaming like he was hurt bad, while Jimmy had no remorse whatsoever for him.

"You hit my *chin,* man! I should beat you the fuck up!" Feeling threatened, Chris pretended to be hurt, but by the time Howard and I got down there, he decided not to fake it so much and got up. Mainly, he wanted to call attention to his spectacular catch.

"Did you see that catch, man?" he loudly crowed. "It was *awesome*!"

Joyfully, I added, "Did you see that *throw,* man?"

High fives were blithely exchanged, and a graceful dance of enjoyment was performed for the benefit of the other team, since we had no spectators. Jimmy laughed, saying, "Okay, you got us on that little play of yours." But Howard was jealous; I'd taken out his highlight for the day. He only moped around, grousing and groaning.

The rest of the game turned out to be easy. Chris and I ended up beating Howard and Jimmy with a close score, but we definitely came home with the win. The only way the other team scored was from Jimmy running the ball, because he wouldn't let Howard throw anymore. Bitter, Howard was grumpy about this turn of events. But I seemed to have scored far more than points; I now had some great new friends.

After that day, time flew past in North Arlington, while school was a breeze for me specifically. I was placed in advanced courses, and my teachers and parents were ecstatic about my high grades. One day, soon after the game, I came to realize that my new, truest best friend was going to be Jimmy. This happened after we sat together, talking for a while after school. He needed help with his homework, and I artfully showed off several new techniques. Jimmy said the only reason he had befriended those two other guys was that there was no one else to pal around with.

I asked him, "Aren't there other Hispanic families in our complex?"

"Yeah, man, but they like to fight all the time." I didn't quite catch the meaning of this, but he said, "Just wait...and you'll see."

Rey and Walter were the names of two of those other boys. Rey was a little older than me, being a privileged 'lieutenant' in the crosswalk school patrols. These were just a bunch of fellows who helped other kids cross the street after school. Wearing brightly colored neon belts, they had a rank system among their order, somewhat like the local police. Rey apparently let the 'officer' rank go to his head, though, he was considered by far the best school athlete, with his father being the coach for his soccer team. This kid was also well-known for his charisma and muscular build.

His athletic capabilities were truly amazing for someone of his tender age. Jimmy appeared to be intimidated by him sometimes, but one thing Jimmy had was that infamous, needful thing: heart. And Rey met his match one fine day, for calling Sal and me 'Indians', speaking in that familiar accent people used to make fun of those hailing from the Middle East. Sal punched him upside the head, and that finished off Rey, who cried like a baby – running like lightning to his older brother, Walter.

That kid was huge, even bigger than Sal, but they were roughly the same height, just not the same build and weight. Rey was my age and had fought with my older brother, so I was fearful, because here came Walter, ready to beat us both up to a living pulp. Sal, as I've said, was a lion with the toughest of hearts. It didn't matter where he went or what he did, in the end he'd show his heart to everyone. But I couldn't figure out what to do; my sisters came to tell me to go inside, as it was getting dark. Wondering what would happen, I dwindled away into the merciful arms of sleep.

The next day, we all saw Walter at school with a humdinger of a black eye. Hanging out with Sal, he kept his arm around him, and they seemed to be the greatest of friends. Jimmy gave me the full report; he said I had a brother like no other, that Sal beat Walter up really fast the previous night, earning the whole neighborhood's respect thereafter. Trembling inwardly, I thanked God for that, because it could've gone pretty badly for Sal, and I really loved my big brother.

Sal remained undefeated, a living champion, reaching a point of self-confidence I'd not seen in him before. Because of the fight, Rey didn't like me at first, but he soon gave up – knowing that I had nothing to do with it. Also, he witnessed me winning the fifth grade graduation dance competition, cheering me on rabidly as I won the small prize of five bucks. Grabbing him and Jimmy, I took them over to buy one-dollar hamburgers, and we laughed and joked all night about the dance moves that made me win, which were 'MC Hammer' style licks.

After that, the three of us were the greatest of friends, and we joked, laughed, and played around every day, forever. Jimmy, Rey and I made a new team, while Sal ventured off with Walter and a whole new crew. The years passed by with a lot of fights that proved we were nobody to be messed with. The entire school knew we were close, and that nothing could ever break us up. We played every sport imaginable together, bettering our skills but never playing formally on school teams.

Rey, on the other hand, played on those teams, getting even more recognition. Jimmy and I were terrific at basketball, especially when on the same team. Rey's most special talent was soccer, and his skills couldn't exceed his demands for trying to get better at basketball. So we all had our areas of expertise, apparently.

I mentioned video games before; Jimmy introduced me to our local arcade, and I found I was hooked from the start. We didn't play at home like kids do nowadays, it was always the arcade's video games that fascinated us. Those things were outstanding! I remember the owner of the arcade – with his strong, dominant features, he could've easily been Afghan. But he played dumb with me, acting like he wasn't. I yearned to let him know we came from the same place, mostly because I thought we might get some credit for free games. He was a 'cheapo', so I let the issue go after the first week.

The arcade was Heaven on Earth, a truly fun place to hang out, but it cost plenty of quarters to play there. I never had much access to money, being from a large and poor family. When I learned that Jimmy's family had the exact same amount of people as ours, this astonished me; he had nice stuff, fine clothes, great toys, etc. I asked him if he was born in the United States, and he said, "Of course, I'm full American."

This got me a little jealous, but I dropped it quickly. I would watch him play video games to pass the time, when I couldn't afford to play; it was enough just to be there with my good friends. And weirdly enough, the very same month, I was introduced to arcade playing, the best video game of all time and space came out: 'Street Fighter Two'. This new game sported awesome graphics and killer techniques, so people streamed in from everywhere, finally more than just kids our age. I saw people there ranging from the age of twelve into way in their mid-thirties.

'Street Fighter Two' was magnificent, on a different level altogether from anything else contending against it. It had to be the first multiplayer game to feature a joystick that moved in four new directions, and six complicated buttons. And it featured a storyline and full plot backstory behind it, making it so much better than the rest of the piddling-butt games around it. The characters were from all over the world, and it brought a kind of cohesiveness to our multi-cultural players. This was a genius concept game; people from everywhere came together to fight in a three-round bout.

We'd sit in the arcade for hours, merely viewing the promotional ads on the video screens, to discover the capabilities of each fighter. The special moves were involved with a combination of the joystick and the buttons, making it way more challenging than all of the other games. This new feature attracted players from various counties in our local region; it created long lines going out the door, and players fought for the honor to be 'on the stick' and prove themselves.

I only had one small problem with the game – it didn't have a Middle Eastern fighter character. This seemed odd, as it had characters from everywhere else. But I played it every chance I could get, regardless. Any dollar or two I had went straight to the game, and I didn't care. The creators of it definitely did their job right, and it still lives on today, going strong with new versions and characters. This game set the standard for the entire gaming industry; all who know about it need to salute the owners and makers of such a remarkable, wonderful game – with or without Middle Eastern characters. I suppose it has something to do with our conflicts.

I catch myself sometimes dreaming of the days when I'd come home late, getting into vast trouble for spending centuries at the arcade. It was the main hangout for us city kids; when you live in the suburbs, a tree house is usually the place to go, but we weren't used to that type of expensive stuff. I did wonder sometimes what it would be like to have your own private tree house, but such luxuries weren't within my reach, and I could only be thankful for the great friends I was making.

Jimmy, my best friend, supported me in each and every single way. I learned immeasurably about life from him and his family – they stuck with us through good and hard times, and we grew up sharing our trials and tribulations. We were never judgmental about each other, only helpful. I'm so glad to have met Jimmy, and wish their dreams to all become realities. It may be one thing to know a good friend, but it's another to know their whole family, enjoying the time you spend with them together.

Where am I? How did I get there again? Am I talking to myself, once more? These memories of childhood burn like brands into my brain, retrieved readily as they give me satisfaction, serenity, and security. Racial issues didn't play a role in my growing up brown-skinned, with people who accepted me as I am. Seeing how similar we were, it was like a mirror image anyway…who was different, who was alike?

Voices echo in my head, multiple people whispering in a deep, hollow room full of walls. The scents perfuming the air bring forth the thoughts I had while growing up, thinking that our American life would never end. The rustling of dead leaves, and the wind swooshing against my skin cause me to envision a place I used to know, which is now forever gone, and suddenly in the mirror, I see how old I've become.

Time fades; I watch the sun settle behind a bigger, much better built city, gazing down as my shadow expands to five times its size. In my dreams, I see myself pacing up and down my old neighborhood's streets. A cigarette burns my lips...back in Afghanistan, I take a long, grateful drag, trying to inhale my death; and then I blow out the rest of my refugee's soul.

Chapter Four
High School Years

'Erratic' is the one word I can find to describe my teenage years. My family moved to Alexandria, Virginia, and my new stomping grounds ballooned to the exploding point with wildly varied, different kinds of human races. To the backbeat of a clanging school bell, my latest digs was the famous T.C. Williams High School, predominantly Black and Hispanic, well known for its football team and iconic coach, Herman Boone. He was brilliantly portrayed by Denzel Washington in 'Remember the Titans' – which many alumni casually mention when representing our ardent, matchless school spirit to curious outsiders.

T.C. Williams was also the only public high school in Alexandria, so it was exceedingly large, jam-packed and overflowing with students. They had to create a separate school for the freshman alone, close by but with a different name. This was weird to me; I'd never heard of anything like it before.

High school was a time where I became deeply involved in lots of different things, exploring bold new personalities for myself and others. Mostly, I planned on making a huge name for myself, which could only happen if I was unique and sophisticated enough. Well, I got a part-time job in a pizza store at least, taking on this sterling position to purchase new, 'cool' and stylish clothes that would garner recognition for me, along with other necessary luxuries that my parents couldn't afford.

It was tough at first, but high school brought forth a new crew of friends. I didn't know who I could trust in the beginning, but a dude I met in Biology started me out, being down to Earth and easy for me to talk to. Melvin was from El Salvador, just one of many people from his country represented at our school. He didn't have a stereotypical image problem, and wasn't the type to hang around folks only because they shared a common place of origin, never wearing a 'gang' bandanna or presenting the image of a streetwise homie thug. Instead, he was a humble soul, who got his thrills and kicks from normal 'laughs', getting drunk, and acting stupid.

Girls liked Melvin, because he always brought humor to the table. I sat next to him, deciding that I was going to cheat off of him during Biology tests, because I tended to randomly skip that class. This was due somewhat to our monotone of a professor, who killed us off with boring lectures and mountains of note-taking – I simply didn't have the patience to sit through it. Melvin never minded this, finding ways to help me out, but I felt guilt-ridden in my teenage angst for 'using' him. His version of getting payback for his troubles was a desire to hang out with some of my homies, the bunch we threw afterschool parties with. No problem; Melvin offered up his house.

Like most high-schoolers, we went to great lengths to gather enough alcohol to fuel our rabid teenage thirst at parties. Melvin was big on drinking, and his family obligingly kept plenty of booze in their home. Cool! We teens had a 'safe' place to drink, ham it up and hang out; this made other teens want to join us, so I introduced them one by one to Melvin, Jimmy, and other choice friends from my old neighborhoods. Everyone got along famously, as if we'd known each other forever. Kids from faraway other counties even crossed state lines to have fun with us on the weekends.

Word about our shindigs got around quick, and I soon met Melvin's little brother Steve. We, as his elders, knew we had to get him started young on getting drunk and partying. And this was easy, as we were a close-knit gang of kids who flocked together, making it known to anyone who cared that we were all from different countries. We were amply proud of that fact, making those who stuck only to their own races and nations look sick, because they couldn't find friends based solely on their charisma.

We had Melvin, of course, and his brother Steve, while Chris was our 'token' white boy. Jimmy was mixed, being from Honduras and Nicaragua. Yani and Yonaton hailed all the way from Ethiopia, while Jose made the scene from Puerto Rico. Edgar was a ripe product of Venezuela, Lee arrived from Trinidad, and my cousins Ahmad and Habib traveled here from my own Afghanistan. This big and growing tribe of terrific teenagers led to scads of partying and tons of accompanying trouble.

We all listened to 'Bone Thugs-N-Harmony', straining to look, talk, and act just like them, mimicking their hairstyles as they were the coolest, sweetest stuff around. Melvin, Jimmy and I got our hair braided, even though we weren't African-American, pushing our images to let everyone know we 'didn't care' about anything outside of our thug-pack. We posed with true thug traits; our very hair screamed, 'These boys are threatening, don't mess with them!' None of us were jocks, so we didn't bother having massive size, just super coolness instead – intimidating others our own way. It worked, believe it or not, as no other foreign kids would think about going as far as our hairstyles did. Our bunch got into fights together, acting like the TV show Bonanza: 'If anyone fights with any one of us, he's gonna hafta fight with me!'

Sharing the same daily habits, if anyone was left out for a single hour, it would deeply hurt their feelings. The entire high school took notice of us, and we were the most popular kids almost overnight. T.C. was such a big high school, it wasn't draped only in the lives of jocks and cheerleaders, which in fact were considered by us to be highly degrading pastimes. We led everyone else to believe that getting in trouble made more sense and was cooler than being famous for sports and stuff like that. We were all about fashion, style, and savoir-faire, topping all others by wearing the clothes that no one else could afford or even find to wear – it took money, and we all had to work, but if you worked hard, you must play equally hard by our code of conduct.

Running the show as a car mechanic, Melvin was the one we could count on for support whenever we had any major or minor vehicle problems. Ahmad and Habib pulled the pizza joint job with me, so that was helpful on weekends, with food, late nights and overall assistance in general munchies. All of us were always there to support each other; making better of our 'team' meant everything to us. You couldn't have that kind of life and not catch some grief from your family, of course. We each had 'issues' back home, and yet we could easily relieve our stress just by 'chilling' together.

Our intricate stories merged with near life and death situations, stretching far and wide, and we remembered them as equals. During our party times, we witnessed many hard days passing, viewing death and life as they blurred together. Melvin ended up having a beautiful baby daughter; he was just eighteen at the time. She was a blessing to his family, and we called her our brand-new 'niece'. Our sweet little gal calmed us down, and Melvin's mom was greatly relieved by that. His parents tended to be favored by our gang, as they seemed to be the ideal parents to us. Not because they let Melvin and Steve run ramrod over them, but because they treated their boys like adults.

Other parents loomed stricter, depending on their cultural norms, but not Melvin's. Due to this, I became super-close with him and Steve, just because I had a great place to go hang out on weekends, often spending the night at their house. School was only a planning spot; we didn't care about classes after the first year there. We were a kid magnet, with people flocking to us, needing to blend in with our crew. It was an awesome feeling, gaining all that prestige mainly from having a great bunch of friends from almost every astonishing sector of the planet.

Melvin and I spent most of our pay on clothes, sometimes buying the same shirts and pants on accident, trying so hard to outdo each other and then failing miserably.

But our Puerto Rican friend, Jose, was by far the best dressed, sporting the same clothes we regularly saw worn in music videos. Stumped, we wondered where the heck he got his fine apparel; he wouldn't let on. Jose was originally from Bridgeport, Connecticut, but his family traveled to New York quite often. This explained how he was able to gather up the sweet clothes nobody else had, beating us to the punch every time.

High school was our 'Project Runway', bringing the trends out of every teen there, and if you weren't great at picking out expensive, amazing outfits, you got left behind. Thinking back on the wildly strange things we did in the name of fun, I can't help but laugh my lungs out! You can never tell a teenager they look stupid or funny because of what they wear; you can only wait for them to grow up and find out the hard way. Older kids compete a lot, and with that came the intrusion into our territory of a rival gang, one which we hated and frequently got into fights with.

One time, we were playing basketball outside, and suddenly fifteen dudes popped in like toadstools out of nowhere, rolling up with bottles of beer clutched in their sweaty paws, half-drunk and totally self-confident. Stopping our game as they made their awful entrance, we looked askance at each other as we waited for their leader to speak. I usually was the one who spoke for our group, but for some reason this time the attention went over to Jose. Maybe it was due to some kid on their side having a couple of words with him in class, which we were just then finding out about. So all those guys strayed into Jose's singular path.

Watching, I really didn't care, because Jose had a good head on his shoulders and was never afraid of anything. He was a white-skinned Puerto Rican, showing where he came from with fierce pride. All the other Hispanic kids didn't know he was Latin American 'til he spoke, flaunting his colorful accent, or when he gamely wore the Puerto Rican flag tastefully on a nice, trendy shirt. He could've passed for a mayonnaise American white boy, but wasn't having any such nonsense. His Spanish wasn't the best, rusty without practice, but he could rap like a superstar 'gangsta'. We all loved him for that; it's one of those special talents not many people have, and Jose used this gift at our parties all the time, making people come closer and seek more out of us.

When the rival gang shoved their way into our group, Jose was the one who first stood firm, his head held high, loudly spouting, "What's good with you?" None of them replied, but this one kid was eyeing him from the moment they appeared on the basketball court. I knew this sucker; he was from another class I infrequently attended, but I'd never spoken with or gotten to know him better. His name was Roberto, and I recall some other hombre telling me he was crazy murderous, belonging to a genuine adult gang, not a laid-back clothes-loving bunch of bananas like us.

This meant he wasn't in high school anymore, thinking that made him tougher than us. But Jose saw no real threat proceeding, as Robert spoke again, "What's all that trash you been talking about me, Pepe?" Jose's nickname was used by us out of endearment, but Roberto knew it would set him off the wrong way, being a sign of disrespect. Keeping calm, 'Pepe' held his head up as their other dudes trudged near, but I got a bad feeling, as if they might all start beating on him at the same time.

One of those guys pulled a bottle up over his head, holding it behind him, and I knew I'd better say something immediately, before it was too late. Dragging on my cigarette, I lightly strolled their way, shouting, "What the *fuck...?*" They all stopped dead in their tracks, even as Jose gazed at me with his patented look of amazement.

Roberto happened to have a close friend who'd dropped out of high school deliberately, just to become a true thug in a real gang, and this kid Lito jumped in front of me, yelling, "Hey puto, don't even try it!"

I murmured, "Okay, well, let them two fight, even that retard...but why does your boy have a bottle over his head?"

Jose didn't see that, but walked around sideways to get away from this oncoming disaster, making me reach the boiling point. I didn't want to see our Pepe be dishonored, and now Roberto and Jose weren't the topic – it was this bastard jumping in front of me. Keeping up walking to him, I flicked my lit cigarette right at his forehead, which flared him up some. I continued talking, but this was soon replaced by mutual hard punches; I yanked his greasy hair at the back of his neck, punching him solidly a couple times, still talking to him a mile a minute. He tried to kick me, but I could see he had no realistic fighting capabilities, so I swooped in for a firm head lock, punching him numerous times in his face, over and over again.

Once I let go, he backed up, frustrated right along with his whole team. They clearly couldn't get the job done, as I took one step backward to get ready – the kid I was fighting backed up about five steps. Breathing through his mouth, he was clearly in shock, unable to pull his thoughts together. I screamed at him, "Lito, you're *lucky* you didn't get fucked up more – I can whale on you *all day*!"

Blasting out with rage, Lito could only sputter, "Don't let…me catch you alone, puto," as I looked fondly over at Jose. Our Pepe brightly gave him the finger, and the bunch of them, soundly defeated by me alone, apparently, stalked away backward, glancing back every five minutes to see if we were still there. A grateful Jose ran up to me, chest-slamming me and giving with a big bear hug. I merely laughed, saying, "Did you see that lit cig burn a hole in his forehead?"

Jose, our Pepe, responded, "Good looks on that bottle thing, man!"

Everyone was flattered that I'd taken charge of things, but Jose and I were marked men after that basketball court incident. We never became paranoid, but we broke jokes like troopers when it was time to go home, all about that weird gang. They were called LH, standing for Latin Homies. I thought this title was lame, and I told them this when we got into a few more fights with them – always a simple fist fight, no weapons. So pretty soon, everyone in our gang chose with one they would fight with, and these dramas led us on for many months afterward. Lots of complications and explaining to do ensued when we came home covered with scars and purple battle bruises.

Our teachers and school advisors were catching on to things, and to who exactly was getting into all the local trouble. We ended up being placed into a secondary school program, aimed at the 'disobedient', but that only drove us harder to fight with better style, and it got us even more respect from other kids. The classes in our new program were a lot smaller, as it was built only for students who either had family problems or serious issues of some kind. One fine summer day, as we all were now attending summer school, we noticed some other gang members fighting. We simply sat around and watched them this time, witnessing a kid getting stabbed straight into his chest, falling down with a hard crash onto his back.

He lay there bleeding against the curb, and I knew he'd been struck in his heart, as every time a pulsation occurred, blood spurted from his chest wound. Watching like an outside observer, I didn't go any closer, because I thought the other gang members would think we were then involved. I just sat perfectly still like a lump on a log, wondering why I was so afraid of weapons, thinking about this as I saw that redly gruesome kid search the skies while knowing he was about to die.

No older than seventeen, he saw his life bleeding away, for no reason. Who was he actually even fighting for? What did he just die for? Was he realizing how his family would react, how his mother would cry out loud for him? Showing no pain or fear, he just kept staring deeply into the sky, maybe seeing something I couldn't, and it was a painful reality check for me. I knew now, I had to change things in my life.

The police swarmed in, and everyone gathered around the boy, scattered. A lot of kids were taken away by the cops, and the killer was tried as an adult, sentenced to life in prison. His life was a death, behind ten foot walls he could never see around again. This was something I had to avoid, a life I couldn't believe in anymore, so I swore to myself that for their sakes, the dead boy's and the living criminal's, I'd stop fighting. I merely felt embarrassment, not fear, and felt sorry for their mutual families.

I had lots of trouble sleeping that week, and everyone told me to relax and that it was all simply meant to be. Those who live by the sword die by the sword. Others stated to me that his homies would never forget him, in either of their cases, but I knew I would never look for fights ever again, and I set out to become a much more positive, law-abiding person. I went back to classes, and began attending school for real, ending up doing well – the teachers saw a marvelous change in me.

I knew that I could be a brilliant student; I was, just kind of, unfocused. My English instructor was Mrs. Moses, and she was a fantastic teacher, great at everything she did. She tracked current events and trends that we teenagers went through in those days, seeing that I had a deep interest in English, as I used to write poetry in my spare time, composing some pretty decent ballads and haikus that she liked. Guiding me like a lantern, she motivated me to start a poetry club. Another teacher, Mr. Vinson, took charge of it, a beloved history professor who had ample knowledge about the entire world. I'd never known before that we had such bright, hip teachers.

Those two professionals became my biggest role models, and I could see through them that having knowledge didn't make you cooler, it meant you had more power instead. My new outlook helped me many times in life, creating a new formula of reason for me to follow. Over time, I added to my new persona, trying to reflect it capably for others – they could be smart and trendy, but I would be bigger and better than them, through the power of knowledge and ideas now.

I began hitting the books; some topics were dry and boring, but some weren't, and I was picking up on things fast. I used to show off to my family how much I knew about the world, history and life, and it burgeoned into a form of competition for me. Our poetry club began slowly, but it took off when I told the guys I knew to come and rap, showing off their 'rad' skills. I relayed to people that rap was really another type of poetry, and to always keep it clean and professional. Mrs. Moses and Mr. Vinson wanted our school to compete, so we decided to create a 'slam competition', where we put our students' poems into a book, letting everyone know how serious we were and how studied, varied and beautiful our poetry was.

The principal signed off on our project, and we started contending against other schools, letting the students be the judges. It took plenty of my time, and my involvement grew into my latest and greatest happiness, as I figured, why waste my time looking over my shoulder, waiting for another gang fight in order to get attention, when there were so many other ways to do things and feel good about myself? I didn't change my appearance; I wanted others to realize that dudes like me into gangsta rap could also be into wonderful, fulfilling writing skills. I believed that no one should be judged by their image, even though being a teen could be difficult in many ways.

Meanwhile, my parent's disputes were heating up madly, and they ended up splitting in two; I was hurt dearly, but for some reason, my folks never got a technical divorce. They did break up homes, and we children decided to stay with Mom. It's hard to tell how much this had an effect on my formerly rebellious behavior, but I think a lot of my angst was caused by my parents' constant bickering and battling. I'm glad to say that my school teachers steered me down a better path. I made the final decision to change, but those two teachers were definitely my wisdom guides.

High school runs hot for many teens, and there are vital moments when mistakes are made that can haunt you for the rest of your life. I'm happy to declare that God launched an angel down to Earth, saving me from turmoil and hopelessness. That angel whispered to Mrs. Moses and Mr. Vinson to keep an eye out for me; it's funny how I can't now remember when the Cold War was, or when James A. Garfield served as President, but I can recall two people who never became famous. I guess you grasp onto the people in your memory who were life altering – they were awesome!

I sincerely hope and pray those two adults got everything they deserved out of this life, as I am also sure I'm not the only kid who benefitted from them or who remembers them with extreme fondness. High school at T.C. Williams was, as Richard M. Nixon once put it, a roller coaster ride – my grade point average shot skyward from a .86 in my sophomore year to a perfect 4.0 during my senior year. I graduated cum laude, tops in my class, and I had nothing on my mind but to go much further in life. My friends followed me on this, and we grew far more mature than before, thanks to that poor, brave kid dying right in front of us. It was a phase we underwent, and unfortunately, many kids never leave it behind; regardless of this, I did, at least.

Chapter Five
The Gym Life

As I began my new job at the gym, worry dogged my heels. I had been told there was a front desk position available; I merely needed to meet with the manager. I passed the interview with flying colors. Most normal paying jobs just require someone with good customer service skills, and I had been instilled with these skills at an early age, as an outgoing Afghan-American. I didn't tend to think it was an 'extra effort' to give a client my undivided attention.

I couldn't take it when I went out somewhere and the service people didn't show me proper eye contact or recognize me for entering their establishment. So many people seemed me to be bitter about their work. I made myself a promise that if I was ever swamped on the job, with a line going out the door, I would deliberately go up to them and greet everyone as they came in. I would let each customer know that I cared deeply about my job and my services, and the gym people absolutely loved that about me. I had to wonder why it was so hard for some people to offer genuine, personalized customer service, making their work days more difficult for them.

One day at the gym, I met a unique man who'd eventually become one of my best friends. Everybody called him 'Big Dee', and we started to have problems from the beginning – when I walked into the gym after my interview and he gave me a glaring stare, reading me up and down from head to toe – his upper lip pushed out in a fowl grimace. This was a look of clear loathing, despite and disdain, so I returned it right back; I wasn't the type to recoil in fear or back down.

Big Dee was a sales representative and trainer, with a stature of about six feet three inches, and weighing about 280 pounds. Only ten percent of this was body fat, as he was in excellent shape, though enormous in his bulky size and weight. Everyone in the gym knew and feared him, but he only made me feel uncomfortable at first. He was an inactive U.S. Marine, medically retired, showing it with his hard-nosed attitude and lack of patience for anyone who made any mistakes in his book.

He didn't say one word to me for days. I kept trying to read his thoughts, figuring he was doing the same with me, as I barely spoke to him too. But he never came up to me and yelled in my face, like he did with some of the others. This upset me, the way he screamed at them, because I only pleasantly teased those who were close to me at the gym. I decided that Big Dee was mostly observing my work ethics, finding out how fast I caught on to the job and my various duties.

I tended to be nonchalant about everything, a tendency I showed when I felt people didn't necessarily like me. Words between me and Big Dee mostly traveled from other employees, just enough to get our thoughts communicated. Eventually, I felt comfortable, like I could do the job however I wanted. One day, the manager went upstairs to the upper level, where all the free weights were placed. Big Dee opened the door with his usual show of self-confidence and authority, and I walked around the front desk to his office, looking up at him where he stood. He didn't make eye contact with me, so I thought he figured I was up to something.

I yelled, "Hey, Big Dee, what's the problem? Is anything wrong, or do you always snub new employees?" Looking down at me with a mean, provocative stare, he asked me if I knew who I was talking to. I told him, "Dee, if there was anything in this world I was going to fear, it would be God, and nothing else." He countered me by saying that I would be better off not approaching him that way, and he basically ordered me to go back to the front desk. Opening up my arms, I stated, "If you want drama and have a problem with me, then please handle it now. I don't mind getting beat up, and if you have something in your heart against me, then let's see how it is."

For some reason, probably because nobody else had stood up to him before, he gazed down at me with a big smile on his normally hardened face. Turning Marine on me, he cried out, "Don't bark if you have no bite, little man!" Laughing at his crude joke, I put my hands up in a boxing position, saying,

"Bring it on, by all means!"

With nothing further said, he rushed me, really fast, thinking I'd turn yellow and run away; but I hard-right hand slapped his face. Big Dee was stunned; I had gone too far, and he simply couldn't believe it! His beady eyes widened, and I knew I'd done something I would probably regret. Now I had to let him know that I wasn't afraid, not just of him but of anyone else whatsoever.

Taking a huge step near me, he put his hand up; I ducked down quick, knowing that if anything landed it would be a big hurt. But he mainly hit me with an open slap, like I'd done to him. The blow rocked my head back, sending me a couple of feet over to one side, and he went right ahead and did it two more times. As I fell into the welcoming arms of the gym's Christmas tree display, the manager came down the steps, seeing the tree fall over with a loud whooshing sound.

Big Dee heard the manager yell his name, and stopped attacking me. My skull rattled a little, but otherwise, I was fine. I told the manger that this battle royal was all my fault, and not to blame Big Dee. Oddly enough, the huge man respected this, displaying guilt at the upset manager, who thought Big Dee was being a bully again. Blithely ignoring the manager, I put out my hand for a friendly shake; Big Dee grabbed it, pulling me close and whispering in my ear, "I respect your courage, little man."

Chuckling, I told him, "I hope he didn't take things the wrong way."

"No, Farid, you're the only one here in the gym who's ever stood up to me, let alone standing up for yourself, so I only have respect for you now."

Things changed swiftly after that incident, though the manager was deeply puzzled as to what exactly had happened. He stalked away from our scenario, more worried about his poor old Christmas display than anything else. "Those idiots better not mess up my damn tree," he muttered in a grumbly way. Smirking, we simply went back to doing our jobs as before – but now we were the best of friends.

Later, Big Dee took it on himself as a personal mission to get me to work there as a personal trainer, telling me that my people skills were 'superb' and that I was made to work that particular job. But I had a problem with it. I didn't work out the way a real trainer did, doing my own routines instead, and I just didn't fit the criteria. Wanting so much to help me, Big Dee really believed in me – he broke down and taught me all about the power exercises, putting me on a tight workout regimen. He made me go from a measly, skinny 140 lbs. to about 175 lbs. of solid, bedrock healthy muscle.

On my own, I caught on to most of the newer exercises. I had worked for the gym as a trainer from the beginning, and I was still the smallest guy there, but now I was working as a personal trainer. The best advice Big Dee gave me was to attract clients by teaching stomach and abs workouts. Nobody else could perform my special stomach tricks that I developed, not without my training; this became my patent property, and word soon got out about it. This was fantastic for me, as most of the people coming into the gym were worried about their stomachs and abs. I was a well-known trainer in less than six months, pulling in more than 25 new clients.

Most of these came through recommendations, but as I was getting paid only the same as I got for working the front desk, I had to take it up to the next level. After I gave it some hard thought, Big Dee said the way to go was for me to 'bite the bullet' for a while, until my clients loved my routines so much they'd transfer to me, if I became a freelance trainer. This was my first major step up; I created a business account, and the clients had to sign a personal contract with me now.

I thought I could keep half the clients at twice the salary, which I deemed a most beneficial risk. I charged $25-$35 per client, and lots of folks came my way, knowing that although it was a higher rate, it was still a very good deal. Yet, I was amazed that they all stuck with me, asking them why they didn't prefer the bigger, stronger trainers. They usually replied, "They seem unrealistically healthy, and look proportionally wrong." This greatly increased my self-confidence, motivating me to do far more.

Working day and night to promote my business, I named it 'Toned Techniques', wanting to let everyone know that being toned, fit and trim was the 'new thing'. It took realistic circuit training to accomplish this. Circuit training is a modern conditioning method used to boost the heart rate by using multiple exercises performed back to back. Each exercise has several variables added, and can be intensified for the different levels of strength each client happens to have.

My particular formula didn't fail, and when my clients left the gym, drenched with sweat, sore from heaving around either ten lb. weights or only their own body weight, my mission in life was accomplished. The more they got used to my exercises, the more I used new, different techniques and heavier weights. All manner of people boasted about my sessions; I was making a name for myself, and it felt sensational. I was now 'king of the gym', and my time there sped by, skimming past like waves on churning water. It got to the point where my clients argued over the best set times in my schedule. I was in high demand, and I loved it!

The minute an hour under my tutelage began, I was on my client like a Marine drill instructor, dogging him to 'move it, move it, and move it'! At first, most of my clients appeared to be shy, asking me to not call a lot of attention to our sessions. But as they got stronger, they gained commensurately in self-confidence. Witnessing their improvement, I brought them even more positive attention as we boldly dove into our sessions. I purposefully kept everything but helping the clients from my mind; the person exercising in front of me was my world, everything I believed in at the time. And I never asked them about their spouses, their lives or their personal stories.

I was hard on them but fair, and they all knew how serious I was about the work we were performing together. Mostly, I put across the image of a hard, fearless personal trainer, needing to instill some type of fear into them. I desired nothing but complete control, but at the end of every session, I received nothing but compliments. Everybody needed to know what 'level' they were on, and I never sugar-coated anything. I told them about their state of fitness and their progress. My personal communication skills were expert, as Big Dee had noticed; it only made my job easier.

I'd wait until a client lost a decent amount of weight, citing how out of shape they were in the past and that those days were gone for good. I ordered them to live a healthier life from now on, and not to repeat their prior mistakes. I measured them for body fat percentages, weighing them at least every month, and I was as excited as they were to review the bountiful results of their physical training.

Another thing I loved about being a personal trainer was witnessing my clients' spirits rise, from being people who'd been in extremely poor shape, never going to a gym or working out, to becoming people who developed a brand-new lifestyle. I'm sure that nearly everyone I trained is still going to the gym, and that they all kept the fundamental teachings I gave them about fitness, body image and health. On top of this, I'm happy to say that everyone I trained was always an inspiration to me, and I think about each and every one of them when I look back on those halcyon days. I've often felt that teaching people is something natural for me – praise is just icing on the cake.

Big Dee by then was my lifelong friend, and we shared our stories and times together as the best of pals. Like me, he was a dreamer, always trying to get into bigger and better things in life. He wouldn't do anything to damage his body, which he frequently referred to as his 'temple'. I respected my own body, but didn't give it half as much attention as he did, doing bad things such as smoking cigarettes and drinking on the weekends. I simply didn't want to be entirely consumed by the gym life, being a firm believer that if I worked hard, I deserved to play equally hard too.

Anyway, my mentor Big Dee guided me through lots of different roles and exercises, and his relationship with me was pretty much that of a big brother. He'd show how much he cared by pushing me to do anything that I dreamed of. When I casually discussed a topic in conversation, he'd jump on me to take it much further. He always told me not to be the best scholar, but to be the best achiever instead.

I asked him once where he'd attained that ideology, and he replied with, "The good old Corps, Reed." He usually shortened Farid to Reed, and I never corrected him. Big Dee was a good old, salty ex-Marine, one who got out due to a knee injury; if not for that, he would've taken his twenty-year retirement. His discipline shone readily apparent – he came to work with a fresh shave every single morning – no shadow of stubble on his bulldog face by the late afternoon.

Things were all coming together for me, and I liked and respected Big Dee for his daily help. Seeing some of the photos in his office, I would stare at them, knowing he had accomplished something a long time ago. He was way ahead of me when it came to the stuff people learn in the Marine Corps. I figured he ruled in the gym as a rock-solid muscle man from the beginning, due to it being instilled in him in the Corps. It was an ingrained part of his life, and he'd never change it. His pride had all the characteristics that Marines were said to have. I couldn't sleep the night after I found out he came from the Corps; it was surely something I would forever want to do.

Deeply yearning for the title of U.S. Marine, nonetheless, I didn't make the attempt to go sign up and become a 'maggot' – not yet. The gym was teaching me plenty, but I needed a higher sense of training and purposefulness. I wished to satisfy my bold ego, and fulfill my wildest dreams. So the very next day, I cancelled my gym appointments and arranged to sojourn off to Italy, to clear my mind and gain time alone to think. My impromptu vacation was well worth the expense of the plane ticket. The clients were a little shocked, but they knew I deserved the time off.

Deep in thought for many nights, I decided that if I was going to have any fun, I had to leave my worries behind in America. But the airport soon brought me back to my senses. Being Middle Eastern looking, I was hassled by airport security, not letting it upset my happy applecart. Those guys and gals were merely doing their jobs, and that was enough to make me smile. I agreed with their requirements for increased security, both in going to and coming from Italy. I returned greatly refreshed; everyone at the gym saw a new light shining in my face. I had left the country with more than a little anxiety, pushing a mental reset button after my time on vacation.

Once I was back home and ready to work, I tested all my clients to see how far they'd come while I was gone. Most of them were 'locked on', and didn't skip a beat. Others had grown lazy during my absence, but I told them to get some rest and come back with renewed muscles, as rest is what every muscle needs.

On a regular basis, I taught my clients power lifts and techniques such as Stiff Legged Dead Lifts, Power Snatches, and Bar Squats – to build up their testosterone and energy levels. My techniques were not aimed at the average beginner, needing deep focus of attention and well-trained coordination. They helped the trained body immensely, but could damage you if they were done or applied improperly. I only took risks with the clients who were sure they could handle more extensive forms of training. Most of my advanced clients wanted and needed to take risks in order to excel, looking at my upper levels of training as a test of how far they could go to develop themselves.

Everybody had different, unique goals at the gym, and it made me seriously proud to see that I could help my people reach their loftiest goals. Watching people come in with low self-esteem and feelings of insecurity gave me the drive to pressure them to make the necessary changes. I could recall my own feelings of doubt, and I really wanted to help all my clients overcome them, driving hard forward so they could enjoy a much better overall lifestyle and a longer, much healthier life.

But lots of folks kept to the same old, dull routines, usually reaching a 'stagnant poin' in their workouts; in turn, that led to their dropping in motivational levels, and they'd often skip out on going to the gym. Meanwhile, I deemed it amusing that in the area where we lived, tons of people would beeline straight to a bar for 'happy hour' right after work – it seemed like society needed you to think that destroying yourself from within solved your stress and burden of work problems. In fact, all it really accomplished was wasting money, getting your brain inebriated and destroyed, potential DUI charges, domestic disputes, and even more stress, ineptitude, and drama.

I could never understand or relate to the 'happy hour' thing; it was a recipe for mutually assured destruction and disaster. Instead, I wished everyone could go straight to the gym after work, relieving their stress and tensions in a natural, healthy way. Exercise releases endorphins, the 'happy' chemicals, making you feel good as they flood your system. This natural, God-given high progresses us, though we're somewhat ignorant about its crucial role in life. You can't take a drug as wise as endorphins.

Throughout the day, as we compress our anger in stressful situations, the only means left at the end is to decompress. Going to the gym lets us take on life's hardships, still maintaining a solid balance. I do not condone drinking, which I did myself, as some like me do it casually and responsibly. But I always thought that if I wasn't hard at work at something, someone else was going to do it, and I was going to be left behind. When I looked in the mirror, I needed to be able to say I was trying my hardest to make my appearance and body presentable to the world.

The gym life can become a daily permanent lifestyle preference, equally open to everyone, no matter your condition or fears. It's the only place I've ever found where any color, sex, shape, or form of a person is fully accepted, regardless of how you perceive yourself and others to be. And the gym life is what led me to boldly make my decision, to finally enter the U.S. Marines Corps.

Chapter Six
Joining the Corps

"Get the *hell* off my bus!"

The bus windows fogged over, while I didn't know if it was from the perspiring recruits or the humidity coming from Parris Island.

"I want a solid line, and your nasty feet on the yellow footprints when you get off my bus – *check*!"

"Sir, yes, *Sir*!" shouted we raw recruits, otherwise called 'maggots'.

We were at the Marine Corps Recruit Depot on Parris Island, also known as the 'House of Pain'. And according to our irately impatient Drill Instructor:

"I will *destroy* you every second of the day from this time on – your soul is now *mine*!"

The intensity, motivation, strength, uniform, pride, honor, courage, commitment, bearing, judgment, justice, decisions, integrity, and dedication…it all spelled out the United States Marine Corps. Not needing any introduction, Parris Island does require an explanation. 'The Island' is where they break boys, physically and psychologically, and mold them into men. Under the onus of a 'wolf pack' of Drill Instructors, not Drill Sergeants from the Army, the pecking order rose from Senior, then Drill, and last but not least, the Kill Hats. These latter regulated and gave birth to future Marines.

The Few, the Proud, the Marines are the legendary warriors who earn everything they have, never being given anything for free. The history of the Corps is too lengthy for any great depth here, but the very name has commanded respect since the days of the Marines' birth at the Tun Tavern in Philadelphia, Pennsylvania on November 10, 1775. There, the First Continental Congress held the first Corps recruitment drive, raising two battalions of Marines in Philadelphia for the Revolutionary War.

I couldn't feel more sophisticated, more sensational, knowing now that my entire life had turned around and changed completely. I was going to earn a title that few people have ever had, or so much as aspired to. And it was an overwhelming feeling to see my 'abbot', Senior Drill Instructor, Staff Sergeant Harris-Smith, in full regalia uniform – the man leading the pack, the one to ensure his platoon crossed the finish line.

The Staff Sergeant's plan was to make his recruits work excruciatingly hard to collect the title of U.S. Marine. The EGA, also known as the Eagle, Globe and Anchor, is the symbol identifying the Marines, and he wanted everyone under his tutelage to proudly sport this honored insignia. Harris-Smith was rock hard, but fair – he hated and despised each of us equally, the exact same way. But the day we earned our titles, he'd love us as one of his own blood brothers; he would gladly take a bullet for any one of us.

The other Drill Instructor, Staff Sergeant 'Bo' Miller, was our basic guide to the formation marching and overall learning disciplines. He helped us prepare our uniforms, showing us how they needed to be worn properly, and assisted us with all the necessary details of regulations. Every item on the list was crucial, related to war or combat as we needed and exercised it later on. 'Bo' was a long-time war veteran, with a world of knowledge about all things Marine. He had no time for any 'maggots' looking around for an easier method or path to training. As for me personally, I enjoyed his guidance and firm stance of never lowering his standards in order to get by.

Finally, Kill Hat Instructor Staff Sergeant Michael McMahon was the fierce, frog-voiced and seriously dreaded 'annihilator', who broke down our bodies and minds, teaching us every lesson the Marine Corps had to offer. He would always say, "When the mind fails to comprehend, the body must be punished!"

At the age of twenty-six, I thought I was already a hardened kick-ass, able to handle all this Marine stuff with élan and ease. But I totally needed to be broken, like all the rest of us. I was still only a boy on my first day at Parris Island, though, I didn't know it yet. Crumbling to pieces under the strict tutelage of the Marines, I tried to stay motivated, but my body was exhausted and fatigued. My Afghan roots were brought up repeatedly; racist remarks were screamed at me daily, only in order to break me so that I could be rebuilt into a new, much better and shinier image.

I couldn't be more proud of anything I did in my entire life. I will forever treasure the saying we shared, "Once a Marine, always a Marine." People used to call me 'Motard', a term used for people who love everything about the United States Marine Corps. It stands for 'Motivated Retard'. I didn't mind being called names like 'maggot' and 'retard', though most people who used these terms were the younger Marines, the ones with a chip on their shoulder, who didn't understand the true meaning of being a Marine yet. Plenty of them were still stuck in the rebellious 'teen phase'.

As for me, I craved all things the Corps had to offer, going after the physical tests with an iron will, and becoming the best recruit there at shooting. I learned exactly how to break down an M-16 Service Rifle, and also how to carefully clean it. Then, I practiced shooting it from 500 yards, hitting nine out of ten targets. Shooting was a trained skill, something I'd always remember. I asked my instructors about anything I didn't understand, keeping my eyes and ears wide open to every detail they set forth in front of me, absorbing it all like a dry sponge that sat in the sun too long.

Time on the Island blew by fast, as everyone tried their hardest to become what he or she required in order to accomplish something big. I'm First Battalion, Bravo Company, Platoon 1109 'til the day I die. A Senior Drill Instructor bestowed the EGA symbol on me, firmly pressing the round, darkly plastic ornament into my open palm, but I didn't cry – unlike many other younger Marines. I was far too 'macho' to get all bleary-eyed and sentimental. Nonetheless, my heart skipped a beat when the SDI bored dead straight into my eyes, saying, "Congratulations, Marine; job well done." I knew it was my time to be somebody in this life, because I'd chosen Death before Dishonor, a popular saying in the Corps. Being a Marine was a twenty-four/seven duty, and I believed in the United States Marine Corps now with every fiber of my being.

My next station after the Island was at Camp Lejeune, North Carolina, working with a helicopter squadron. But I had yet to know why and what I was doing; it made no sense to me. Fate had brought me there, and I met many Marines, but my Sergeant Major was the one God intended me to see. He was an alpha male that ate, slept, and breathed the Marine Corps, resembling a full-grown pit bull that had been in one too many fights. This Sergeant Major was a six-time combat veteran, bestowed a Medal of Valor for his honorable acts in war. He was with the Light Armor Recon team, known far and wide for their bravery in going on missions in places that conventional Marines couldn't go.

The discipline of this Sergeant Major was outstanding, and his tolerance for the high standards of the Corps were stressed significantly. I was hugely proud to have finally met a leader who'd ventured into every type of duty the Corps had to provide, from Drill Instructor to the Marine Security Detail for Embassies worldwide. Checking in with the Sergeant Major is one of the first things you do as a Marine when coming into a unit. I wasn't afraid, merely excited in wanting him to know I hailed from Afghanistan, joining to go to war in order to serve by using my language capabilities.

When I first entered his office, I stood at parade rest, a semi-relaxed position that tenders a respectful way of standing in front of your superior ranking personnel. But the moment I opened my mouth to say, "Good morning, Sergeant Major; Private First Class Hotaki, reporting as ordered..." he fist-slammed his desk resoundingly, screaming,

"*No,* hell no, get the *hell* out of my office! *Nobody* walks in here reporting at parade rest! In this man's Corp, we report at the position of *attention!*"

Before he could even finish, I spurted out of the office, smirking slightly, wondering at how stupid I felt for forgetting such an easy thing. Running back in, I stood at the position of attention, with my body locked in place, head up, and shouted with a fierce, unafraid voice the same exact thing I'd yelled earlier. The Sergeant Major jumped up from his desk, true Devil Dog that he was, glaring at me up and down, making me feel like a brand new puppy in a dominant dog's territory. He examined me sidelong, inspecting my uniform for any microscopic errors, such as threads sticking out. Once he was sure I was squared away, he said, "Tell me something about yourself, making sure not to whisper at me, like you want to have my baby or something."

I knew not to laugh, as he was testing my Marine's bearing, to see if I'd unwillingly crack a smile. Ignoring his remark, I leapt into some motivational talk, finishing up with how I was different from the rest of the Marines, more needed because I was born in Afghanistan and could speak their languages fluently.

In answer, the Sergeant Major bent over, inspecting my shoes and slacks. Suddenly, he jumped up, eyes opening wide. "What, are you, a damn *Haji*?"

Not knowing exactly how to reply, I figured the term referred to someone from the Middle East, so I said, "Yes, Sergeant Major, I am."

"Tell me this, *Private First Class,* why the *hell* are you in my squadron? Have you taken a *language* test yet, PFC?"

I stammered in response, "They...told me I had to wait first...to get to my unit, Sergeant Major." When addressing anyone in the Marine Corps, we never used names, just ranks – it's been a long-time tradition, reminding us that problems never arise from using a time-tested ranking system with very few intrinsic flaws.

Telling me to sit down, the Sergeant Major spilled his stories about what he'd done in his lengthy career, and I listened with intense interest. I always loved to hear about war stories and career accomplishments, starting with those of my Dad. I told the Sergeant Major that I wanted the same kind of life as his, and that I needed ample help and support to attain it; but he stopped me with a motion of his hand.

"Listen, PFC, I need you out there helping my boys in the field. You don't belong in Logistics, and you also don't belong in this helicopter squadron." I agreed; Marines usually beg to leave these types of units, and do the things they signed up for. "You have a very rare talent...with both the Marine skills and being a Haji...it should set you up for a lifetime of success. Your risk level is already elevated by telling me about yourself, but you don't look too young. How old are you, PFC?" I told him my age, and he replied, "Good, that means you can handle your training, and still be mature enough to roll with the big dogs. I'll set you up with your officer in command, and get you started down the correct path. Say, what's your physical fitness test score?" Proudly, I informed him it was 295 out of 300, glad to be at the highest level. I also let him know I was expert in the shooting qualifications. "Good, PFC, very good...we can work with that."

However, I was soon learning that things don't happen overnight in the Marine Corps. I waited day after day as months passed, getting impatient because my job in the squadron was a sick joke – I couldn't fathom how such work existed in the Marines. But I also learned that support elements were crucial for the guys on the ground, while I really thought I deserved to be one of the guys in the field. Ground and field Marines were called 'Grunts', the best type of warriors, what I was used to hearing about when I was growing up. This type of dude would fight, joke, laugh, cry and die alongside you, and was part of your family. In America, though, they hated each other and fought every weekend – but when abroad, we were a tightly knit wolf pack.

I respected them, feeling like I was with my brothers or dearest friends back home; it was the most camaraderie I'd ever seen. Joining these few groups of Marines, I realized now what everyone had talked about concerning the war stories. I had read tales of the troops and how they interacted, but I didn't see that type of thing in the support element groups. It was the guys who got to go outside the wires and live in people's homes that were the closely 'together' ones. They taught me valuable skills that neither boot camp nor combat training had taught me, and these people displayed the skills for adapting to anywhere that we ever went.

I picked up on matters so quickly, they called me 'Old Bastard', as I was always enraged – I finally got my true alias. The Marines also gave me the call sign 'ROC', an acronym for 'Raged, Occasionally Calm'. I loved it, running with it madly. I razor-shaved my head off, having the right, many Marines didn't have to grow my beard out, because I spoke the local Afghanistan languages.

My first tour into the war zone engendered feelings like no others. I was in a country I'd left behind twenty-five years ago, and I didn't know what to expect. My fellow Marines joked around a lot, teasing me about being an Afghan, but the one thing I learned the most was to never be thin-skinned. It only showed weakness. As I was older, I could pull jokes back on them, because I had more life experience.

I didn't know what to expect, my first deployment slated for early 2008, but I got all my gear together. My family wasn't there as I left, just the same as when I graduated to become a Marine at Parris Island. So I was alone; this was true during a great deal of my life, as once again, I traveled out to have what I thought would be a life changing experience. As I sat alone the night before we headed out, I reflected upon my past close friends and family members. It seemed like I was nothing to them anymore, and a saying repeated in my mind until the day I die came to me: 'Misery needs company.'

Yes, I was truly miserable, but I tried to deny it by going to school and then attending several dead-end jobs. I started to turn into someone who would say 'I almost, could've, should've...' and I really didn't want or need that. I hate regrets, and as I grew older I knew the time would come to burst from my cocoon. Everybody needs some space and alone time in order to grasp life's actual worth. I'm strongest when it comes to being alone and mixing it up with new groups of people; I've always been a strong leader, but it gets old when you're among the same peers while growing up. The biggest challenge is when you can mix it up, when more variables are added.

I knew I had to make a difference in this world, leaving my footprints somewhere important, somehow significant. I had to prove to myself that creating a legacy wasn't as difficult as it might seem. Being a hero or superstar, or famous in some way, is something most people desire; but so many of them don't anywhere near deserve it. Needing to come into my own time to shine, I was through with people telling me that I could've done so much more, and why wasn't I doing this or that.

Taking control of my life, my formerly suppressed inner dialogue finally turned into the 'real' me. I artfully let my identity, which I sometimes felt insecure about, become part of my new formula to take charge. It was now time to show off my leadership skills, and move expeditiously but cautiously. There wasn't any room for mistakes or repeating errors from the past. Not truly owning my destiny yet, I was seeing the light, and decided to steer my way full-out toward it.

The winds of change weren't going to blow me away anymore; I was wolfishly hungry for knowledge, respect, and showing everyone the true spirit of the Marines. During that time, I had little sleep at night, and I still experience the blood pulsating in my veins when I see another Marine, or hear things that trigger my soul. The mission of the Corps' Rifle Squad is, "Locate, Close Width, and Destroy the Enemy." I've taken this from the Marines and used it on anything I do when it really needs to be accomplished, whether it's a problem in life, at the gym, or anywhere else. I substitute the 'enemy' portion with my goals, which I want to be my end results.

Many similar things are taken from the Marines, useful later in life, derived from the brilliant teachings, training, and spirits imparted to the troops. Most people keep these things sacred for life, though others can't wait to become a civilian again – but no matter how hard anyone tries, it never leaves you fully. The traits of the U.S. Marine Corps are deeply instilled in you; it takes years upon years to ever change again.

Chapter Seven
Back to Afghanistan

As a fully focused, capable U.S. Marine, my tours in Afghanistan were the most exhilarating times in my entire life. Looking back, I readily recall my first destination – landing within my native hometown of Kandahar, at a massive military base loaded with war personnel and surrounded by unfriendly locals.

Kandahar has figured immeasurably in Afghanistan's tribal, divided, and extraordinarily violent ethnic history, while its country has sustained lots of noteworthy rulers, monarchs, sultans, emperors, and kings. Widely known as the nation's capital in earlier times, Kandahar is the second largest city in Afghanistan, a traditional seat of power for over 200 years; the region around it is one of the earliest human settlements, laid out by Alexander the Great in the Fourth Century BC. The capital was moved north to Kabul, due to threats emanating from foreign countries, way back in the 1770s. So Kandahar had a rich, tapestried history, but what we Marines immediately knew it for was shit. Literal shit, not just a bad word or swear tactic…just *shit!*

Out of six U.S. military bases in Afghanistan, our base was mostly fabled for containing a large 'pond' featuring all the feces from every bathroom nearby, filtering straight into it. That caused the entire base to be a smelly, demeaning, nasty place, as it spouted four percent breathable fecal matter in the air. The Marines poured into Afghanistan when our participation in the war started in 2001, right after the September 11 attack, but we didn't show our faces there again until much later on, turning into a conventional force to move into the neighboring West Province. This region was known as 'Helmand', a place noteworthy for its beautiful river, a perfect place for crops to be raised – a virtual 'farmer's heaven'. Helmand didn't offer up wheat and corn, but instead lushly grew in ninety-five percent of its native lands…poppy plants.

Poppies produce a green bulb called a 'kuknar', with its shape growing straight up the middle near the top of the stem. They reach roughly four feet in height, with lovely rose-pink petals clustering around the kuknar. But inside this deceitfully delightful plant is where the lucrative 'black tar' is formed. Black tar is raw opium, the strongest drug in the world, sent illegally to labs to form a superior drug – heroin. This means hundreds of billions of dollars to those concerned, so the war from the terrorist side has always been driven from this innocuous-seeming plant's cultivation.

Heroin money funds all the Improvised Explosive Devices, ammonium nitrates, the weapons caches, and the funding of the release of detainees in the rampantly corrupt government structure of Afghanistan. The innocent, pretty little poppy is the single most important problem causing the war to be hard, fast, steady, and long fought. It's said the attack on the World Trade Center was only a 'mask' for the Poppy Wars.

The Marines had a huge task to fulfill, needing to set into the biggest province in Afghanistan and try to assist the interminable British forces there to not get overrun, while killing as many members as possible of the local terrorist organization, the Taliban – an Islamic fundamentalist movement, spreading into Afghanistan and forming a kind of underground government, ruling with Kandahar as its capital. But starting in 2001, they began to be a part of ancient history, albeit a livelier sort of that, due to the American presence there. I'm proud to say I was a part of those matters; our goal was pretty much to kill all of the terrorists, as their goal was to kill all of us.

The province itself was a crazy quilt of mixed terrains; you could see deserts stretching out for miles, mountains several acres high, trees, grass, and the green river waters flowing freely, crashing hard into their lush, jungle-laden banks. This new country, to us, was wild, pristine, amazing me – I could never have imagined it. Such a gorgeous, bountiful place, while the most hazardous things occurred here, endangering the lives of the entire world – when you consider the nuclear quotient.

My first day in my once native nation exploded in my face, showing me that it was time to be forever on the alert, as we proceeded into combat, firefights en route to Helmand Province. Our forces were large, superior, and we had ample manpower; it was mainly a case of the Taliban 'letting us know' they were there. I got to see how we reacted to small arms firing, as the push inward was through small, armored Humvee trucks that eventually went out of usage, due to their vaporizing from the massive explosive devices being used at the time. Sadly, we didn't have anything else proper in the way of heavy equipment, so we needed to learn our lessons the hard way.

Usually, matters only improved through trial and error, a method I was used to from exploring in my younger days. Strangely enough, we, as a united strong force, tended to underestimate the normal, old-fashioned farmers' capabilities, to our vast devastation, deaths, and injuries. Quickly, I had to learn precisely where to tread in the fields, and where not to go. Talking to native villagers was crucial, because relaying messages from the local standpoints always had to be completely accurate. If I slipped up or didn't pay the right attention, my whole team's methods were in jeopardy. It was clearly in my hands now, to save and preserve our and their people's lives.

I was in the enlisted ranks; when I was in Afghanistan, nobody seemed to pay much attention to my ranking, though. Instead, they saw me as a means, sometimes the only means, of communication, involving finding the enemy or getting our own guys to safety. It felt great to have such an enormous amount of responsibility, and I definitely yearned to show all the Marines that I was there for them, any second of any day. My fellow Marine Corps 'grunts', or the infantrymen, showed me things I'd never learned before, and I saw that I was indeed feeble to most of their jargon, or way with words. But it turned out to be an even trade, as I used my linguistics to assist them; the more they trained me, the more I could be of service to them.

Telling them that I didn't want to be out in the field on patrol and not know the right techniques, or in other words, slow them down and mess things up, gained their deep respect – there were other linguists, but they were all local nationals. Our boys couldn't trust those 'farmers' any further than you could throw them, it seemed. So they used me a lot, too much in fact, and I started getting burnt out by the job.

I couldn't show them how exhausted I was from mounting four patrols every day and Sunday with no breaks, as they needed me so badly, and that's all I cared about. I kept myself on eternal vigil, on high alert each day and night, encountering my comrades dying and losing limbs from the first month we arrived in Kandahar. I ate nothing but 'MRE', or meals ready to eat, bland food containing enough preservatives to stuff a dead horse; it never went bad, sealed up tight for consumption in a day or a year from now. My fellows warned it would 'back me up', and I didn't use the bathroom for three whole days. Being scared, I talked to the one doctor on base, and he dryly stated in an acrid Southern drawl, "No worries, bro...you'll be fine, just eat some of that wonderful cheese they packed for you. You only need something greasy, and when it comes out, you'll feel pain...but your body's getting used to it."

Damn, he was right; when I finally made chocolate, it felt like giving birth to a blue whale through my butt. Glad I'm closer to women for it! By the way, our bathroom was only a spot in a dirt-filthy corner, where I defecated into a Ziploc-closing bag, then immediately threw it into a fire pit. We didn't have or use a proper military latrine. To me, this was the nth degree of stupidity, but no one else appeared to care. We all had to share the basic living styles here, so I gave up commenting on embarrassing situations. I knew we were all 'one', as the Marine Corps called it. But when the days dragged along, the grunts tossed small rocks at guys taking a crap, just because they were helpless when taking a shit and adding to our general 'air pollution'.

One time, we took over a mud compound that held about five rooms. It was fascinating, with livestock surrounding it, inhabiting the world's smallest farm. We shared our new home with three chickens, one rooster, one sheep, a goat and an anorexic looking, fly-covered, burping horse. At this point in time, I had yet to come face-to-face with the enemy, but always knew in my guts they were lurking somewhere nearby. You wouldn't believe how difficult it is to sleep when you know nothing around you is secure, and that only the guy on post standing there is your 'savior' for the night. That's why discipline and decent, appropriate bearing, plus many other things we learned in boot camp were so important, the undying embers in our burnt-out minds. You need this when looking out for one another in a foreign country during a war.

Once again, I felt the Marine feeling well up in me; I knew I must relax and trust the nightly guard, and then I'd be able to watch over him another night. If I didn't trust him, not only would I not get enough rest, I could possibly fall asleep during my turn on post, and that's exactly when the enemy is surest to strike.

I remember our 'Gunny', formally a Gunnery Sergeant, crowing proudly, "Believe it or not, these bitches watch out for you *twenty-four seven*! You better be on your toes, Marines!" He was dead right; any moment we got too loud or felt too relaxed, that's when something wrong would happen. It's called 'complacency', the biggest threat to military service; even in the States, when people get too relaxed, that's when they usually are robbed, killed, or something else terrible occurs.

On the lighter side, I was elated to meet local farmers who shared features like my own family members back home. If I took any of these folks and put them into American clothes, you couldn't tell them apart from my relatives. And you wouldn't believe how many of these villagers desired a more peaceful Western ideology, but they never could speak up – from fear of the terrorists. The Taliban made them pray and worship to the exclusion of all else, using techniques that fostered God as a scare method, telling villagers that we were 'infidels', that any interaction would cost them their lives. Out of this, most locals didn't care to approach us, or help with our concerted hunt for the terrorists. Trying to win the 'hearts and minds' of a group of scared, religious, local villagers can only be done by conversing closely with their head elders, in spite of what any American government officials have to say about it.

Anyway, Afghans always hold deep respect for their elders, supporting almost anything they say; so we kept our focus to that for quite a while. However, that country's elders sometimes played double roles, just pretending like they actually cared and gainfully desired to help us. Often, it was merely to bait us into trouble, another lesson we had to learn the long, hard way. Having thirty-six other nations on our side in a war was a difficult enough balancing act, trying to regulate who was who every time, who exactly held sway and power over what or which territory.

Local Islamic nationals faithfully sounded the prayer call five times every day, their clergymen or 'muezzin' loudly calling the 'azan' at the 'mosque', or religious church. There, they always had one clergyman called a 'Mullah', who would normally have a sermon playing, either inside the mosque or by broadcasting it over a microphone and speaker, with the message booming out from the mosque's 'minaret' – a tall, semi-hollow spire with a conical crown, also useful as a primitive air conditioning device – up on top of the mosque. This was so that everyone in the vicinity could hear the Mullah's all-important religious words. But we Marines grew suspicious about said speaker, and what he was genuinely preaching. Sometimes, I overheard their words, and as I understood it, they were broadcasting that 'foreign mongrels are in the area'. It didn't happen everywhere we went, but some locations were worse than others.

Oddly enough, a few Mullahs would reach out with open arms, actually assisting us in our undertakings. This was however a very hard game to play, and it got tiring in about twenty seconds. We were each burning out, with what all the security patrols needed, and training the Afghan forces – such as their army and police. The Afghans tended to want anything they could get their hands on, never bothering to do lots of work for it. Some of them were honestly hard workers, but these kinder folks got burned out too, toiling away in the hot weather and harsh conditions.

Most of them just laughed their color-turbaned, salt-stained, sweaty male heads off, stroking their lush, black beards in a wise-guy way, looking for a free ride, only performing needed or requested tasks when forced to or pressured. They're practical folks, men who wear their turbans or 'lungees' for identification purposes; unlike what many ignorant Americans think, it's a similar extra cloth called a 'patu' that they find useful for multiple daily hygiene and weather purposes, such as wrapping up against the cold, sitting on them to protect their butts from dirty or muddy ground, tying up their animals, or even carrying some refreshing water. And the various different Afghan ethnic groups – there are quite a few – sport a variety of lungees, in different hues and patterns, although the standard seems to be grey, striped, or white.

I understand in much greater detail now how these men harbored their own frustrations, as they typically had few goods to work with. They also recognized that the Marines possessed no real luxuries or resources either. Laughing loudly, they'd say, "How come the infidel American Army has money, and so much supplies, but you nobody guys never get anything?" They were talking about simple hardwood floors for a tent, real food instead of MRE rations, and what about a generator for heat or some nice air conditioning? Our weather was forever extreme, so the locals thought it was insane and rather suspicious that we had nothing to our names but weapons and ammo.

And we never used standing showers or baths, making do with simpler stuff. It was considered 'the Marine way of life'. Poking holes into water bottles, we spurted them as treasured mini showers, only caring about vital areas of our bodies that led to infections, if they weren't properly bathed. From this, I learned to appreciate the things you normally take for granted back in the States. Laundry wasn't done out in the field, and salt streaks overlapped slickly on our clothes. The smell was as horrible a one as you could imagine when you strolled into a tent full of sweaty Marines.

Using that 'get used to it' attitude, it was our own form of leverage with the natives, to either sound 'tuff' or loudly state we were only about the mission and getting the job done. This caused those laughing locals to at least view us as strong-willed fighters, 'real men' in other words. To them, we appeared to be about as bad off, or worse still, than they were. The only problem really, once you got past their defenses, was getting them to adopt our styles of warfare. They couldn't or wouldn't grasp the concept of patrolling, or doing it multiple times per day to meet and ensure security levels – they thought one patrol per day was sufficient, either in the morning, on hot summer days, or later in the day on cold winter afternoons. Stressing to them that the enemy doesn't wait for a comfortable time to strike us or do something wrong, we said we couldn't wait around to do the right thing at all times.

Many soldiers on the local side quit, returning instantly home during the first harsh invasions of broadly critical territories. But a few others stayed, sympathetic to our side due to us all taking heavy casualties, at least from both sides. Wondering, I saw the locals taking their likely deaths and those of others pretty calmly, not showing much emotion, while on our side, it killed our morale, making us fall down and stress out frequently. The only times we got our minds off death were when we made 'a great kill' ourselves, our only wretched form of psychological payback.

Sitting hunched together on logs around the campfire at night, with our uniformed bodies, the only other thing keeping us warm or cool, we'd either tell jokes on each other, or tell stories of whatever we missed back home. It's funny – when you're deployed, you talk about nothing but home, and when you're home, you talk about nothing but deployment. The same goes for civilians who gabble about going to the bar, and when they get there, they go on at great length about work, which I mentioned around the fire to some peals of hoots and laughter. Seems like every Marine has a tale or two about love, or a sexual encounter, of course.

Going into history, the Germans called the Marines 'Teufel Hunden' or Devil Dogs, for how we speedily killed them during WWI, and nowadays, it's used motivationally, better than 'retard' and 'maggot', I guess. According to legend, Germans were describing the Marines fighting in the Battle of Belleau Wood in 1918, as we slaughtered them with such unabashed ferocity that we were literally 'Dogs Straight from the Depths of Hell'.

You couldn't tell that from our bunch of bums at the campfire. Marines prepared new stories during the day, for airing out with each other, waiting for another patrol to happen. We were easily amused, loving to learn the languages and cultures of any countries we visited, it seemed. Marines are famous as the strongest, most dignified individuals back home, taking pride in their state-side regions. I learned about places I'd never been to just by listening, and of course, the other Marines' 'love lives' got played out maximally too – who knows what was real, and what was fiction? Wives and girlfriends missed us greatly, because we deployed so often. This in turn led to late night yelling sessions with spouses, and probably far worse things also.

We Marines tend to be overprotective of our significant others, and jealousy will make our blood pressures rise merely from a wife stating she's going to the mall, although others were a bit less fortunate, hearing about their spouses seeing other men in a Marine town back in the States. I hated this, having no respect for either males or females having a loved one serving their country, and then cheating on them behind their backs. It made my blood boil; that just *wasn't fair,* I inwardly screamed!

So many stories about couples breaking up right in the middle of a deployment…I was alone, and liked my life for that reason alone. The only people I contacted or were close with were my friends now. They were positive, wanting to hear a lot from me. Seeing a fellow Marine down at the mouth, sometimes I would attempt to shed some light, joking around and showing my love through teasing people. I was pretty good at it, as Marines swiftly learn to make fun of anything from race to your overall body structure, and any sign of weakness is insurance that you will get 'picked on'.

Being too close with your brothers also meant arguments from tight quarters. Thankfully, I never fist-fought anyone while I was deployed, but I witnessed many fights that appeared to serve as tension release valves. Things didn't rage out of control, but everyone would provoke a coming fight, like we were in a Roman coliseum, gleefully watching the gladiators go for it. I didn't care; I loved everyone too much, knowing I could lose any one of them at any time, and also knowing the fight would break up in minutes, with differences set aside and something new to talk about around the campfire that night: "Did you see that *punch*? Wow!"

I should mention that we studied mixed martial arts for training purposes, so what better way was there to test our skills? Grown young men with no sexual relations for half a year tend to build up shitloads of testosterone; it makes them into wild-hearted suckers, both day and night. I'd just sit around and give haircuts to Marines, scoring some cigarettes, my own patented method for easy release. Money wasn't available, but the few dudes with cigs passed them my way when I gave them a nice new hairdo – I learned how to do it years ago, and it helped like crazy when I was deployed.

It was a lot like what I've heard about jail, trading skills for a pack of smokes. Other times, I sat on the roofs of local houses we took over, entering a daydream world, observing the beautiful scenery of my native country. Lost in serenity, viewing animals roaming like children without a care, I mused: how could a place with such beauty, full of local wisdom and charm, be at war for unmitigated centuries?

I knew the neighboring countries had influence, but didn't get how Afghan people were able to deny their neighbors and become their own independent country. They regained their independence from Britain in 1919, starting up diplomatic relations with America shortly afterward. Predatory neighboring nations were a fact of life throughout the country's entire history; in its defense, Afghanistan has tried everything from isolationism to outright resistance. But all I ever heard from villagers and so-called 'normal' civilians, was that Pakistan and Iran were seeking an endless war, so they could keep right on sending weapons to their troops and paying off 'our' local people, in order to continue performing the most heinous of acts.

Reflecting, perched on a rooftop like a rooster lording it over his coop, I thought about a villager who had twelve kids to raise. Desperate enough to do anything to feed his growing family, he was wavering on the fence. I told him in Pashto not to sell his soul, which wasn't the answer – dealing with evil people was wrong. Maybe I didn't grasp the whole parent thing, how far a father would go, but morals are simple fundamental aspects that should be recognized at an early age. Knowing what's right from wrong should lead a parent gently into swallowing his national pride and finding another means to make enough money to get by – no excuses.

Many stories differed, but at the end, I thought better decisions could be made; maybe going through thirty years of steady warfare, being uneducated, and keeping overly religious could cause simple decision-making skills to drift out the window with the harsh Afghan winds. The Marine forces I was attached with used to question me frequently about how the villagers treated their women, how the little girls were handled in a Muslim country. But I never won the right answers for them. It was a mystery to me too, about why women were treated like second-hand clothes, worth nothing sometimes in the eyes of their husbands, brothers, and sons.

I already knew that in the Middle East, their views about women were completely different from ours, including their dress codes concerning exposure, but I hadn't realized how bad it was in Afghanistan for women and girls. They were always fully draped, wearing a virtual thick army tent termed a 'burqa' by the locals. You could barely tell they were human beings when they wore those all-enveloping things. Fully covered, they talked to no one but their own families and husbands – which was fine with me, thinking they must be protecting their women, leading to a sense of national pride. I understood how male honor was an issue in times of war and uncertainty, but saw that it was the 'female rights' that deeply puzzled everybody.

Women and girls weren't allowed to go to school. Trudging down a dusty, dirty road one glaringly sunny day, I came upon two young girls, blood-drenched from the neck down, with daypacks for school under their dead backs – tiny throats sliced from ear to ear. A yellowed note fluttering on the ground caught my eye; I picked it up, stifling some extremely heartfelt sniffles. They were *so young*...maybe each *ten years old*...and so dead. The note blared, 'Girls attending school is forbidden, and anyone who tries it will see the same results'. This was obviously done by the terrorists; no one else in the area was that cruel. My pounding heart sunk rocklike into my stomach.

I could smell the girls' bodies decaying in the midday heat, but showed no emotion, as a true Marine should do. I stared insanely into the distance, believing fervently that if I had a chance to slay their murderers, I wouldn't leave any evidence. I'd kill without compunction, no trail leading back to me or the Marines. Now, I truly comprehended why negotiating with the enemy was out of the question; a job such as mine was highly important, concerning *any* young person's life.

Whether in Afghanistan or America, I really thought that jail shouldn't be an option for some 'offences', if they involved taking vengeance against such remorselessly obscene oppressors. Death was the only way to deal with these monsters, and I was okay with their being judged by God for their cruelties, if I was to find them. Two innocent, beautiful girls gone, because they wanted access to knowledge through education to better themselves and their families. They were ready to risk death to endure their dreams, and as I daydreamed on the rooftop, I swore I'd avenge their souls, risking death or anything else if it stood in my way. *They looked just like my nieces!*

From that day on, sleep became problematic. And I saw loads more deaths of innocent, fascinating, funny, kind, proud civilians. I never understood the Taliban, why their way of life was so great and wonderful regarding having sex with little boys and molesting them for years, while shooting women in broad daylight for 'fornication'. It's as though they took a perfectly good religion, twisting it to fit their liking, bringing in a score of false pretenses to justify their blatant acts of sheer idiocy.

These things forced me to be shocked and irate early on in my deployments, and flared me up to the point where I aimed my heart, body, mind, and soul to find any 'bad guys' who I could kill and get away with it. Largely, I seemed to be losing my mind, becoming a cruel killer whose subconscious drove me to believe that certain people were brought down by God into the world to eliminate 'the Devil's helpers'.

Chapter Eight
Becoming a Love Spy

As my first tour reached its anticipated end, the Colonel of our Marine Expeditionary Unit called me into his pristine, air-conditioned and oddly welcoming office. It was so hot in Afghanistan, any reprieve from the all-encompassing powers of the midday sun was fantastic, even for someone born in that country, like me.

The Colonel, a major ranking officer, had heard about me requesting to stay in Afghanistan, even after a relentless, nearly deadly eight-month deployment. So he questioned my motives, while I stared proudly at his uniform, taking into account his full bird eagle rank, thinking how wonderful it was to be called to sit in front of a high-ranking officer in a combat zone. I was finally being found worthy by the Marines of something like a higher calling, possibly for a new mission as well.

Immaculate, the Colonel's desk contained no mound of paperwork on top, just a simple clot of unmovable Afghan desert dust. Ignoring the potential for danger if I stayed on, I told him that I deeply enjoyed what I was doing, being a capable linguist for the Marines, making feel like much more than low-ranking enlisted personnel. Due to the amount of respect I was getting, because I was heavily important to my Marines out in the field, the Colonel avidly begged to know in greater detail about the various things we were going through. He'd only heard everything secondhand, so now he wanted to know an awful lot more.

Some of the higher enlisted men tried to bother him with petty questions, but he simply dismissed them. My being native and potentially foreign didn't seem to bug him any; instead, he was extremely intrigued by my words. I carefully couched things into easy-to-read mental pictures for him; I thought he was trying to collect enough info to see if it all panned out with the stuff he'd heard previously.

By the end of our conversation, he appeared to be satisfied with me. Leaning over, in a deep, strong, and almost overly clear voice, he said, "I needed to hear you speak, in order to thoroughly evaluate you. You seem to be good to go, so I'm going to fully approve this measure. Gunny, get your stinking ass in here!" This was the first time I'd heard a Gunnery Sergeant ordered around like we were, in such a derogatory manner – usually, the Gunny defamed us enlisted dogs. It was all I could do to keep from smirking or laughing out loud; hey, I was getting *noticed!*

"Take Lance Corporal Hotaki here, and handle his needs and paperwork. Make sure everything's set up, and he gets issued a brand-new weapon, because the armor has to handle his back from now on." Speaking up proudly, without any spite for me, the Gunny seemed happy to get tasked, responding with, "Roger that, *Sir!*"

Swiftly leaping to his feet, Gunny probably thought I was going to follow him out of the room. But I made an abrupt about-face at the door, turning back around to face the Colonel at the proper position of attention. "Lance Corporal Hotaki, requesting permission to be dismissed, Sir." Waving in the air offhandedly, he gave me permission granted. Gunny stopped dead in the hallway ahead of me, probably thinking: who does this foreign dude, one of those Hajis, think he is? But it's true that the Gunny followed the Colonel's orders and helped me get set up.

Staying on now, I watched the Marine group I'd entered Afghanistan with, fly away home on a huge C-17 aircraft. Going back to my tent, I had to stand by for the new group to come in a few hours later, soaring via similar aircraft. Reflecting to myself, I heard my mother's voice, saying, "Watch out, son; you keep knocking on the Devil's door, he's gonna answer you, sooner or later." Was I risking too much in this harsh multi-sided, multi-country war, full of grisly explosions and swift death, bringing in unlimited casualties? There are reasons Marines don't stay that long in combat roles, because our deployments are intense, demanding, more tiring than those of other service groups. It pounds a great deal of wear and tear into your mind and your back.

Taking a heavy, deeply dusty breath, I thought about my Drill Instructors and the Sergeant Major, hearing their commanding, stout voices: "Locate, Close Width, and Destroy the Enemy! When the brain fails to comprehend, the body must be punished!" But I couldn't understand much, nor can I tell you here about everything I was assigned to do while in the Marines, as my message can be easily intercepted by hostile outside parties; so I just had to push my body until I could gain the answers to my most devout questions. It was like I was amped up all over again, wanting to meet the incoming Marines as a kind of mentor and 'zookeeper'. I knew that they'd trust me, needing more things than the outgoing group did, and I was highly excited about their arrival. I was going to more than fulfill the role of a big brother to them.

When I joined up with the new unit, I met new civilian interpreters, although I had yet to meet any American linguists – these guys didn't know I was Afghan until I freely spoke Pashto in front of them. Telling them I was born in Afghanistan only brought me disbelief; they thought I'd learned Pashto in the services. But my dialect was proven to be the target language, so nobody could deny me that, as my version wasn't taught in any courses or Marine outlines. The northern dialect of 'Pakhto' only separated the 'sh' pronunciation to a 'kh' pronunciation – I *knew* all this stuff!

I figured we'd be stationed in the same spots as my last tour, but was wrong; things had to keep moving, so I was being uprooted. I learned real fast to let go of old knowledge and to update my information. My Sergeant Major told me once, "Intel is similar to eggs...eggs got a *short* shelf life!" Things that were important yesterday meant next to nothing tomorrow. Meanwhile, to assuage my nervousness, the forward operating bases, the combat outposts, and the patrol bases remained pretty much the same, while people on base continued to have only the essentials available, whether they were male or female. Devil dogs is what we were forced to be, with the girls treated no differently than the boys. And around this time, I began to notice more of the incoming Marine females, support techs, and the civilian or local women, too.

I was proud to wear a uniform by now, more so after meeting up with the American Civilian Linguists, who appeared to feel I'd achieved an incredible amount of work in a very short span of time. I only knew it felt good to carry a weapon, where the rest of the linguists weren't allowed to do so. Called non-combatants, they were brave and courageous in my sights, because they traveled to every dangerous area or zone and weren't allowed to defend their own lives like I was. This was extremely honorable and valorous to me, all by itself. And they asked me why I didn't do it their way, because they were paid radically well for their particular services.

Demand was high, and the job threats were higher still. Soon, they brought in a Female Engagement Team, to set the cultural ties for enabling our women to talk and investigate the Afghan women. Their culture didn't allow for any male, U.S. Marine, or Afghan Army interaction with local Afghan females. Searching houses on a regular basis, we had to 'engage' with females sometimes, especially since the Taliban males would often wear female burqas in order to conceal themselves.

I mentioned the burqa before – they were usually a light blue or darker blue color, draping over their entire bodies, with the only way to see into them being through a small, mesh net covering their eyes. You could only view these ladies' hands and feet, and it was easy for the Taliban men to hide out this way. I recalled my mother's early family photos, and she was never shown wearing a burqa. I thought it was the most miserable thing you could do to any woman

– but female engagement soon brought me a happiness like no other, especially since I couldn't talk to anyone about what I was doing. I had 'top secret' security clearance now, having to keep it to myself about a lot of things. So discussion of my job was out of the question...but what about *love?* With so many females around, what did that word mean to someone like me?

The greatest light in my life came from the lack of available women, not the presence of them. All the men on base out in the field, distant and far away from town, hadn't seen a female for a long time. We tended to crave feminine company, in whatever form we could get it. Things changed fast with the other Marines in their usual offhanded ways, with them showing off to get noticed by both the new Marine women and female civilians, any way they could to get some feminine attention.

I loved it. It made me smile, seeing a female visitor or someone new coming in, making profound changes and new attitudes occur. One day, I noticed a linguist complaining about some small problem, presumably defending her rights. I was always being told how the linguists do things to avoid being tasked to go somewhere, and I heard other putdowns of females on base as well. It made me kind of defensive, as I fondly remembered my sisters who'd tried to help me back home.

This one female complaining linguist – apparently an American – presented a very strong demeanor. Idly observing her, I was distantly fascinated by her ability to not give in or give up on her complaints. She was prattling a mile a minute to a Gunnery Sergeant, and must've been a civilian, I reasoned, as she didn't know what level of respect needs to be given to higher-up enlisted or officer personnel. She wasn't afraid of the Gunny, or willing to back down by any means. I enjoyed her style; she flared up like a popping Afghan firecracker, defending her side of a long-winded story.

Grumbling in disbelief, the Gunny soon gave up trying. I couldn't see this interesting lady up close, as she wore a light red scarf, partly covering her face. Something about her told me that hidden visage was impossibly beautiful, and well worth seeing, if I could just get close up enough to view it. I had no intention of talking with her, mostly from every sharp-pointed kind of mortal terror. To this day, I can't tell anyone my whole story, about my life when I became a spy for the Marines. It's a lot of privileged info. But I couldn't resist seeing this important lady civilian; I needed to play it cool, so I attempted some distant eye contact. I lucked out, as she suddenly waltzed right by me – there she was, right there, across from my line of sight, and I was completely correct. My heart dropped – she was flat-out *gorgeous!*

Big, immaculate, beautiful, blacker-than-night eyes peered curiously into mine. Feeling like I stared into the liquid depths of outer space, I was a kid once again, smiling at her sheepishly, while she cocked her head to one side, saying 'Salam' as an informal greeting. Responding so softly, so sweetly, she moved past me all too quickly, to reach wherever she was headed. I nodded, returning her Salam or hello, and that one aching look back over her shoulder kept me awake all night long.

I entered a point of no possible return; I thought about her every waking minute of every day, how strong, capable, fascinating she was! Someone on her level of beauty shouldn't be anywhere near such an ugly thing as undying war, which is how many people perceive the Afghan conflict. She should be defended by her men, not drawn into this ridiculous service of things like constantly checking out people, peeking into burqas and houses to see if she could discover any hidden Taliban. Being an Active Duty Marine and a full-time spy was daily punishment enough; it boggled my mind to also wonder about...*her.* What was I doing? I didn't really know her – why was I acting like a pizza-faced teenager from middle school?

Weird feelings coursed through my Marine's veins. Was it a simple crush, or was it true love at last? Was I mostly confused, mistaken, abandoned somehow by women enough to daydream about one of them? Heading back to a rooftop, I thought about what qualities a real wife should have, and how I would go about seeking them. Catching myself, I knew I had to be discreet, polite, and truly respectful in every way. Being hot under the collar and bloodthirsty, I didn't think that in place of war something like this could happen. It might be a sign from God; I always believed God set up a plan for me, and I had to read into these matters to find out more. Was it because I was on the road to becoming a remorseless killer, seeking nothing less than blood vengeance? Was God deliberately placing this incredible lady nearby, to show me that love was still a thing I should strive for? Frowning, I knew I had to do some research.

Shama was her blessed, sacred name. She descended on me like a bird of paradise emanating from the skies, her eyes captivating me in one moment's time that I'd recall infinitely, for infinity's sake as well. Back in my past, the 50th anniversary magazine of National Geographic featured 'Sharbat Gul' – her name meant 'sweet flower', as she was displayed on the book's cover. Her picture was taken at the time of the Russian War in Afghanistan, one of the most iconic photos ever published in an American magazine. Oprah Winfrey tried to investigate her, longing to find and discover more about the enigmatic lady on the cover, known to have the most intriguing eyes. Clearly, I had found my own Sharbat Gul in *Shama!*

Wearing a scarlet scarf on her lovely head, showing off her shiny black bangs in the front, she kept me thinking and reflecting on her image. This was a lady wholly set on serving her country – I fell hopelessly in love with her from Day One. I couldn't hide it, or fool myself anymore; I had to enter the reality of this happening, and take on this fervent sign from God straight into my lover's soul.

Seeing Shama a couple more times, I tried hard to play it cool, but crumbled up inside each time I was around her – the funny thing was, she did the same! What did this mean, now? Why was she gazing back at me that way? By then, I figured I was great at speaking, and you know a ladies' man works hard on his appearance. But I never felt love like this before, it was so new to me; she was almost within reach, keeping an arm's length away, casting that look of hers over her shoulder.

She'd cook local food for the team she worked for, which was of course ludicrously welcome next to MRE rations – we all fell madly in love with her. Offering up food, she found me accepting it with a kind of studied glee. Over a short while, I landed the honor of sitting with her and the other interpreters, garnering info from general conversation, never directly asking about anything for decency reasons. I couldn't sit with the local women, not unless they were together for meals and everyone else was showing up. Chow time was gathering time, and there was no harm in that.

On a lonely night, as I searched through the wide array of stars in a cloudless, unlimited sky, I composed my feelings for Shama. It formed into a plan to write her a simple letter, declaring my love for her in a poetic but reasonable fashion – I knew it would either work, or backfire profoundly. Some people hate that method of communication, but it felt like I wouldn't get the elementary school two squares to check off whether she liked me or not. So I groped for a writing utensil among our limited supplies, finally discovering an ancient pen, covered in dirt and muck, which had obviously sat around in the bleaching sunlight for years.

It was down to its last mark, showing through the plastic. My next step involved finding something to write on, as my resources, to sum it up sucked! An empty carton of cigarettes filled the bill; I peeled it oh so slowly around the edges, until it opened up evenly as a flat piece of paper. Slicing off the corner tabs, I had a completely white solid sheet, while the pen took some time to actually release any of its ink. I licked the tip off, uncaring if God knows what nasty germs were stuffed into it; I never seemed so determined to write before. The thoughts rushing through my fevered brain spurted out, like blood bursting from a wounded chest, or a butterfly emerging from its broken, unneeded cocoon. I mustn't lose my train of thought, I reasoned.

Loving poetry, as I mentioned before, and free verse being meaningful to me, I skipped the 'roses are red' rhyming routine. What started to pour forth was pure, whole, and well, and I didn't let my lust or instincts control my feelings. Shama was the one, like I'd known her forever, as she readily related to my job, the war, and our mutual mission in life, the hope of Afghanistan. I had to let her know this. Starting off, I nicknamed her 'Shysta Gul', meaning 'beautiful flower'. Writing in an old-fashioned cursive style, I forced my trembling hands to keep steady, as the ink painfully trickled out, flowing in a belabored, slanted manner. It was similar to the times when I had so much trouble with stuttering, but the pen finally began behaving.

What should I say to mold Shysta Gul into my true love? Marines, in our dress uniforms, cut a profoundly romantic swath...how could I keep it that way?

"Love...is a timeless emotion...that gets our thoughts running for an eternity. It creates a blindness...that is accepted and feels good, regardless of any situation. It deafens us to the point where we can't hear reason or logic. It takes every inch of our control and rationality, and throws it out the window. Love makes everyone we ever knew in life wrong; it can be soft with its warm, fuzzy feelings one day, and then it can turn sharp like a knife, piercing through the main valves in our hearts.

The light love sheds, wakens us in the morning and gives us the peace to sleep easy at night. It can be mad, fierce, can set our blood pressure to boiling, making us sleepless and tired instead. Love carries its dramas, like death carries its fears. Love is like a disease, and once you get it, you're incurable. It has no known antibiotics, and no relief for its pings and pangs. Love is airborne, and tends to catch us at the moment we don't risk looking for it. It lingers in the air, and hides softly in the shadows.

*Love can make you grow wings, and set you to flight –
even when you're not ready to fly. It puts you in the front of
the roller coaster, and forces you to throw your hands up,
when you never wanted to go on such a ride. Love turns
seconds into years, and years into seconds. Love holds a
power no man or woman could ever attain on their own,
because it is always sent straight from God. It can start or
stop a war.*

*Many have fought and died in Love's name, and
everyone can try to explain and translate it, but no one can
really define it as yet. Minds, bodies, hearts have all been
consumed by love; it is the owner of many names, and is
instilled universally down to the atom, as the positives and
negatives ensure a life. And the unexplained things in this
life usually involve love following behind them.*

*The substitutes for euphoria and the things we do to
intoxicate ourselves can easily be replaced by a simple small
dosage of love. Its strength can unite souls to become
everlasting, and even create another helpful soul. Love can
never be denied, and cannot be destroyed, abolished, or
changed altogether. I say now, Shama, that I share a love
with you, which you know; and God has given me this
bounty of love – it is simply you. I will never say anything
more, if I don't receive that present as strongly as it came to
me, but I had to share my gift with you, my love, as you are
my love..."*

I rattled on in a sublimely sentimental style like this, in
as great a length as that cigarette box wrapper would let me.
My writing didn't pause for a second – it was that simple
and honest of an experience for me. Nothing wasn't the
truth, and that was all I could do. I wasn't going to let myself
down, start 'romancing' things, or give any false statements.
And I didn't want a girlfriend or someone just to replace my
loneliness from deployment, which is infamous in the
services. I wanted to truly love, and I wanted it for life,
without ending. Shama was destined to be mine, by any

means necessary, and I promised myself this, second-guessing her a little as that's in my nature.

Soon afterward, I saw her working with the female Marines, for they had missions to engage with Afghans in a variety of hostile environments. They were teaching her about uniforms and wearing them correctly, which she abided by firmly. Marines know it's a great honor to display our outfits, whether they're the familiar dress blues, every particle of them ironed, stylish, and neat, or only our field green khaki costumes. And Shama appeared twice as proud to wear one as a civilian. I really loved it; she was damn *proud* of the Corps, and the role we were playing in serving our country!

When the alarm sounded in the Basic Aid Station, where the injured were usually taken, I jumped up, thinking our patrol base was under attack...I heard plenty of yelling, and things churned into utmost confusion in seconds. Running over to assist with the commotion, I saw Shama blurting her words loudly...darting in and out to help some kids and a blood-covered female local. An interpreter sprawled in the doorway, thinking he was injured – he was only fainting at the horrors of war, which turned out to be a mother and her children. They'd been returning to their house, where an Improvised Explosive Device (IED) awaited them in their own backyard. The cursed Taliban had rigged it to slaughter the entire Female Engagement Team...including Shama!

Breathing heavily, she stayed fearlessly focused on telling the children they were gonna be okay. I helped move the unconscious interpreter, getting him out of the way in order to improve the flow of human traffic. Swooping over us like the angel she was, Shama read the whole stressful situation, taking a moment to smile at me. My heart bled, seeing how strong she was, her unit equally so – they were all a real team, in an environment where women weren't expected to do such crazy things. My poor heart pounded in my mouth, while Shama had me look after the kids.

She held the probably dying mother's hand; shrapnel and jagged pieces of bloody metal thrust out from that dear lady's chest cavity. Pouring out gobs of goo, she thoroughly stained our clothes, while we tried impossibly to keep everybody sane. The mother kept right on calling out for her youngest child, and I could barely stand to look – there was only a small, gory limb wrapped in blood-stained cloth on a table. It was obvious that the baby had been vaporized in the explosion.

There was this one little boy I was forced to comfort, deaf, now, in both ears, while Shama continuously soothed the mother: "The baby will be okay, continue being calm." Long gone, it was yet another victim of the Taliban's irrational tyranny. The boy I held was missing an eye, its socket spilling out blood, with one leg blown off. His Achilles tendon and bone hung on by meat threads, dangling together like shredded wheat. This made me drift in and out of consciousness, daydreaming fervently as I sat there for hours; no, years, watching keenly as the medics came in and did their jobs.

Watching Shama, never making myself apparent, I saw how much she cared, how hard she was trying to help people – with no concern for herself. She and the other women strained mightily to always be an equal asset in the war, and eliminate the stereotypes going with being a female in the field. The guys talked badass about every woman walking on base, saying things like: "They don't need to be here," or "She has sex with anybody, she's a skanky whore." Fact of the matter was that most of these ladies were more skilled than the normal infantrymen, or could save far more lives through their linguist and reporting skills.

A lot of these female interpreters did exactly the same as Shama, but she was the one who got special to me, growing right through my heart. I couldn't let her go. She had two sisters who also worked for the Marines in Afghanistan, and their level of interpreting was on a much higher level than ours, so their jobs didn't entail going outside the wire, like Shama's and mine did. Nonetheless, I was highly honored that those ladies were out there, serving under the bleakest of circumstances. I'd *kill* anyone who called them names, or didn't pay them the greatest respect for their work!

Shama's older sister had a son who came to Afghanistan, working with an elite team of Marines. 0321 – the Military Occupancy Specialty Unit of being a Reconnaissance Marine. This son of hers was called 'Mo', and he grabbed the Marine ego right up, building on it with due speed. He mimicked everything we did, picking up on our lingo, and we all loved him because he spoke impeccable English and knew every Afghan dialect too. He was incredibly useful. He made up one needed asset, and so he became 'expendable at any means', which caused deep respect from me. I grew close to him, as he knew the full story about his Aunt Shama and me.

It was amazing. Shama's entire family seemed ready to serve their country. But Mo's mother talked to me late one night, when we spotted each other leaving the crowded chow hall. Crying and sobbing wildly as she came up to me, emotional as many people can be when they're hard-pressed. She said that Mo was taking on the worst missions, the most risky ones. Dabbing at her eyes daintily with her scarf, she implored me to guide him away from volunteering for death patrols.

I didn't know what to say, thinking her son and I were simply cut from the same cloth, as I too volunteered for dangerous assignments. How could I lead him down a sane, safer path, when I craved to go out on riskier missions than his? Shaking my wooly head, I slowly came out of my thoughts, agreeing to work in an informal manner. I saw Mo the very next day, and we chatted about his heading out, with me offering some sage advice on being what we call a 'hard target' as versus an easy one.

Agreeing to forever remain vigilant and maintain his composure, and to not always volunteer for every suicide mission, he was pretty darned smart for a nineteen-year-old kid, surpassing his peers by light-years psychologically. I did my best to not be preachy, using school slang and cursing like we Marines do, which he liked for no apparent reason. He definitely felt I wasn't overshadowing him, and that I was giving him full respect, which was mutual. I told him how proud I was of whatever he got involved with, considering he wasn't receiving the full Recon Marines training.

His next mission set out the next morning, and I was put en route back to my patrol base, the one Shama was stationed at. Mo didn't know any better, but his mother must've seen something in her dreams that led to her coming up to me in tears, begging for my help. While out on foot patrol, the Marine right behind Mo stepped on an IED, and it ripped both his legs off. Mo flew down ten feet forward – flattened by the powerful blast, swimming around consciousness, he heard the man behind him bellowing in agony, lost to insanely wild screaming. Shrapnel pierced Mo's lower back and arms on his left side. What saved him was an extra backpack full of medical gear the other Marines carried, helping them wrench his organs away from the hot metal.

Mo and the survivors were medically evacuated, their tour ended. He and the other badly wounded Marine survived, but his mother and sisters were devastated. The legless man was awarded the Purple Heart, but Mo got nothing due to being only a civilian – I know they were both heroes, out on the combat field, ready to sacrifice not only their lives but their sanity as well. Awards don't make *the hero!*

Hearing the news from her older sister, Shama rushed to support her family. That's how pure, kind, and noble her heart was. Her nephew was important to her, as she broke down in tears, clinging to my arm in a faithful-seeming way. I let her know I'd do anything I could to support her, if she needed it. They boy's aunt told her she didn't need to leave – the war needed us, and there was nothing else but that.

Mo was hurting, but set to recover, albeit slowly. I spent hours with Shama during what we called 'ruff times', and we bonded, growing ever closer, going out on missions, now together. People assumed we were married; but we were joined at the hip, head, and heart, destined to laugh at each other's jokes. "We'll puke up our buttholes driving through that jungle area," we'd laugh…thinking a death blast would surely occur any second. This was serious stuff, but fatalistic joking kept us alive.

Shama was inordinately shy, speaking furtively to me about her family, due to her great sense of national pride. Letting her pretty jet-black hair down, she admitted how proud she was of me and her being involved with the Marine Corps, in any capacity. She put herself freely into danger for our cause, witnessing firsthand the topmost level of threat every day. I told her she was a lioness, the best thing that crossed my path.

This was my moment, the time to take my place. So I stopped her right in the middle of something she was chatting about, regarding fixing us dinner. "Shama…will you marry me?" It was that simple – she could've said 'no' in seconds.

"Yes!" came back, without a single blink. "Of course I will!"

Skipping a beat, my heart raced along with the dialogue in my head. The way life steers us is crazy. who'd think that 8,000 miles from home, here in the middle of a war zone in the arid, flattened desert, among wrecked buildings made of crumbling sand, that I'd receive my true love's hand in marriage?

Not knowing what else to say, we sat hunched together for a couple of minutes, not saying a word, just looking lovingly at each other. I had no fancy diamond ring, no nice clothes as my dress blues were miles away, and I'm sure we smelled like a Marine's used tube socks. But you couldn't tell that from how we were acting.

Love will hit you at any time. We stared deeply into each other's eyes, lost in the middle of nowhere, knowing that it would only happen for us later, but for the moment we could combine our two souls. That night was the most beautiful one we ever shared, and I could see most of my life ahead with her, watching her cat-like eyes view the millions of stars displayed by a boundless desert sky – unpacked with tall buildings that normally block the view. Nobody could take our sweet love away, though many have tried. But in front of people, we never so much as held hands. Respectful of the codes of both countries we were serving, we carefully made everything secretive between us, until we could make more formal arrangements.

Marriage wouldn't require any fancy headaches, after all. We didn't need to date or go out to expensive restaurants and movies. She didn't need to waste her precious, valuable time on the weird things society tries to make us do before marriage. All she did was to trust her basic instincts, along with me, as we each felt the same way.

Time spun faster than whirling cotton candy, with us getting busy on our respective work teams. Soon, the wretched day dawned when she had to leave me, without our knowing where our next days, or if we'd get to have any, would be. Shama worried incessantly about me, and Mo was still recovering in the States for a short time. Our reality was enabled solely by pure chance, in spite of my weapon and the training, because those things don't begin to help you with the unexpected explosions – you only accidentally walk on them, or ride over them. The main threats and highest casualty counts are totally impossible to avoid. Merely hearing a door slam punches you in the stomach. But I needed to stay alive now, for Shama.

She meant everything to me and secondly, after God, I made my promise to stay on my toes and somehow wend my way home through death itself. Time slowed down to an ant's crawl when we separated, maintaining only telephone contact when we were sent to the major bases, which at least had phone support. Mo got in contact with me almost constantly while in the US, telling me that his mother had nothing but kind words for me, and that his uncles each wished me well.

This was a *fantastic* stepping-stone, as I always told anyone who'd listen about Mo's story of bravery and courage, cloaking my love for his aunt under wrappers. Mo respected me as I was respectful for Shama, and I was incredibly glad to be close with such genuine, wonderful people; he saw how pure and true my love was for her, that she was the light I needed in my heart. Shama was set to be my soul mate.

Wanting nothing in life but her, I committed to doing anything in my power for her, getting on my knees over and over again to thank God for her blessings. Life held a purpose for me now, and I swore that I'd never spend it alone, ever again.

Chapter Nine
Home is the Marine

Afghanistan, in spite of war, is a fascinating place to live –
the hot deserts and cool mountains stretching out
wonderfully wide. It's too deadly nowadays, aside from any
alleged 'peace talks' with the Taliban; and yet, you can
stretch out and sleep peacefully under a spectacularly starry
Afghan sky. But by the end of my fifteenth month there, I
was definitely proverbially homesick. My beard, full, black,
and lushly scratchy, was as horrible as possible, thriving
with mange like a worm-infested, flea-bitten mutt's scruffy
coat. This was not altogether wrong, as I was supposed to
look like, smell like, and closely mimic the enemy, in order
to draw close and get them to divulge their worst secrets.
But it was nasty, painful, and embarrassing to walk around
looking like the Taliban, while I copied their moves and
methods of carrying themselves.

I was far more than ready to go home, thinking that I
might be greeted as a hero or glorified in some way once I
was back in the States. Packing up our things, we troops
needed lots of time to reflect; I felt a little depressed,
favoring mixed feelings. Somehow, it was as if the war
couldn't go on without me! Everyone in the Marines knows
his or her role, and it's lousy to simply drop everything –
only to return to a place where nobody really knows what
you've been experiencing.

All the single bums blabbered about the bars and clubs,
how they were going to beeline there first chance they got,
while the 'marrieds' talked about the Disneyland vacations
they planned to take with their loved ones. But I had none of

these finer feelings; I just kept on thinking about the women and children I was stuck leaving behind. Who'd be there to help the victims? How could I turn my uniformed service back on my own Afghan people? Their screams flowed through my mind, fluxing back and forth in a raging ocean tide of sound, along with visions of blood and gore. A background of rap music seemed to play sometimes, illustrating my hardest times.

Retrograding to America was equally difficult for the rest of those who served during the most heated times and battles of the war. Shama crossed my mind constantly; how I was going to have her hand in marriage soon, the only thing I really looked forward to. Before landing in the US, the long ride home wore on my soul, filling me with guilt feelings dotted with small spots of relief. Whenever I shut my eyes to nap, I heard the rotors on our helicopter churning, and my mind drifted further away, blowing around like the billowing desert winds. Every minute of turbulence caused memories of our soaring into the negative battle spaces, rushing in with armed force weapons, and taking over local compounds. I would jump in my seat, feeling a bullet graze my ear, or a Taliban agent stabbing me – these were only vivid nightmares.

My aching body was righteously sore, from carrying heavy bags mostly, and it affected my dreams and ideas. When the bell beeped to buckle up our seats, or someone else got a request from the flight crew, I startled, envisioning waking up in a truck, hearing similar beeping sounds and noises. The different days and moments passed by each other in my head, mingling like clots of butter melting slowly together.

My Marine brothers and sisters I'd spent tons of time with out in the field returned to their original units; I had to wonder how many of them would remember me, counting me as one of their own. But landing in the state of Maine was incredible, as a clutch of aging veterans assembled at the airport, there to support us troops. Those salty ol' vets from prior foreign wars brought cell phones for us to contact our families immediately, letting them know we were all home safely. And they applauded for us too, as we roared in with our big, heavy green duffle bags, uniforms reeking of sweat, desert dust, and other alien filth...faces glowing through the muck with pride.

Every Marine smiled as we shook those old coots' hands, ecstatic that they cared about us so much. Only expecting a few people, I was shocked to see Maine show its patriotism with throngs of spectators; but mostly I lounged around in the tiny-seeming airport dining facility, so much better off than our mess or chow halls, munching on a long-awaited thick slab of cheesy pizza. No more MRE meals for me! At least, not for a long time, although Afghanistan dwelled on my mind. The sauce from the pizza burned my avid tongue, but I didn't care, chugging down an icy cold fountain drink that sloshed invitingly in my welcoming hand, popping and fizzing in my mouth!

Crowds of veterans and civilians begged us politely if we needed anything, making quick conversation, moving on to the next Marine each time to show how grateful they were for our service. This felt fantastic, until I recalled Vietnam: how their troops were treated by the civilian population. I wasn't born yet, but could review the TV news scenes in my head of witless protestors reviling the returning troops, throwing garbage, rocks, and protest signs at them. I was proud that Americans had come far since then; whether Democrat or Republican, all the civilians showed great respect and love for us, while the war was going strong and showed no signs of stopping.

Just being able to walk on normal floor tiles and concrete made such a big difference to me. Blowing on my neck, the air conditioning brought to mind cool summer breezes, while I heard in my mind the Drill Instructors yelling, "Bring your face to the *chow,* not the chow to your nasty *face!*" Long, stringy mozzarella cheese fell onto my chin, making my taste buds orgasm. I tasted freedom in each bite, didn't want to leave the inviting, awesome airport, but our next flight came up fast. We hung out for roughly four hours there.

Cigarettes ran fourteen dollars a pack in Maine, a steep hike from what I remembered; later on, I realized we were far North, and cigs wouldn't be that much once we got back to good ol' North Carolina. Smokes there were under five dollars. So once home, I smoked them back-to-back like a chimney.

Meeting the officers and enlisted Marines once again at the Helicopter Squadron the next morning, I checked in to show the old crew that I was still alive, handling some needed administrational work before getting set to undertake my combat leave. My Commanding Officer was brand-new on the unit, and so was the Captain in charge. I was deeply hesitant to meet my Direct Commander, but he welcomed me home with open arms – a big, fat, hairy grin splayed across his clean-shaven face.

Hailing via Louisiana, he was a giant linebacker who knew everything about me from my records, which led to a truncated, brief introduction. I guess my staying in the unit called out a lot of 'talk' about where I was, what I was doing. My CO told me that the Sergeant Major had described a Marine en route back to the States from a long deployment tour, going by the call sign 'Gumbo'. Grumbling, the DC said I had to take combat leave immediately, seeing that I was highly 'wired'. I didn't know what he meant, keeping up my end of our conversation. Highly intelligent, he was a strong, capable leader, one I was glad to enjoy while returning home; he glibly said that he was proud of me, and that I would be the Senior Corporal in the Logistics shop.

But before I could tell him anything much, a loud, vicious voice rang out from the other end of the long, vibrating, metal-lined hallway. It was my dearest *sweetie,* the Sergeant Major, giving out the loud war cry of 'EEEEEE*yuuuuuuuttt!'*

Glancing quickly at my Captain in charge, I knew he already saw what I had to do, so he smirked, saying we'd talk later on. Grinning, I yelled back at the Sergeant Major, running straight at him, saying, "Corporal reporting as ordered, *Sgt. Maj*!" Nothing had changed with him; no matter how many tours I underwent, he was more respected than I ever was, for always having and doing more than I did. Well, at least he didn't give me a big bear hug or wet kiss on the cheek; he merely gave me that hate stare of his, up and down and sideways, snarling, "Get the fuck into my office!" I wasn't looking for a hand job, nor did I need any sweet, tender loving. The Sgt. Maj. knew it because he went through it, many violent times before. I just needed that good ol' tough love, and so he ordered me to have a seat as I stood in front of his desk, once again at the desired position of attention. Silently, he poked at the buttons on his computer and phone for messages, being in his sweaty physical training uniform, returning from a long, health-inducing run. Once he spoke, I was ready for any questions.

"Listen, Corporal, I will ask you this only once, and you better not *fucking* lie to me, or else I will destroy you slowly: when was the last time you slept for more than three hours?" Brought up short, as his tone had turned somewhat to concern, everything that came to me flew out the window. Not knowing how to answer, my eyes flared up, giving a non-verbal gesture of straining for an answer.

So he slammed his meaty fist on his big, wooden desk, spouting, "Exactly!" Speaking with a firm voice, he stated, "You're fucking *wired,* Corporal! So wired, you dunno you've been in transit for more than 72 hours, and you can't even remember your *time of sleep*? This is exactly why I wanted you to come home *sooner*."

Completely confused, wondering what the hell this had to do with anything in reality, I finally vented my frustration. "Sergeant Major, I am *fine,* just happy to be home, that's all…"

"No," he shouted. "You're wired, on *crack* right now! These are your first signs of post-traumatic stress disorder (PTSD)!" Nostrils flaring, breathing growing heavy, I still had no real response for him. He witnessed my confusion, calming down, saying, "I see you dodged the bullets and explosions, coming back in one piece."

Lying somewhat, I said, "Yes, Sergeant Major, I'm fine and feel outstanding," straining to let him know I had no such stupid symptoms. But he entered a hail storm of questions, making me snap my replies loudly at him, like gunfire on a game show. I was being tested for my knowledge as he leaned over, stopping me, telling me that good things were forthcoming on the way.

Having no idea of what he meant, I hoped there was an award or two in this for me – apparently the Sergeant Major hears and knows all, no matter where his Marine is at any given point in time. His final question was whether I'd spoken to the Gunny in administration about my combat leave. I responded that I hadn't, and he screamed again, "Gunny, get your ass in here!"

The Gunny rushed in, with, "Yes, Sergeant Major, what can I do for you?"

"Handle Corporal's leave, quick, fast, and *in a hurry!* As for you, Corporal, go back to D.C. and see your family – don't be loitering around here, telling *war stories* and all that *shit!"* Smirking snidely, he then yelled, "Get the *fuck* out of my office, Devil Dog!" Unbelievably, his behavior meant that he held the greatest respect for me in my profession, or at least that was what I was being led to think.

"Roger that, Sergeant Major!" I roared, a bit limply.

Stepping over to the old Logistics shop where I'd first started, I thought my time was growing close to getting out of the Marines. I met the other enlisted personnel in the shop, and my Captain introduced them, in a line all together. They glared at me weirdly, as I was wide-eyed, beat down, and scruffy looking. I'd at least managed to get a quick shave in, and my mangy Taliban beard was long gone – but they seemed a little fearful as I spoke sternly to them – three female Marines and two males. Last I could remember, it had been just the Captain and me in that office.

This bunch was their own crew, and I was utterly new to them. It seemed like I'd been away for too long; it was hard for me to talk normally again, instead of sounding like a robot landing straight from Mars. Anyway, they paid full attention to me, settling me in real quick and giving me the 'warm and fuzzy' approach. The part freaking me out most was that they all used only first names to refer to each other. This was way, *way* beyond my norms list, and I tried to put a stop to it immediately.

I was just about ready to check out of the unit for combat leave when I realized I needed to go see the medical officer, which led to a world of amazing, disconcerting new matters. There, they performed all types of tests for Marines coming home; but when I complained that I'd received a slight injury in Afghanistan, the doctor got awfully worried. I'd only sprained my knee; coughing, he insisted I get an MRI, stating that something didn't look altogether right. I didn't think it was anything that bad, but finally had to admit that I'd been hiding a little something to myself.

There was that day I'd been in the mountains, and we Marines fell into a battle, fighting back with casualties against a much stronger Taliban force. It continued sinking into my mind, as I stood in front of the doctor – the time I was absolutely gonna die. In the middle of a mountain-top's slippery slopes, firing my weapon at an invisible enemy, I sprawled, tumbling down a small cliff, dodging repeatedly rapid fire. My buddy Eric and I were the only two left on the mountain, against a savage group out to kill us, knowing our gun force was on the other side of the mountain, capturing those of the enemy who fled. The Taliban were gutless cowards, always fighting at a good distance, running into nearby fields, pretending they were peaceful farmers to get away.

When I fell, I dropped from a pretty short height, roughly ten feet – but with the amount of gear strapped on me, it made things intensively dramatic. And who knew what a fully automatic 7.62 caliber rifle could do in the way of damage; but I wasn't gonna wait around to find out! Whizzing 'ping' noises right past my eardrums, dirt flaring up in patterns alongside me – these things told me I was being shot at directly.

Lying there at the base of a cliff, my M4 rifle had gone one way, and my radio to somewhere else. Groping around in mounting panic, finding both items in the bushes, I did my level best to call my platoon leader, rallying them back in for our support. Seeing Eric, I flipped him a hand gesture, locating some small manholes – wide enough for the enemy to crawl into and shoot at us. Red-hot sparks flying from front-end barrels were our signs to see where the gunfire spewed from; meanwhile, Eric, outstanding 'war pig' that he was, handled his own shooting skills precisely, killing two Taliban charging straight downhill and trying to close in on me.

Dazed, I knew I had to get up and assist Eric. I raced over to some plant cover, not even feeling the damage to my knee, and began unloading magazine after magazine; but all of the shooting suddenly stopped. We frog-leaped down the hill, one after the other, to get each other's back and keep safe. Eric was hitched to get married, so I planned to never let my good friend down – if anyone got hurt, it'd be me. But Eric thought the same way, while we were each putting our lives in more danger than we could realize. Coming up short, I found I'd lost a top secret cell phone carrying vital info, as it got away from me during my fall, screaming, "I have to *go back,* Eric!"

The enemy, once they had possession of the phone, would take out names and info they'd use to kill several Marines and civilians. I couldn't let that happen, so I launched my hurting body straight uphill, to find it – along with this 'brave' move came an array of gunfire, straight at me – they must've thought I was suicidal. But I found the phone, lying there covered with pebbles, in the rubble of the mountain rocks.

Grabbing it up, I sprinted to a happily available services truck which came onto the scene through some miracle. The platoon leader had enough of my actions, roaring at the tops of his lungs: "You will obey *orders,* Roc! You will *not* run into enemy fire unless *ordered* to do so!"

With no breath left, I squeaked, "Roger that, *Sir!"*

Our side stood our ground, firing at the enemy from the trucks which had gracefully appeared, further air support rushing in minutes later. All these things flashed through my head in one second, as the doctor expressed concern about my injury. It only swelled a little; I'd walked on it freely for six months. But gamely, I went to get my MRI; once it was reviewed, they stated that my right knee had taken internal damage. I sported a torn anterior cruciate ligament, torn meniscus, torn cartilage, and my tibia or lower leg bone was bruised badly, all the way down to the shin.

"Sorry, son," Doc soothed me. "We have to do surgery...tomorrow."

Hell, *no!* I wanted to go right home, but this had to be done. I didn't understand; how could I walk around for half a year with this? The doctor said it was normal, it's only a bit painful, but I remembered only complaining vaguely until I got used to it over time. I guess the Marine saying, "Adapt and Overcome," got to me. But the Marines weren't going to keep me unless I had this surgery done. And if it didn't heal fast, they wouldn't let me get released after my active duty time ended.

I'm hugely grateful to the kind doctors and my friends from the shop, who took great care of me, looking out for me during my times of worst pain. My new pals in the Helicopter Unit, Natalie, Adam, Tara, Bryan, and Jessica were there for me constantly, whenever I felt weak, brittle – like a sick ol' Taliban scurvy drone. These people were living 'stateside' Marine lives; having civilian traits could be a good thing. I learned plenty from them, and will forever remember them as my best friends.

Meanwhile, Eric returned to the States, recommending a Navy Achievement Medal with a Combat Valor for me – due to my charge up the mountain to fetch that important cell phone. But I was mostly concerned with walking normally after my successful surgery. A Three-Star General in Afghanistan signed off on the award – he put me in for it a few minutes after the fight ended. Gleaming, the medal was pinned neatly onto my breast pocket in front of my unit, my Sergeant Major, and Eric. I didn't feel like a hero for some unknown reason, like I hadn't done anything beyond usual expectations. But the Marines were congratulating me now, shaking my hand one after the other, like well-mannered ducks in a row.

Unable to let me get ahead of him, the Sergeant Major boasted on how he'd won the same exact award back in his early days. I was duly fascinated, having yet to hear about many of his courageous acts. The Marine Corps, though you wouldn't know it from us, is a service branch that doesn't hand out awards easily – rightfully so! I honestly didn't understand why I'd gotten one of that stature, as so many others had done far more than me. Supposedly, it's because others view your acts as beyond what you can imagine by yourself, when you think about it.

Well, that was the size of it. I headed out finally, buying scads of things at the Commissary, our local one-stop shopping spot on base, leaving the unit for my time actually at home – spending it with my family. I had to prepare for marriage, ready to see Shama again, as her civilian contract ended at around that time. Not telling the others in my unit about our wedding plans, I was going to make it into a stupendous surprise. I spent what little time I had with her, doing my main rehabilitation back in my home state of Virginia, ready to ask for her hand formally in front of her family. To my vast surprise and satisfaction, they instantly accepted me as their incoming son.

Having saved some money from deployment, the time was right. Shama and I got hitched in Virginia, without a big, formality laden, or spectacular wedding. We just wanted to start our lives together, keeping things simple and our vows heartfelt. Shama was incredibly excited about her homecoming to Jacksonville, North Carolina; but I told her it wasn't anything worth bragging about. Needing a vacation, I had a few days, so once we got the chance, we flew to Cancun, Mexico for our honeymoon. It was the best time I've ever had! Cancun was a paradise on wheels; we hadn't a worry in the world, next to what things had been like in Afghanistan, of course.

Taking our subsequent days slow and pleasant, as she'd worked far harder than me, we were so proud of each other – we could converse on any subject, and it made complete sense to both of us every time. The warm, richly Mexican air ran its soft hands over us as we laid out tanning on the beach; this made me realize there was such a thing as life after the war – God didn't need me to get killed yet. I could take it easy, and Shama repeated our axiom that when you work hard you must also play hard. But after multiple miles through mountain ranges, I couldn't comprehend relaxing, eating steaks every night, sipping a bottled Corona, and doing nothing. The words of the Sergeant Major floated on the wind: wait, it will come to you, maggot.

He'd really told me nothing more than, "Corporal, if you take those shots once at the bar, you'll feel good for a while; later on is when you're drunk as a skunk." Maybe I was feeling too good – the rest would sink in eventually. My lovely wife caught me dazing off somewhere, sometimes, snapping me sweetly out of my daydreams. To me, everything was talk, talk, talk; I always lived by the 'movie rule'. One person will tell you that a movie totally sucked, but until you watch it you can't judge it, because often when they said it sucked, I thought it was brutally awesome. I handled my entire life in this exact same manner.

Also, I had yet to know what PTSD was, until I saw it in action. To me, it sounded like a sign of weakness, a way for people to feel sorry for themselves. As our wonderful, too-short honeymoon came to its end, we heard about a kid who killed himself before returning to our unit. So we held a ceremony, and the Chaplin, or some active military officer Clergyman, said his words and listed briefly some very awful sounding suicide statistics – I had no idea the numbers were that large. Apparently, service members were offing themselves in *droves!*

Rising to his feet, the Sergeant Major called out a couple Marine names, and they stood up at the position of attention, replying they were present. At the end, the SM called out the dead Marine's name, getting no response. He called it off several times, as if he stubbornly insisted there should be an answer. It was still quiet, as my heart sunk, and I recalled the ramp ceremonies in Afghanistan for my fallen brothers. The thing that hurt the most was that dreaded name being called out repeatedly; it made me focus on what had happened, and it dug deeply into my Marine's soul.

The sound of the Death Horn or Taps doesn't affect me, viewing a dead body or bodies doesn't get to me, but the stubborn calling out of a fallen Marine's name will forever haunt me. That wasn't the first or last ceremony for a deceased serviceman who committed suicide, for the hardest thing for us is to deal with is what we went through during the war, or to find someone we can talk about it with. Many, such as me, can't speak about our involvement due to security reasons; but most of us simply have trouble mentioning anything to others. These dark secrets eat away at the returning service troops' insides, etching into them the acid of echoing memories.

One time, we were called to investigate a dear friend of mine, who'd been deployed with us in Afghanistan, as someone caught on that Dan was going to hurt himself. We were taking classes with lessons concerning the signs of mental disturbance, so we were able to go check on Dan, knocking on his door late at night. No one answered; we pounded away, thinking he might be asleep, but somehow I didn't believe it. Going over to a window, I tapped on it, calling Dan's name out. Worried sick, I lightly edged the window up. The curtains caught a draft of air, letting me see inside.

My heart stopped beating, for Dan's feet were sticking out of the kitchen – he was unconscious on the floor! Turning around, I yelled to Corporal Roman, wrenching open the window and squeezing inside, screaming Dan's name at the tops of my frozen lungs, over and over again! When I reached him, he was pale, stiff as a board, his high and tight haircut flawlessly intact, his shirt tucked in. You can always tell a Marine; even relaxing at home, not a hair or piece of his clothing was out of place.

Well, he wasn't relaxing, he was…gone. Roman, screaming, "What's the matter?" stepped forward, diving onto Dan's body. Crying and shouting epithets, he asked Dan if he was okay, obviously in shock – unlike me, he'd never seen a dead body before. Holding back sobs, I scanned the area to see what Dan had used to kill himself. There was a bottle of pills scattered on the floor, so he must've overdosed.

Calling the emergency line and then my Commanding Officer and the Sergeant Major, I decided not to mess with anything inside the house, for forensic reasons. I also needed to calm down the others, especially Roman. He wouldn't let up, though I stared at him somewhat harshly and tried to hold his shaking body down. My trauma levels for experiencing death were higher than his, being fresh from Afghanistan; I thought about Dan's family, going into my 'zone'. My ears always go deaf for a couple minutes, as my blood pressure drops too. Somewhere in the distance, Roman was performing a shrill tirade against the Taliban or something; but during this time I spied a note on the table, not wanting to touch it. Highly puzzled, I couldn't take my eyes off it, slowly reading it and discovering that it was poetry composed in a letter.

Death Poem by a Suicidal Marine

Finally, back home but all alone 0300 awake and in the zone
Cold chills run down my vertebrate bone, 13 missed calls on my iPhone.
The TV's on with media cameras and microphones
Anchors are talking like we lost drones but they weren't unknowns.
My life, was it really meant to be this way? Stressed out I smoke cigarettes all day.
I pray I should've been dead, floating in the clouds – yea, I'm proud
Bred from a wolf pack mixed with night owls

The memories of burnt flesh and bloody towels
Life turned out to be...so foul.

"My adrenalin was amped up, about 1200 watts. We marched in staggered columns like some battle-ready robots. Woodland camouflaged backpacks on the side, strapped one sleeping cot. The choppers had gone in its time to bust some shots. All day, I heard heavy rounds, blown-out ears, deaf from too many loud sounds. My mind isn't right, state life is just a long-ass tunnel, but no damn light..."

Just tell everyone I will be all right.
Under my pillow, I keep a monster Rambo type knife.
This letter is for my beloved son and wife.
Tell them I can't stay here, because I fear my devil is near.
Sometimes flashes of suicide, late night I grab the keys and take a ride.
Why my ball cap is always low and why am I always trying to hide?
I think about all nine and why they had to die.
My brothers are on my mind, every single stride.
Moving on is hard – I fucking tried!
Now it's time, like Hammurabi's Law, an eye for an eye.
My Devil Dogs, I cry for your loss, fallen but not lost.
We sacrificed at any cost.

"So much isolation mixed with devastation looking in the corner and their seats are still vacant. Why do I have so much aggravation, and no fucking patience – and how is that God gave me the right to take his own creation?

They won't and can't *ever* come back! Every way I turn, it seems like a damn trap – and yes, emotion is what I lack. Fuck everyone, my best friend is now a bottle named Jack. Relapse after relapse, and no one can fill these gaps. My men taught me real life facts; we had each other's backs. Fuck, frustrated, I'm about to collapse, what the hell am I going to do with medals, ribbons, and plaques?

My warriors learned killing as an art, and warriors, your names forever are engraved in charts. Hand salute, the 'Colors' fly for you, my brave hearts. I'm sorry; this inner dialogue is ripping me apart. This liquor and brew has me thinking non-stop about my team and crew. Guess what John, your little son, he just turned two. Who knew that your little brother joined the Corps too? Black combat dog tags and the shrapnel is still embedded here in your last name, Calvin James.

Right around now, you would've been promoted new E grade. Reality, or is this a stupid game of the untamed? Blurred vision non-stop, just thinking about that rocket, and in my back pocket I carry Sam's ripped bloody Gore-Tex jacket fabric. I guess this is what it means to be posttraumatic. Helpless, I can't breathe like an asthmatic, bipolar but can't unmask it. Tom, it's hard for me to smell burnt clothes or plastic. Don't ask if my fucking deployments were fantastic, no just tragic, harsh, and drastic.

Yeah, I'm sure you don't like my answer, then you shouldn't have asked it.
Think – is it your friend in the casket?
Tell me why my brain can't surpass it!
I'm going to be ok because now my body is flying
No more crying,
And no need for lying,
As my brain starts spiraling.
Euphoria has come…as I start dying.

Frowning, my brow furrowed, I noticed the letter mingling with my tear drops splattered on it, after reading every single line and vowing to remember it, knowing all too well about every single thing Dan had been going through. I finally wept, not for Dan's stiff, dead corpse lying right behind me, but for his living soul, crying out to us in this carefully composed soulful poem of a letter.

Roman darted to the door, calling out to the ambulance. A parade of medical personnel stomped in, so I took up the letter, kissing it, praying for Dan's soul to be forgiven by God for his transgressions – if there truly were any. Bending down, I put my hand on his forehead, said another prayer, and kissed his cheek dryly, telling him softly that I'd see him on the other side someday. Maybe soon. I gently closed his eyelids, briefly protecting his bright, blue eyes. They'd already faded away.

Catching a sob in my throat, I stuffed the note into a back pocket of my jeans, keeping it secret, so the media wouldn't run amuck with the story, using it to embarrass Dan or his family. They'd never be able to understand any of this. But I planned on giving it to his wife, and copy it for our command later. I read it over carefully two more times before I turned it in, and that poem of death would ride to the grave with me, as I promised myself repeatedly.

To me, Dan was lost somewhere else, stuck in his own thoughts. I felt for his family, wishing them the best, trying hard to get them over to the family advocacy group, so they'd get the proper kind of assistance. Roman, oddly enough, was able to move on right away, but it was harder for the rest of us, as we realized how true the stories we heard were now, coming your way when you least expected them.

Too late for Dan; like in the war zone, we didn't want to leave a Marine behind. But this time, there was no way in Hell to save him, something we'd never forget, though I promised myself that I'd find a way to avenge his death. I was right about that, but tucked the letter away...this is the first time it's been read by strangers.

Chapter Ten
Intro to the Agency

"Shut up! You don't know *anything,* woman!"

This was one of my lighter-side comments, after suffering through months of depression and anguish over Dan's death and other, similar matters. I argued incessantly with Shama, while my time dwindled down in the Marine Corps; I flared up multiple times for no good reason, really.

Shama, aware of what I was going through, stayed silent, helping me on numerous occasions. Instead of arguing back, she'd rub my shoulders, purring softly, insisting that I calm down, and then not paying attention to me when I yelled unbelievably rotten things in her ear. You couldn't ask for a better, more tolerant spouse; she was always there for me, understanding about the adverse impact from the war. But I felt like a total pile of crap at home, yearning to return to Afghanistan and help those people; some part of me was convinced they'd die without my assistance.

Everyone but Shama thought I was losing my mind, asking me frequently how I was doing, apparently afraid I would end up like Dan, sooner or later – dead as a doornail from my own hand – someday. To help me in my journey, my unit strived to land me a better job, one involving me heading into a counter-intelligence billet, rewarding me with a huge money bonus if I resigned from my Afghanistan military contract.

Confused, faced with deserting my 'home' country in order to better my family, I frantically talked with Shama, who said I could do a lot more if I left the military, being worth far more in civilian life. So I ended up denying the

Marine Corps, mostly because I'd grown older and had undergone extensive knee surgery. Having to face facts dead on, those physical tests were getting to be quite a struggle. My Sergeant Major, however, saw things differently, sitting me down across from his perfectly squeaky-clean desk after confabbing with my Commanding Officer. The SM wasn't thrilled about my decision to leave, spouting that my physical scores were 'beyond good enough' for my age and training levels.

Not liking the spreading confusion I experienced, I told him, "Sergeant Major, you once ordered me to never lower my standards...I need to pass those scores and tests with absolutely flying colors..."

Blasting at the speed of light, the SM blared, "Shut your mouth, *Corporal*!" I froze in place, knowing what would come out loud and proud after that first blurt of my SM's wit and wisdom. "Listen, Corporal, you're good fucking *gear* (he plainly thought of me as a commodity, not a person), and my Marines have a stock *demand* for that!"

Never having heard myself referred to that way before, I decided to memorize the word 'gear' and use it on someone else later – hopefully not my wife! And I maintained my listening posture, but the SM was tired, not wanting to fight with me anymore. He knew that Corporal Hotaki was getting old, and that the system isn't made to serve maturing Marines like me. I was set to leave, staying on as a civilian; he couldn't argue, realizing that if I returned to Afghanistan, I'd be serving with bigger, better teams, and would be utilized on a far greater scale than he himself had ever been used.

Taking a long sigh, much like a drag on a busted ol' cigarette, he said, "Corporal, if that's what you want...c'mon over here and shake my hand. I'm proud to have known an excellent Marine such as you." Slowly, I rose, shaking my Sergeant Major's sweaty hand for the last time, feeling mostly overwhelmed – not because he was such a tight leader in our unit, but for what he seemed to think about me as a person.

My last days in the unit went well, and I got my DD214, the paperwork for ending active service in the Marines. Glancing it over, profoundly shaken by the turn my life had now taken, I felt proud at least about the words Honorable Discharge – written plainly in bold typeface. I'd done it, becoming a Marine and paying my country's dues; I had greatly loved it, learning tons of things I'd never be able to forget. But it was clearly time to move on, going forward with my new family's life.

Supporting me all the way, Shama accompanied me back to Northern Virginia, letting me go home again – which I didn't think would ever happen. I was so sure I'd be killed or maimed in Afghanistan, but I was going home in one whole, albeit shaken, piece! Less than a month went by while I ended active service, and I was suddenly in another government job, hired out as a contractor linguist, much as my wife had worked before. This told me it was going to be a matter of doing another tour, back in the saddle again, while Shama and I settled into a profound, non-argumentative silence. During this time, we were blessed to find out we were set to become parents – just as I was leaving for deployment, once again, to Afghanistan.

Now I had to worry twice, no, three times as much as before, although things were a bit more relaxed for me as a civilian contractor. But I had to undergo the loss of respect, no more wearing a uniform, with the troops out in the field, not really liking the contractors, too. We made more money for doing virtually the same jobs as them, but I was proven to be right about my new missions, starting to do things at a much higher speed, with different and much better trained new groups.

Stomping through Afghanistan, venturing into wildly new provinces, I was moved around everywhere by the Corps. I woke up multiple mornings not knowing where I was, or even which side of the war I was actually on. Flashbacks from previous deployments slid snakelike through my brain, as I lived off energy drinks, coffee, and cigs; it just wasn't the same as before – nobody knew now that I'd ever been a service member, as my close comrades of before were utterly missing. Strict work schedules made things impossible at first, seeing other service members who worked under completely different rules than the Marines. Swiftly, I picked up on the new jargon, later discovering that it wasn't the civilian contractors' fault, it was my own stupid ego leading me to think that because I'd been a Marine, I supposedly knew more about our work.

I'd overhear stuff people mentioned about the Marines, deciding to accept the competition and not get bent out of shape, changing my outlook; my new teams eventually opened up to me, while the jobs got harder and harder as the days trickled by, desert sands blowing back up the hourglass, making time longer for me. Of course, the war hit its own turbulence, all over again, with the burning of holy books and the religious men lashing out at women and girls. I hated those people, also the ones in the States who were safe, having freedom of speech to back them up.

Mostly, some American idiot burned a holy Muslim Qur'an, uncaring about the repercussions on our troops' safety. This is not a gigantic wrong in itself, but not caring about the effect on our armed forces, doing something to put us all in danger – this is the most abhorrent of evils. I despise those who ignore us when we're abroad, serving both them and their country, who can't keep their simple opinions to themselves; they're only media whores, while we're biting the dust on a daily basis.

Society's losers, no one remembers their names – hoping that one day, they can use religion to strike anger into the minds of those they've won over – they only get negative results, making the overall situation much worse, every time. We don't need that kind of 'newsy' drama when people's lives and limbs are at stake!

Anyway, as a contractor, I was meeting other civilians, creating a vast new network of great people and wonderful job opportunities, learning about the support missions that 'civvies' got when joining the Department of Defense. I knew I must make something happen with my job soon, so tired of being out in the field, months at a time, with no end in sight. There must be better positions, I realized, so I learned all the languages I needed up to the government's top levels of translation. I had the necessary skills and experience, and could burrow into a major base office job!

Through with 'playing Rambo', I met a couple folks who guided me to the right contacts, pinning down a much higher level role with an intelligence background. That was my right line of work; I dismissed my civilian contract, as you're allowed to do that, not like in the military where you usually have to complete it. The nice thing about contracting 'at will' was you didn't get any negative repercussions. I spent my time, six months in, coming right back out without missing a blink. Shama, having gone through it before herself, took this in stride, agreeing to it for the time being.

Able now to spend more time with her, I gleefully noticed that she was six months into her pregnancy, appearing to glow, looking every bit as beautiful as before. She went to stay with her mother, to make things easier for me. Groaning playfully about leaving her again, I told her it was a six-month break time in our marriage, happily chucking her lovely chin. The pay was so high, she couldn't dispute me on it, as it would only help our family to be doing so much better and in a much safer way.

Coming back again with a totally different company, I met a charismatic younger gentleman on one of the forward operating bases, named Chuck Star. He was a former active duty Marine, an enlisted Sergeant who'd mounted his own back-to-back tours in Iraq, leading him further into the war in Afghanistan. He showed no signs of weakness to me, being highly outspoken, and I observed Chuck cautiously – he presented lots of good qualities, and I admired how much we resembled each other when we spoke. He was forever straining to impress you with his fine words, bending over backward to make you feel welcome and liked. Clearly, he was a strong, capable leader, which made me want to learn more about him, encountering exactly who he was.

Well, he made a charismatic ladies' man, standing straight up six feet three inches, an all-American dude with blue eyes and a smooth, Elvis Presley-style persona, greeting anyone who jumped in front of him with a big 'Hallllooooooo!!!' This was my type of guy, and I drew closer to him, to see if I could learn anything new. He ended up taking over the team leader position, becoming my boss in the intelligence field – which I unfortunately can't discuss in a lot of detail, as mentioned before. But I was finally moving up, from all the mountain climbing, long patrol walking, MRE barf eating, sore muscles, boot rot fungus feet, bullet dodging, IED alert butthole puckering, no showers or baths, extreme weather conditions, sleepless nights, no real bathrooms…you name it, if it was good, it was gone, if it was bad we had it in spades. Now, I enjoyed a much improved deployment life, needing to research this side of things and see what I could accomplish, helping to serve my country on a much higher level of personnel.

Mostly, I met with the big provincial and district governors, including their higher-ranking Afghan Army people and police officers, needing to use a greatly improved set of linguistic skills. Loving what I brought to the table, they totally supported me, and Chuck and I grew closer every day; we hung out late nights on his second deck's balcony, talking about the amazing things we had in common. He was always looking around, and you could see his brains moving whenever you spoke to him, noticing his impatience to get in his own response.

Through Chuck, I learned that smart people have plenty of good things to say, but those who listen attentively and speak at the proper times, who carefully gauge the correct moments to speak, are the ones people desire close conversation with, making it much easier for me to communicate with Afghan officials. Great speakers and conversationalists go full out to pull a fantastic story from you, one strand of yarn at a time, just to learn something they never noticed or understood before.

Chuck exhibited everything you could imagine as the righteous qualities of a noble, caring leader, working on his physical image every time for the good. As a tall man, he did seem to need to add some muscle to his gaunt frame; shortly, I told him that I used to be a gym trainer, coaxing him into working out with me. He thought initially, that I was too small to lift heavy weights, going into shock when he saw me bench press 225 pounds ten times, like it was light as a feather. I reassured him, casually mentioning that I'd been lifting since my early twenties, teaching him more specific exercise moves. I showed him I could talk and move fast, while he absorbed everything that interested him like a gigantic but skinny looming sea sponge.

I didn't realize at the time that it was because Chuck was a spy. He boasted four other legal names, playing four different character roles, elaborating on how he thought I could be perfect within his three-letter agency. I knew he was part of something big, but not that he was a full-blown spy, befriending me mainly to recruit me. Looking into my paperwork, he'd checked over my clearance and background, asking if I was interested in following him into his 'course of maneuvers'. Chuck never got around to telling me his real name, and I never expected him to do so. But after the day he admitted to being a spy, letting me in on the ground floor, I told myself to be highly cautious of the people I interacted with, extremely careful when it came to sharing privileged information. I needed more time to think about things.

Meanwhile, Chuck and I carried on with our daily tasks, which amounted to trying to catch the bad guys on both our parts. Learning about how he worked, I slowly became conscious of things that people in our organizations said, after he told me about a couple of important matters. I figured he was more than smart enough to fool me, so that meant that I would have to bow down in respect, same as if he was older than me in my family. I didn't know yet about how the three-letter agency worked, or what the method of joining it was; but every moment passing by with Chuck made the job more intriguing to me. I thought deeply about my life, how it would change my outlook to become a spy, thinking about the intriguing things I would get to do – helping to capture more bad guys, assisting my country in ways no one would ever find out about, probably.

Considering myself to be an 'old salt', ribbons, plaques, and medals were literally the furthest crap from my mind…as you grow up in the war zones, you realize the truth about the 'fresh boots', mere posers who want the glory and the trophies. I didn't care if a Four-Star General awarded me anything; for what, serving my country in some dangerous manner? It was normally like that anyway – why care? My particular egotism was fulfilled by any new challenge coming my way, so I told Chuck one night to give me his contact info. Strangely enough, he demanded that I put him down as a reference; I didn't know if he was just being helpful, looking for a special bonus, or had been scouting me for a potential spy the entire time he enjoyed spending with me.

Well, I said lots of good things about Chuck, whatever his real name was, not thinking or caring about his being a spy. I only take in what I see, like most Afghan-Americans, reading between the lines in conversations. Sometimes it's better to trust the other person, fully accepting whatever they have to say. I gladly agreed with Chuck, thanking him for his assistance in noticing something useful about me, and he mentioned how not only did I have the crucial skills of speaking the war's target languages, being a person who loves to talk with people, but that I was also taking a major step upward – beyond the purview of most normal, ordinary citizens.

In his sharp, harshly northern Ohio accent, he told me lightly, "Believe it or not, Farid, many people get the jitters and freeze up when talking in front of crowds, or when speaking outside of their comfort zones." I agreed, nodding and actively listening, and he continued, "Take the chance when it arrives; maybe I was the person to fool you into seeing this life at more than one angle. See, Farid, we're cut from the same cloth, born twice in this life...once involuntarily from the womb, and again into reality, when something happens in life that wakes us up."

This was beginning to sound like the first Matrix movie, but I just said, *"Damn,* Chuck, that's deep!" Like me, he only wanted to play verbal chess games, analyzing a person and bringing closure quickly to see if you have enough info to keep things moving. He smoked cigs, and also like me, he'd stare into an imaginary distance while creating his verbal points. I believe Chuck learned plenty from hanging out with me, feeling that very few people who were younger had anything real or honest to teach me. But he was the exception.

Basically, Chuck opened up a whole new world, one where I could respect his words, giving him due credit for what he did at such a young and tender age. I told him that I was the type of person who needed no empty promises, as in deployment life, everybody blathers on how they should meet up when back in the States – I never told anyone except my wife that I'd ever see him or her again, because I considered it to be a pipe dream. This was a hard fact that I learned fast, losing close buddies to violence in Afghanistan; out of sight is out of mind for most people.

I worked closely with Chuck for four months, taking as much from him as I could, while he did the same with me, helping me contact the right people and letting me know exactly what to expect over the long haul. Going for it, I blitzed through my paperwork in the office, saying I'd deal with the rest of it later, as I finished up my tour. Office life wasn't any different from state-side life, except that everything seemed to be coated with 'moon dust', and color shades were always a variant on tan. Most infrastructures were made out of four-by-eight wooden boards, and we had to pound nails into everything to hold it up. Five-fifty cord is very strong string, 'yuck' green in color, as thick as yarn; it can hold weight of up to 550 pounds. Inhabiting a place with no windows constantly drove me crazy, claustrophobic, but I reasoned that the grass wasn't greener on the previous side.

My new intelligence field produced and sported a whole new line of characters, people who regularly quoted popular movies, holding weird outlooks on what was currently happening in our country. We did pretty strange stuff to pass the time. I started thinking I was in prison; there's not much more I can say. But after Chuck left, finishing his rotation in Afghanistan, I figured it was also time for me to finish up, trying to advance under his advice in my career.

So, I completed yet another long headache of a tour, probably the very worst one, coming home to be surprised by my brand-new baby son, Zmaray...it means 'lion', of course! Shama, thankfully, was okay on that name; the baby gave me warm feelings of gooey goodness, filling me to overflowing with love and support as I stood there holding and rocking him. I would kiss him on his forehead, thanking God repeatedly for this miracle.

Peering quizzically into his deep black eyes, which he had plainly stolen from his mother, I felt his strings of drool running down my proud chest, thinking that those fat little cheeks were forcing his tongue and saliva out. It was wonderful to come home when he was still an infant – I was never happier in my life than when I held him, while Shama cried copiously at seeing us bonding for the first time.

I'd sit on the couch, shirtless, while his little fatty head sunk into my chest cavity, passing out to silent sleep while listening to my loud heart beating. Coming over to sweetly kiss me, my wife said that people declared how much he looked like me, nicknaming him CC herself, for carbon copy. I burst with pride, having a son as my firstborn, fulfilling male Afghan tradition; all of Shama's sisters only had girls as their firstborns – not that there's anything wrong with this!

My time with Zmaray passed by faster than no other; I thought daily of all the things I'd teach him and expect from him, while Shama just wished we could remain together for much longer, and keep getting to know each other better. Holding my little wrinkled ol' man everywhere we went, I noticed how much attention you get when carrying around such an attractive little bundle of love. He was so cute; all I ever heard behind me at the supermarket was cooing women – and he'd reach out to hold them, so I passed him onto them sometimes, knowing how excited he was. He was just a big ol' flirt, because I never saw him smile at men, only women. So I nicknamed him 'little pervert'. But I got used to the Daddy thing, spending my days learning stuff on how to be a better parent, until the day Chuck magically appeared on our land-line phone.

Picking up gently as she always does, Shama talked to Chuck briefly, but you could tell she wondered who the hell this dude was. How well did he know her fine, still Marines-oriented husband? I already knew it was him – he was the type who used your name repeatedly, and I could hear him over the line. Stepping over, I waited as he asked question after question about the baby, asking also if Shama was getting back into the swing of things. Finally, I grabbed the phone, handing Zmaray to Shama.

"Chuck old man, where've you been hiding, brother?" Chuckling, he laughed longer than usual, saying, "Farid, I told you I'd *make* shit happen!" He'd splashed down again in the U.S. and made his calls, boosting and promoting me to his case officer, claiming I was perfect for some missions they needed to promote to their boss – but they didn't have the right person lined up for this yet. Well, Chuck knew they'd get whatever they needed with me, handing the phone over to his boss. This older, experienced-sounding man took over the line, stating very sternly: "Farid, it's great to hear your voice; I'm grateful you finally made it home again. I have a few things I need to discuss with you if you have the time…maybe we can meet in my office."

Game as ever for new, exciting anti-bad-guy work, I replied, *"Any* time, Sir!" The boss put Chuck back on – he planned to stop by our apartment soon.

Starting to give him the address, I heard him laugh, "I got it already, *dude!* I'm en route, gimme thirty mikes," and then he abruptly hung up.

'Thirty mikes' is agency talk for thirty minutes, which didn't stop Shama from getting all worried. "What's this about, my love?" she sighed in her most caring voice. Telling her not to get upset, I mentioned that it would probably be a great opportunity concerning that new job we'd been talking about recently, the one with the three-letter agency. She caught on quick, asking me if she could go get cleaned up a little, but I could tell she was nervous. This type of work actually meant more risk than before, and that I might have to leave home again.

So she washed herself and picked up the place, putting Zmaray down on the floor to sleep – he caught onto how anxious she was, and stayed up playing with his toys, always trying to strengthen his skills, holding and chewing on every object within reach. Meanwhile, Shama inched away from me, as I followed her around not saying anything, obviously aware that something was wrong.

Finally putting a hand on her shoulder, I asked her about it. I thought she'd be happy that my level of work was moving up, with greater pay attached. But silently, she kept making things tidy, stopping for a moment to think. Coming behind her, I wrapped my loving arms around her thimble of a waist, and she broke down crying.

All I desired in this life was to please her, but she clearly didn't want the money, fame, glory, or even to fight the bad guys anymore; she needed her loving husband at home. Crying louder, she hugged me tight as a vise; I could feel her heart pounding like a sledgehammer into my chest. "Why?" she moaned. "Why is it *always* this way…why can't I have my hubby more than *two weeks* out of the year? Why are you always doing such *dangerous* things?"

Not knowing how to respond, I could only reason that my wife was still proud of me, but was worried sick about me dying on the job. Well aware of how ambitious and passionate I'd become, she had her own problems with living alone, telling her girlfriends about her brave husband serving our country. She forever fronted for me, excusing my lengthy absences. I didn't see at the time how I was being selfish, because we had tons of money, a splendid place to live, and two expensive cars, all from my deployment pay. I just kept wanting and buying more, with Afghanistan developing into my 'drug fix', making me addicted to the rush of doing crazy, risky things, with my one persistent comeback being that everyone else who stayed home went to college and ended up with a dead-end boring job, not like mine – which was *exciting!*

Pouting, her face streaked with lines of tears, she begged me, "When, Farid? How long are you gonna keep this up, 'til you die of old age, or get killed?" Bending over, clutching at her stomach, she inexorably screamed, "What about *Zmaray?* You have a son now; you have *responsibilities* here at home!"

Whimpering, I was caught dead. I didn't throw her my usual flip answer, sensing that this somewhat paralleled a husband found cheating – whose wife enforces the awful truth. Her stare of shame, and that look of hers that she'd never change her mind, making our surroundings freeze in place, goaded me into stopping cold. Flashbacks of decades of time, seconds worth of jaded memories, raced through my soul; my heart was ready to burst, my blood pressure shot skyward, and I clenched and unclenched my bunching muscles and fists. That overwhelming desire for death, some way to make up for all my fallen brothers and sisters in the Marines, slapped me hard in the face. So I stormed out of the room, onto the balcony, sparking a cigarette in my shaking hand.

Walking slowly after me, Shama could tell I needed to be alone, so she went back in after Zmaray – he could light up any situation with his innocent little face, that toothless smile, and those gurgling sounds. Looking over my shoulder, I saw her sweep him off the floor, hugging him tight and singing to him. As I stood there, I reflected on what I'd tried to accomplish for our family, only to make our lives better and much more fulfilling, and myself more of an outright success. I loved my wife and son, so I knew that even if I experienced full blood lust, craving vengeance for all those I'd lost, who were innocently subject to the Taliban's insane rage – so be it! I couldn't stay motionless, sans power in my home country, without doing something.

God gave me my gifts, and it meant I would sacrifice anything for God – this special calling came straight from Heaven. And I thought about how deeply a man like Chuck could reach into my face and my mind, just as the doorbell rang. I flicked away my second cig, while Shama opened the door, as that tall, slender young man in a suit waltzed in. I could clearly see Chuck in Afghanistan, straining like crazy to look great; he wouldn't appear any lesser now. He couldn't see me, as the reflection off the glass balcony doors blinded his view, but he resembled a model from GQ magazine, or that cologne 'dummy' who you couldn't tell whether he was gay, straight, or just incredibly handsome. He didn't wear a tie, but had that 'stockbroker look' written all over him.

Undaunted, Shama gave him a warm greeting, striving to sound professional, as her job was once deeply related to mine. Taking Chuck's hand, she led him over to the balcony, asking if he needed a drink. He gratefully accepted her kind offer, showing that he wasn't shy the first time at our house. In moments, Chuck and I were laughing, clutching ice-cold beers and talking once more, as I calmed down a little, not knowing how to handle things but giving Chuck a big bear hug, just the same.

Grabbing my biceps and giving them an earnest squeeze, he commented on how healthy I looked: "I see you made it back again, *in one piece*!"

I responded with, "You came to sell cars, Chuck, or hang out?"

All of a sudden, he stopped laughing, but he simply said, "I see…you're starting to learn, now."

"Game *on,* bro," I warbled. "Shama, 'kay if Chuck and I fart around?"

She knew that meant I was busy, and she left us completely alone. That was all I needed to say, as the person I kept cloistered deep inside insisted. Chuck was a hard call, a caution when it came to conversation: it involved roleplaying bundled with acting, and I had to stay sharp and remember story lines, things about my characters, never stumbling once on my words. It all had to be completely natural, and Chuck realized it was my time to re-enter 'spy mode'. We downed our beers, had a small conversation, and then he told me that John Rogue needed to see me as soon as possible. I dressed similar to what Chuck wore, but he said "*Shit,* I didn't get threads like yours 'til I got *in,* looking sharp, Farid...you're a born *natural!*" Understanding how my mind worked, he could plainly sell water to fish. Soon heading downstairs, not looking back at Shama, we climbed into his Mercedes, lighting straight out to the District of Columbia.

During the ride, I asked a gamut of questions about my upcoming interview. Guffawing, Chuck gasped, "You're not applying for corporate America, *Devil Dick!*" We hadn't left the Marine Corps behind, still sporting potty mouths and unfashionable humor, as he shouted into the wind, "You're a *mad man* now, and I got you there, so don't forget that shit, *Farid!* Don't fuck it up, get soft and pussy on me. Just be Roc, and leave little baby and Shama out of the loop, you'll be fine."

"Is there anything you don't have a fucking answer for, Chuck? I mean, holy shit, you're a fucking *soulless demon,* brother!"

Laughing our fool heads off, we wove in and out of traffic, with Chuck chanting, "That's it, Mr. Mushy Pussy, put some dick and balls into that treble clef of a voice again! You're like a bad-ass *girlfriend,* man!" We went on and on like that, a car trip of two Marines laughing, cursing, saying things that would make an average person cry, or beg to stop the car. But for some unknown reason, Chuck suddenly got deep, saying, "Listen, Roc, we weren't meant to be normal, nor were our jobs; you can't stop or control things, you have to accept this shit..."

"Chuck, this isn't fucking *Fight Club* – you fake Brad Pitt motherfucker! You're trying to get *pretty,* and that hardcore thing going, *huh*?"

At that moment, Chuck lost it totally, not stopping laughing for five whole minutes; he had someone verbally slaughtering him, making fun in a smart, savvy manner that he could deeply appreciate as a spy and a hardcore ex-Marine. The others he worked with were just lame, square, overall boring types. I knew I'd latched onto a nerve, just as we reached our destination, with Chuck spouting, "*Good* times, Roc; nice one bro, I will get you later." Yet, he accompanied me through the building's lobby, showing Security his badge and getting me a visitor's pass. Farting around was over for now, maybe for a long time.

The government building was massive, tiled everywhere – shiny, flat, square tiles coming up halfway on the walls. You couldn't tell if you were in City Hall, or the world's most humungous restroom. I had to analyze my surroundings as we strolled down the hall, and Chuck couldn't resist throwing in one last joke, whispering, "Stop being *suspicious,* dude, you look like a fucking *bomber!* We gotta thin out your eyebrows, you're *way* too Middle Eastern to be here!" Smiling, I lost myself in this new, palatial-looking site; we'd walked so far, I lost track of where we came in.

Without warning, two double doors opened right in front of us, cubicles lining up in rows to either side, and we stalked quietly past them like thieves in the night, pacing straight ahead all the way to the back. A couple of work junkies stared at me, I got some stares in right back at them – and then, ahead of me, I saw the word ROGUE written over an office door. Rogue – wasn't that some type of video game warrior?

Chapter Eleven
Collecting Souls

Heart pounding in my ears, I quietly entered the small office without any idea of what to expect…from what could only be called a group of spies. I can't tell you which three-letter agency they represented, not yet. My mind speed raced like a car in the Daytona 500, stretching to its limits to dope out what to do, disputing whether I should stand at the position of attention as before, or behave normally. Going with my brute instincts, I decided to remain normal, imitating Chuck, who was hanging around the unassuming office desk of Mr. Rogue with his hands in his jacket pockets.

Already standing up to greet me, John Rogue obviously knew how and when I was going to walk into his office – timing it out to the second. The man was precisely what I'd envisioned: Caucasian male, in his mid-fifties, going over to the side of plumpness, hairline receding fashionably with more white than dark left. Also, he wore a pair of thinly wire-rimmed glasses, and was so nondescript that he almost vanished into his own office; he didn't speak at first, but I could tell he was analyzing me. Gratefully, I noticed we were about the same height, five feet seven in my case. In the military and during government work I met hordes of six footers who uncomfortably towered over me, which I always took as an unintentional putdown.

Swiftly stabbing my hand out in greeting, I waited to grip his fist in the expected, dominating male handshake posture. Without skipping a beat, he grasped mine tightly, saying, "Farid, it's a pleasure to actually meet you in person." But we didn't smile at each other – I wasn't there for a customer service job, wanting to show Rogue nothing less than my best skills and tactfulness, and my ability to deal properly with conversation. In seconds, he was firing multiple questions at me, and I shot my answers right back, keeping them short, simple, and to the point each time.

Meanwhile, patting me on the shoulder, Chuck simply stated, "See you in a little while," after Rogue told him we needed the time alone together. I sat down, leaning forward into John's desk, carefully situating my cuff-linked forearms against the expensive, glossy wood. This desk was the most expensive one I'd seen in my business dealings, solid mahogany with detailed, ornate cherry trim, apparently some kind of nineteenth century antique. These guys *owned,* and it showed!

"Listen, Farid, I won't waste either your time or mine..." he began, but I interrupted him with,

"John, one thing: please don't sugarcoat anything, and let me know exactly what you need me to do in Afghanistan." Laughter unexpectedly burst from his lungs, filling up and echoing in the large office.

"Call me *Rogue!* I like that name better, Farid." Well, I didn't give a shit about what his fat ass liked; I wanted to know what I was going to have to do, but wondered if maybe I'd gone too far. Rogue clearly needed something in particular, and the reason he laughed was because this brazen Marine had suddenly inhabited his office, looking for 'the business'.

I wasn't too concerned with his money – I already had the funding to do whatever we wanted – but I didn't need him to smell any weaknesses. Turning away for a sec, he instantly spun back around, saying, "Okay, listen. I can hire you on a GS grade, and that comes with a full package of benefits."

Now it was my turn to chuckle, boldly stating, "Rogue, can you skip the foreplay? I like instant gratification."

He'd surely learned about me from Chuck, that I was a battle-driven type, going through plenty of Hell in my time. So he let my impertinent demeanor slide, putting his cards on the table. "Fine, here it is: we require your skills for a special hostage case." Whoa, I thought, *hostage* is a pretty strong word. "Lay it down, Rogue, give me who, what, and where, in great detail." I could tell he was trying to make things professional, while I had ample experience in matters like this, working on prior cases for other, similar officers. Time would be a factor, as it always was.

Rogue might chew me a new asshole and kick my big brown butt out his spiffy office if he got upset with me, as nondescript as he looked. I could tell a primitive fire smoked behind those glasses-concealed brown eyes. But no, he needed me, and I had the upper hand now, or at least I could speak freely. "Slow down, Roc," he muttered, using my call sign alias. "Let's get to basics first." Like many, he knew me as Roc, though I never gave him that name – using it to bring me into 'war mode', to get me thinking like a killer again. It's funny how a nickname you started out liking grates on your nerves and brain over time and through misuse, too.

Anyway, Rogue stopped talking, plunking down behind his pricey desk and pulling out two manila file folders. Scanning the room with a casual air, I was keenly watching him, noticing the pictures lining his desk front, those which a normal business executive's desk held: his wife and three cute kids, two sons and a daughter. Showing off at an amusement park, they all wore bathing suits, coming off the water ride. Next to that main pic were snaps of the same group in multiple vacation areas, letting me know Rogue was into 'spoiling' his family. Daddy surely wasn't around loads; this was his method of taking that one-month break and getting away with it.

Also, his minor obesity led me to believe that he spent a lot of time behind his desk, ordering 'take out' Chinese food every day, or eating on the run. Well, as he strummed through the first file, it spread open to me, showing my picture and a layout of my general background info. So he began detailing my life and jobs, step by step like I hadn't known what I'd been doing all those years. Digging into the languages I took in high school and college, he mentioned that I'd studied German and Spanish, coming around to the salient fact that I proficiently spoke 'Pushto', the Southern dialect of Afghanistan, as fluently as any native speaker.

This shocked me; I'd been waiting for him to pronounce it 'Pashto', the way most Americans said it. Pushto was actually a closer notch to the way natives pronounce it, so I figured he was trying to impress me with his knowledge – heck, I *was* duly impressed! After reading a portion of my life story to me in a dead monotone that sounded exactly like how he looked, Rogue calmly reached for the second file folder. Parking one knobby elbow on my chair's rail, I leaned onto my right side, giving him my infamous Pose of Wisdom, where my index and middle fingers glance against the temple of my forehead, with my thumb sliding easily beneath my jaw line – hoping he noticed how deeply attentive I was to his every single word.

He knew how impatient I was to get the details of my mission, and that this wasn't an easy line of work that he was still in the stages of offering me. Nonetheless, I was highly intrigued that they'd chosen me for such an important sounding task as something involving hostages. This was a heavy-duty political matter, and without letting him know, I was absolutely on fire to be in on it – although briefly, I pondered Shama's crying spell, wondering if I was only being selfish and should take up something a lot more like a sedentary desk job. Playing with Rogue a little, I made it seem like I'd already found a good gig in the States, working for an intelligence department that accepted me for my lengthy prior experience. The only problem, I told him, was that my expertise was needed on the desk side of things, which I subconsciously couldn't stand – it's too boring and normal, I said. Rogue, smiling, replied that his job offer would be otherwise than commonplace, in any case.

He then stated that I had to go on yet another six-month deployment. Again, I inwardly moaned? I thought this was set to be something *different!* But next, he added that I'd be going completely undercover. Interrupting him, I asked, "So that means what?"

Coughing into his hand, glaring over it like I'd asked if I could have sex with his wife, he only replied, "Be patient, Roc; I will read you all the details. Just sit down and relax." But I felt like I was on Mission Impossible now; "Your mission, Roc, if you should decide to accept it..." I probably gave off a false impression that I wasn't interested, having taken in more than what I was expecting.

Plopping both file folders down on his desk, Rogue told me about two different hostage situations, and how one of them involved our own troops, while the other one pertained to a foreign ally country that required our full support. Due to how time-sensitive everything was, I had to accept his proposal immediately, and they'd send me out the next morning on a luxury first-class flight – first to Dubai and then on to Afghanistan, back to the Southern region. But I wouldn't be dealing with the military, or landing on any bases, so at least this was going to be different somehow.

I was set to play a local national, which I'd done before, once I landed abroad. Rogue would supply the documentation I needed for the mission, including various types of passports and Afghan identification docs. This included a 'Taskera' or valid local ID – acceptable even by the Taliban. In every way, Rogue was showing me why he sat at that expensive desk and held that important, vacation-laden position. His image projected a sullen, fat, lazy bastard – but you could tell that's why he made a fantastic spy. He totally fooled the untrained eye into thinking he was a CPA or something boring, uninteresting, someone you just passed over without thinking about it much. He'd plainly done his homework on me, and that was all that needed to be said; now it was his turn to sit back, mirroring my body language, and wait for my response.

Once again, I gazed off languidly into eternal nothingness, aching to know if I was ready to take on this type of important job, thinking a lot about how I always took on the toughest obstacles while everyone else had enough time and training to back their jobs up securely and wisely. I was being thrown face-first into the deep end again, without any realistically related experience – but if I wasn't a good swimmer, at least I could tread water, thrusting my screaming head above the oncoming waves.

I was a verifiable jack-of-all-trades, master of none. What would this new project add to my existence? Every time I resettled into America, Afghanistan jerked me backward, a distant echo in the dark, wind gusts traveling thousands of miles to blow me their way. Whenever I moved up professionally, it was into a less well-armed and far more risky, death-defying position. Suddenly, I rocketed from my seat, grabbing the hostage file that Rogue was poring over, telling him I'd be at the airport during 'zero dark hours'. Not letting him shove a word in edgewise, to baffle his mind, I sprinted out the door before he could gasp, "Glad to have you aboard, son!"

Waiting a couple doors down, Chuck swilled his designer coffee, pursuing conversation with a good-looking office vixen. She was a brilliant redhead, obviously dyed, with breasts and ass galore. Chuck wasn't gonna like me, but I pulled him away, telling him, "This is *crazy* shit, man! Nonetheless, I'm hungry; I could eat something *bigger* than her tits!"

Blushing, the vixen stalked away, staring at me over one skinny shoulder. Nodding his head from side to side as I walked by, Chuck groused, "Fucking *Marines!* You better watch your six," meaning my ass.

Probably due to this, the ride home wasn't the same as the halcyon one to Rogue's office. Pulling my mind together, I had to refocus, realizing that in a few hours, I'd be taking a fourteen-hour flight back to the Middle East, my home away from home. Not bothering to joke around, I didn't even talk to Chuck, who rambled on gregariously about code names and what I was thinking. "Why are you shutting up?" he mumbled, guessing that I was too busy reviewing the office file about the hostages.

With a look of vast concern displayed on my rapt face, I was going through the photos of people that I was supposed to assist in finding, and the areas that I had to reach eventually, in order to help properly with the mission. Every page was stamped 'Top Secret', and after I was done, I told Chuck to take the folder back, just as we pulled into my driveway. He looked at me like I was insane, saying, "Roc, are you bailing out on us now?"

I responded with, "No, Chuck, I got it. I've been to all the related places, and I don't need Top Secret level paperwork sitting around my house. So return all this shit for me, so my poor wife doesn't have a cow when she sees this. I'm good, trust me, I remember everything I read there. Just make sure you drop off my plane tickets at zero two hundred hours. After that, I'm on Zulu time, okay?"

Frowning but compliant, Chuck didn't say one word, giving me his hound-dog look of being proud but a little wary about how to take in recent events. Watching him leave, I stood around outside our place, wondering what to tell Shama. She wouldn't have expected me to drop everything and leave, but after my review of the paperwork, I could now only think of those hostages. Deep down, I knew how many risky raids I'd been on, how much intelligence I'd collected for all the branches. But one thing for sure was that with foreign hostages, a lot of innocent civilians had been locked up, thrown away to rot, and were likely to be killed if I didn't intervene in time.

I wanted this job, not only for the people involved, but for the thought of my saving them all at once. However, my big question was: should I risk death for this possibly uncertain mission, giving up Shama and Zmaray for people I didn't know from Adam? Hitting an outside wall with my flat hand, I eventually walked inside – Shama wasn't even there, she'd left for her mother's house, to get some baby supplies. This gave me a chance to move faster, as I had to pack up my special stashes of Afghan clothes and my related military gear. Being a typical Marine, I was usually 'on point' when packing up stuff, keeping to a uniquely organized manner; but this time, I floundered around, lost and struggling. The phone rang – Shama called, saying she was returning to the house in minutes. She got there just as I zipped up my last suitcase.

When she came in, she found me sitting on the balcony, smoking a cig and gulping down a cold brew, which was sweating from the warmer temps, much like I was. Cooing softly like she meant it, she eased onto my spread-out lap, having left Zmaray at her mother's place. Kissing me sweetly, she gave me her big, beautiful eyes gazing fondly into mine, for a few precious seconds – asking how my job meeting had gone, while I responded with a prolonged kiss. Looking around, she saw that some items on the balcony had been moved; being incredibly smart, she forever noticed such small things, always able to gather her own conclusions. Her favorite joke was, "A *real* wife investigates you lots better than the FBI."

Too good at it for even me, she saw quickly that my military gear, sitting in cardboard boxes out on the balcony, had been relocated. Sobbing, or at least suppressing an outright sob, she hugged me real tight, crying without making a sound. She wasn't the type to yell, scream, or fight, when she knew the battle was already lost. Her version of dealing with the inevitable was to savor every moment with me, staying close to me all through the night. Shama, totally savvy to the ways of most government affiliations, knew that I couldn't tell her anything about my new work, where I was going, or what I was planning to do when I got there. All she understood was her hubby was leaving again, and once more, it would be a case of my possibly not returning.

I couldn't sleep that night, dwelling on what loomed ahead, what to expect in order to collect the needed info for people that I didn't necessarily inwardly trust, although they might trust me, due to the things that fell into place. First and foremost, came my clearance level, and next, being a native speaker helped me out an awful lot. Who else but me could qualify for such tasks? Believe it or not, native Afghan speakers who are also American are anything but a dime a dozen; in my experience, we had a solid two of us in the Marines, at one point of time anyway. I'm sure there were more somewhere, but not close to the East Coast or anywhere near Washington D.C.

The three-letter agency hadn't taken the time to filter me through any experienced others; instead, it was all about the network Chuck had built for them, how he had a keen eye for exactly what I could do. Giving up on sighing, I placed my group of bags by the door, calling a taxi, sitting on the bed near Shama. Leaning over, I found her wide awake, probably having been so all night long, and she was still crying softly – trying hard not to bother me or make me feel guilty. Stroking her fine, long clumps of black hair, I kissed her on her tear-streaked cheeks, over and over; but too soon, I scanned my digital watch, telling her it was time. She faithfully escorted me to the door, and we hugged like we meant it, kissing with passion and mutual concern, with me telling her that I loved her more than life itself and to take care of our little prince of a lion.

Over again, like before, I was gone – on the way to what I anticipated as my most dangerous mission, not unlikely to end with my demise. Under the front doormat, I found the reserved airline tickets that Chuck had stowed there. Early morning's chill enveloped my body wetly as I stalked down the concrete steps, noticing every sound. But I barely heard the door squeak open as Shama silently watched me leave, with me unable to turn around to give her one long, last lingering love stare. It would've hurt too much, as I needed to push all emotion away from my mind.

Outside ahead of me, I saw the last bits of stars glowing through the lit-up city skyscrapers, viewing the constellation of Orion – following me everywhere I went. It's a group of stars that form an image of a hunter, which meant me – I was going to have to hunt down those who'd taken the hostages, without much outside assistance.

My taxi cruised in mere moments later; I was already back in my head zone, striving in my mind to return to the

Afghan character I'd have to become. Not having any special training in this, I was once more jumping into a field which normally requires many years of work and schooling. What I actually had was the experience of going after and actually capturing the bad guys, many successful times. Believing what Chuck had told me, I thought of myself as a natural, so to *hell* with training – who needs it? Any such classes I'd gone through didn't lead to what the overall cases turned out to be in the real-life stomping grounds of the Afghan fields.

Beginning with posing for the cab driver, I put on a show for anyone else who wanted small talk, getting in a couple drinks at the airport to ensure a nice buzz to settle me down for the long trip. My plane was slated to take off in the early hours before dusk, and fortunately, it came in right on time. Making my way through the airport was easy, as I showed my special passports that got me swiftly past every checkpoint, being fully respected and on a much higher security level than usual. The flight, as expected, was excruciatingly long, full of crazy dreams of death and defiance – crossing the Atlantic Ocean had turned into a normal thing, with my battle-weary brain growing accustomed to turbulence, nasty airline food, and unexpected occurrences.

We landed in Dubai, where I changed my apparel, wearing the traditional 'Camise Parthoog', better known to westerners as 'Man Jammies'. In other words, I looked richly robed in men's pajamas, while I also had to use the Kanahari traditional cap, flip-flops, and the 'Longowta', or turban-style head wrap. Taking a glance in a wall mirror, I could see a whole different person there, smiling, reflecting to myself, "*Shit,* you look so suspect now; let's *do* this, *Farid*!" My attire caused no concern at the Dubai International Airport, as Terminal Two contained almost nothing but 'foreign' passengers from the Afghanistan and Pakistan regions.

Getting out of there, I soon landed at Kandahar International Airport around mid-day afternoon, with the sun merely starting its attempt to slowly cook the sandy grounds into a hot mess that burned your bare feet, if you didn't wear shoes. I stowed away my American passports and documents, deep inside a hidden compartment in my main bag – lovely spy stuff galore – going through Customs logically enough. This little, almost invisible half-ass airport is located nearby a major military base I'd been stationed on for great lengths of time. Nervously, I figured nobody cared about anyone coming into the airport to Afghanistan, the focus being mainly on those leaving for some other country. I found only a couple of taxi drivers, sitting around drinking green tea, thinking that humans don't change much anywhere you go; it's just the cultural norms that separate us, like green tea instead of coffee or beer.

The drivers were in no hurry, as just four to five flights roared in every day, so I walked over to a driver, starting to use the Pashto language with a positive voice. I carefully altered my vocal tone, doing my best to impress the driver by using simple, easy to understand speech terms. "Who's going to be the lucky man to drive me to the picnic?" I inquired, smiling like a tourist. "Sir, come right this way, please," he answered, making me feel relieved that my put-on was proceeding reasonably well. I knew he needed this run, as I had a good amount of Afghan currency on me, being able to exchange plenty of dollars over – breaking the denominations down and keeping most of the smaller bills in my deep pockets.

Asking me where I was headed, the driver grinned when I told him to go straight to the nearest city, and that I needed the nicest possible hotel. He sized up my clean clothes and well-maintained appearance, deciding that I'd come from America. I explained that I'd completed a trip to Dubai, and that was all he asked of me. Really, I couldn't let anyone know exactly where I'd come from, and I wasn't emotionally prepared to open up to anyone yet, especially such a sneaky, dingy-looking cab driver.

The sparking radio tinkled with local show and nightclub tunes; I asked the driver to turn it up so that I could better enjoy my ride, to divert him from asking any further questions. An explosion somewhere set off my fluttering heart, startling me profoundly as the driver, eyeing me in his rearview mirror, guffawed – this only helped me, making it seem like I was unused to such things.

Seeing that I was upset, he turned around, saying: "It's a normal occurrence out here; you'll get used to a few distant bombs." Frowning like I meant it, I ignored the disturbing sounds, entering my twilight zone but skimming my gaze past the mountains, the stores, the people passing by who never seemed to change or appear to be any different than they'd looked for a thousand years. This colossal Earth could shift, with fashions consistently remade, but most Middle Easterners remained the same.

The three-letter agency and the Marine Corps kept drifting into and out of my feverish mind, which reviewed every place, every hell-hole I'd seen. The Sergeant Major and my Drill Instructors were once again yelling at me, overwhelming me, as I experienced all the time and effort I'd put in: the crystallized blood, sweat, and tears. My family of origin I'd left behind could never understand my life. If I'd stayed home, I'd doubtlessly have become a loser drunk at a local bar. Instead, over a hundred thoughts spewed through my mind in a matter of seconds, as the driver's rhythmic, nasally accented voice broke me out of my panic-stricken reverie.

"Five hundred Afghani, Sir," he said, toting up my dues.

"Since *when* did prices get so high?" I grumbled, reaching for it.

"It's only ten American dollars, Sir," he chuckled, taking the money. But I handed over seven hundred, telling him to keep the change. Grinning sheepishly, he piled back into the cab as I surveyed my new surroundings, which were mediocre.

The hotel was every inch a $60 per night room like in the States, but upon closer inspection, it actually did appear to be pretty nice. Immediately, kids raced up to me, helping with my luggage as I softly moaned, 'Little *turds*'! They sized me up as rich enough to pay them plenty. I doled out big wads of money to split between them, as I really did love kids, and that was that! Who cared what country they came from, or if they were good or bad? They were just kids. Mostly, they reminded me of every innocent I'd seen vaporized, cut up, or blown to pieces by the war. And now, they also reminded me of my young son, who might have to grow up without a dad.

Truly, I was only violent to the demons who fed off the innocent and less fortunate, hating those who had no capacity for reason and logic for their gruesome, obscene acts. In the country where I was born, instead of fighting the people, I was more than ready to fully accept them for exactly who they were, mostly in order to collect vital information that would be used to save other human lives.

Checking in at the hotel, I signed on for two weeks, giving me time to get assimilated and maneuver around enough to make a few friends. Mostly, I was hungry, not too tired, and happy about the fact that in a major city, blending in was easier, as I felt like many eyes scraped over me. It was my paranoia talking, forcing me to think that I'd bump into a familiar face; but this city was populated enough to make that unlikely, and to keep me relatively safe for now.

Any small things such as an aircraft flying overhead set me off, memories of the military and my Marine's uniformed existence still haunting me. Also, I seemed to be missing something, reaching for my sidearm – but of course, nothing was there. It really hadn't hit me yet that I wasn't there to fight, that I was trying to leave that former life far behind me. I merely desired peace; I needed it for my overall wellness, wanting my soul to breathe freely and become more at ease. Definitely, I was having problems with Post Traumatic Stress Disorder, like so many others before me.

I'd grown slowly over time into an adrenalin junkie, calming my nerves with slews of energy drinks, cigs, and loud music or white noises. And I'd over-analyze everything and everyone I ran into; anywhere I walked, I'd hurriedly scan every face, my mission being to do it before I had to make eye contact. This technique made me think I had the advantage – and I always desired to be on a higher raised platform, to see over the people around me. At shopping malls, I made straight for the second level, avoiding the first or ground level, to make myself feel complete.

If I walked somewhere, slipping into daydreams or not paying attention and someone observed me deeply first, I entered a blue funk for the whole day, saying with a calm whisper that "I got *sniped*!" This was my way of believing I'd be dead if I didn't mind my manners. I took it very seriously, psychologically beating myself up, calling myself weak, slow, and underprepared. Punishment time for this revolved around the gym, making my workouts really hurt me, because what the mind failed to comprehend in a timely manner, the body must pay for in spades.

Recalling Jimmy from my childhood, he was someone I knew who lived by that creed regularly. I missed him and the competitive games we used to play, even as adults, for we'd find games that made grown-up sense to us. One time, I bought a pack of 24 grenades online; they rattled loudly when you pulled the string. After they arrived at my door, the game was on – I was gonna 'get' Jimmy a good one.

Adults and children play reality games with the finest graphics and toughest weapons, which to me was purely feeble, with the adrenaline rush too weak for me to bother with them. This was okay for kids, remembering the days when I was a game junkie too, but adults need a better fix, I figured. Those grenades consisted of 24 chances to kill off Jimmy's ego, taking planning and time in the process. My first idea was to introduce things smartly, so I had Shama hand-wrap a grenade to look like a nice, clean, immaculate gift. I gave her the story line, simple and easy, telling her to walk over to the hospital where Jimmy worked, going to the phlebotomy office and finding his boss.

Shama thought I was out of my mind, so I said, "I need a decoy for the workspace," deciding all the rest of the 'kills' were up to me. She spurted that I was being childish, seeing that I got frustrated easily and agreed with her. Apparently, she could see through my inexpert plans of toying with Jimmy. But keeping with it, I told her to let the boss know that her grandma was at the hospital for over a week, finally making it home safely. But during her stay, she loved the help Jimmy had given her, wanting to thank him, while still unable to leave her house. She wanted to send warm thoughts, leaving a gift for Jimmy, having the boss personally give it to him as a 'thank you'. He could even pull a 'pop smoke', leaving in a hurry so there would be no embarrassing moments.

That very afternoon, Jimmy's boss shook his hand, telling him that he was doing a fantastic job and that a very nice young woman had left him a gift. Jimmy was astonished, never having gotten such a great compliment before. That part of my plan was to 'bait' him in. According to Jimmy, he waited for only a few seconds, going to a back room to open it, the thoughts he encountered probably being feelings of pride and accomplishment. I can only think he must've felt pretty damn *good!*

Smiling as he opened the package, he was confused by the first little piece of the device, as he kept going, thinking it must be some old antique thing – maybe worth a lot of money. Then he opened it up all the way, seeing that it was a pineapple grenade; reeling from total hot confusion, he read the little note inside:

"The moment you get complacent is when you die...1-0, you've lost your lead on me!" I'm sure he laughed his fool head off, realizing who'd done this, having nothing to say about it but respecting me for plotting such a detailed, annoying little plan. He texted me later, saying that I'd 'done it now', repeating after me that the game was once again on. That kept me looking over my shoulder daily, you *bet!*

Walking down the crowded streets, lost in my daydreams of home, I ignored everyone; for some reason, it felt good to be a stranger. Wearing that hot, sweaty old turban or lungee, well-known in Afghanistan, was foolishly weird. It caused too much fussing on my head, as I perspire heavily whenever anything's up there. It'd take some getting used to. I also knew I had to get around town and meet someone, moving out of the hotel. Visiting convenience stores and buying everyday snacks gave me the chance to mingle; eventually, I bumped into a bored, store-owning gentleman who craved conversation as much as I did.

Trying like sixty not to talk too much at the beginning, I was the type of person who couldn't hold off for long. I'd surely go stark staring crazy if I ever got detained or had to spend time in solitary. We talked about local items and cultures at first, moving over to vehicles passing by on the street. My old job as a mechanic came in handy now, as I asked him if the car parked outside his store happened to be his, calling out the year and make of it before he could even tell me. This gentlemen was deeply impressed, especially since I also pointed out that he needed to fix his wheel alignment.

"Really, the tires are the issue, not the alignment," he sighed.

I responded, "No Sir, it's the tie rod that needs adjusting, and the tires are merely the outcome of the initial problem." This amazed him, as I had just saved him from spending a lot of money on the wrong problem. He told me that he'd been buying new tires on a regular basis, and now this would save him the trouble.

"I'm...Abdul," I lied, hoping that such a sobriquet didn't seem too obvious. "What's your name, friend?" He gave me the famous Arab moniker of Karim, which made me feel better; it was as if 'John' had met 'Dick' in America.

To hold onto his presence, which was hugely cheering for me, I fired off responses to all of his mechanical questions, to attract his attention and stay in his good graces. I was making a great first impression; finally, my chance came to ask him where he lived. Karim said he was staying in the city, and I asked him if anyone he knew had a room I could rent. He said their house was small, but he could see if his family was okay on me staying with them. Blushing and stammering slightly, I stated that it wasn't a problem, testing him by backing off, saying, "Really, you wouldn't mind if I intruded on your wonderful family?"

Insisting that they needed a good mechanic, he decided to check with his folks, and we agreed to meet later on. But I didn't return the next day, to appear less eager – I didn't have anyone else to handle my loneliness and communication problems, but couldn't let him know that. Instead, I returned in two days, with him shouting, "Hullo!" like I was his dearest friend. I simply gave him a hug, asking where God had taken him the last few days. Laughing, smiling, and pounding me on the back, he said my problems were over with, and to come home to meet his father for full approval.

I told him I had to go get my stuff, coming back when his shop was about ready to close. Grabbing up my hand in a friendly manner, he walked me over to his vehicle, pointing down at his tires. He'd bought four new ones after what I'd told him, and gotten a new wheel alignment as well – saying his father was contented, wanting now to 'take care' of that mechanic. Nothing but happy for Karim, I nodded as he thanked me, profusely and repeatedly. I didn't think much about his car or the tires; my mind was racing like an engine, trying to understand why he was holding my hand without letting go of it for such a long time. I guess it was a normal cultural thing.

"Karim," I breathed, "You are a funny guy…you *really* are!" He laughed, not really knowing why, locked into that moment of happiness. He was clearly a kind-hearted soul; nice people usually don't make it too long in Afghanistan, because of the probable exposure of getting hurt. Extending my other hand, gripping both of his in a warm handshake, I cried: "Karim, if you watch my back, I'll watch yours!" That simple, elegant man gave me his firm vows, as I looked deeply into his black, fathomless eyes, peering into the endless depths of his effortlessly loving soul.

Chapter Twelve
Religious Lessons

There we stood, Abdul and Karim – you'd never guess we only recently became friends – with me saying whatever I could think of that might create any data concerning finding the hostages. Once I landed a solid lead, it would immediately be ferreted to Chuck and Rogue; but right now, Karim was my first and only means of getting into the area's villages, full of the local people. Info tends to travel like a wildfire in rural Afghanistan, so all I needed was one really super-good break.

Staying in a hotel wouldn't get me anywhere soon, and Karim was obviously interested in me, asking to know my family's tribal name. The agency hadn't assigned me one, so I made one up, based on a sub-tribe the Taliban was somewhat involved with – telling Karim that I was from the "Noorzai Tribe."

Quickly, but not wanting to appear panicky, I asked him if that was okay; he only smiled in return. "It doesn't matter, dear brother, you're still Pashtoon at any rate."

There are multitudes of different types of people in Afghanistan, and it matters if you're from one of the major tribes, sort of like being in an American gang; if you're caught in the wrong part of town, you're vulnerable to bad events. The Pashtoons are the major group, with these minorities following them: The Hazaras, Tajiks, Uzbeks, Farsibanans, and Bulouchis. There are many more, but I've listed the ones the Pashtoons like to deal with the most. Predominantly, the Taliban comes from the Pashtoon tribes, which are the leading forces in the whole country.

Asking Karim what tribe he hailed from, I got a respectful nod. "Popalzai," he stated, bowing to my laughter back.

"Wow," I mused, "You're a descendant of the President's tribe; that must be nice!" However, Karim said it was much harder to be a member of that tribe, knowing you're a target due solely to your lineage. The Taliban went freely after anyone close to any government figures, much like the Mafia does when they're pressured about getting caught. What better reason to drop a court case than when no one in the family is alive anymore to be a witness or to prosecute a case?

Definitely, this meant a troublesome life for Karim. I saw why he seldom washed now, preferring to remain country-dirty and appear to be a simple local farmer. The poor man feared for his life on a regular basis! So he shared my paranoia, but at least this might mean that he had some of the info I was looking for about the Taliban.

Standing medium height and showing a normal build, Karim's most prominent feature was a thick bunch of bangs hanging over his eyelashes. He was stuck shaking his head constantly, in order to force the hair out of his eyes. His mid-level, standard male Afghan beard playfully tickled his Adam's apple – he really appeared to be quite typical. Thinking it would be best to look somewhat like him, one thing I apparently needed to get used to was wearing the same clothes for two solid weeks, to look and smell just like a native Afghan citizen. Not wanting to stand out, it wasn't much of a problem for me, as nobody actually smelled all that bad when bathing infrequently; it was just a way to show how you weren't living lavishly, that you were an anonymous type who wouldn't be associated in any way with America.

Also, I didn't desire to attract attention, as I sat by Karim's store for a while, watching a few suspicious bad-guy types on the street. I had prior experience in picking the wrong sort of people out of the crowd, so I knew these dudes were up to no good. This was one reason that Karim didn't want to wait any longer for me to move into their guest house; so about three days later, he agreed to have me come rent out a room, actually pushing me to move in with them. Trying to appear casual, I told him I'd visit his shop, and we could leave from there without a lot of onlookers.

I carried with me a small cell phone that Chuck refilled with minutes as needed, and it would give me ample 'talk time' to give him any info I was collecting, going directly to him on a daily basis. He would text me, asking to know what was going on constantly, but he didn't realize that in Afghanistan, things are slower than in the States. Also, I couldn't pull out the phone on the street, because the Taliban feared cell phones, thinking that users were giving info to local officials; it was a major security threat to them. To fix things, I kept the phone off 'vibrate' as it buzzed noiselessly in my pocket, soon climbing into the repaired car with Karim, heading outside the city to a more opened-up space of desert-hot but still fertile farmlands.

This whole area reminded me of Indiana's vastly spreading farms. I had the freedom to talk openly now, as I continued my conversation with Karim, asking him if there were a lot of 'bad sorts' around where he lived. "Abdul," he knowledgeably sighed, "There are evil men everywhere you look, my Brother. Just remember that God will always protect you, and that I will also take care of you. Of course, this is not news to you, as you say you've lived here through the current regime."

Laughing, almost having as much fun as before with Chuck, I shook my head – more in compliance than anything else. Yet, in the back of my mind, I was paranoid and fearful; my hands and knees shook as we neared his village, seeing dudes standing around the market stores, loitering outside. I immediately noticed three suspicious types sitting on barrels, drinking green tea – with AK-47 assault rifles slung over their shoulders, not even trying to be inconspicuous. Plainly, I was once again in the midst of evil people, as my blood pressure rose – what was I in for this time? My American brain loudly babbled that *everyone* knew I wasn't from there! But Karim steadily yapped it up, while I dazedly dwelled on my fictional story line: what to tell his father about why I was staying over there.

My tall tale was already in place, dreamed up during the car ride, and I gave Karim only short answer replies until he cried out loudly, "*Abdul*? You okay, my Brother?"

Smirking into my sleeve, I sighed, "Yeah, I'm fine; got a little headache, though," as we pulled up to a sand-tan colored mud-built compound, one with high walls and an old, metallic blue gate – completely rusted out. This brought to mind memories of how many of those gates I'd crashed through to enter an Afghan bad guy's house.

Popping out of his seat like a jack-in-the-box, Karim forced open the screeching gate in seconds, driving his car inside, where zillions of little kids ran around, up and down, yelling and screaming – and two adult women in full burqas were cooking flat bread over an open fire. This rustic scenario made a smile break free from my aching cheeks, showing my teeth involuntarily, as my family-loving heart melted from the sight. The two youngest boys were bare-ass, and every child was dirty and sand-infested, but they all seemed to have not a worry in this world.

Staying safely in the car, I watched as Karim strolled over to the women; I was just wise enough to put my head down. He told them he was bringing home a guest, a 'new family member' as he put it. The ladies quickly left, going to their side of the compound, where Karim's father was staying. Waiting, I fidgeted fitfully until he returned, keeping my head buried in my chest, as if I couldn't see anything. Opening the vehicle door with a great big smile, he asked me, "Are you ready, my Brother?"

Sighing again as if very tired, I replied, "Yes, my Brother, whenever you are, and many thanks to you." Meanwhile, the kids proceeded toward me, a pack of lion cubs seeking fresh bloody meat, swamping me whole. Happy as a lark, as these kids were no one to fear, I dropped to one knee, opening my arms wide to give those I could reach a great big ol' hug. Running close to me, they all suddenly stopped – I heard the fateful sound of crickets chirping in the stillness – and none of them actually came up to hug me. Apparently, they were wary, curious of who I really was.

"Where are your *manners?*" Karim spouted. "This is your *Uncle Abdul!*" In spite of his reassurances, the children didn't make a sound, staring at me like I'd suddenly landed from Mars, right in their front yard. Heaving one last sigh, I decided that if anyone was likely to blow my cover, it would sadly be these kids, because they could turn anyone transparent with their sinless souls. So I started talking fast, making my way over to the little girls, knowing they'd grow friendly faster than the boys.

Pulling out a couple pieces of gum, I handed them around; still silent, they at least accepted my peace offering with no worries. Afghan children love gum more than anything, which I learned long ago, always keeping some on me. It's a favorite with them, because it can be chewed all day long, even when the sugar runs out. They each grabbed a piece; out of nowhere, shrieking arose from their collective little throats, and they went back to playing, ecstatic to be enjoying a brand-new treat.

Karim stared at me the entire time. "How many kids do you have, Abdul? You are certainly highly experienced with children." Hauling out my cover story, I told him that my children and wife had died from a huge blast, when I lived in the neighboring province of Helmand. Not saying a word, care outlining and etched on his face, he said: "May God forgive their souls, and may they rest in peace." Pretending it meant nothing to me, an emotionless state which male Afghans tend to display, I asked him to show me the room, as I was considerably tired from our journey.

Karim tenderly put his arm around my shoulder, walking me through a door carved straight out from a mud wall. It led to a small, cozy little courtyard; in its corner was a thick building structure, no bigger than twelve feet by six feet. Upon close inspection, it held little but a huge, thick Afghan rug splayed across the dirt floor, so that dust wouldn't whoosh up. Karim ducked in first, coming out quickly, and I followed him in, knowing I didn't need much of a tour. He pointed to a small internal door, exactly the correct height for midgets, stating that I must use it to both enter and exit the compound – his father's wives were on the far other side, and needed their privacy.

Agreeing, I told him it looked simple enough for my tastes. Karim then handed me two tiny metal keys for two small locks on the room's door. Sliding them into a deep pants pocket, I warmly shook his hand. Smiling at this form of a 'thank you', he stated, "Food is included in your rent payment, and I or the children will bring you at least one meal every single day." Stammering, I said I didn't know how to repay him for their Spartan but generous hospitality. In local custom's style, he slapped my face lightly three times, saying, "Stop thanking me, Brother, this is a good deed for me...hopefully, God gives me the credit for it." Literally blushing this time, I assured him that God is merciful and gracious, and that he would certainly receive all the credit due him.

Asking me now if I was hungry, Karim ordered one snot-faced little boy following us around to go rustle up some food for me. "That is my oldest son, Rahim, and he has three sisters and two younger brothers."

Blown away by this, as Karim appeared to be quite young, I said, "Wow, you're certainly a *busy* man!"

This had us both laughing our fool brains out, and once we paused, Karim told me, "After you eat, you can meet my father, Haji Sahib. His name has a long, respectful history."

Karim was right; one of the five pillars of Islam is to travel to Mecca, a journey better known to Muslims as 'the Hajj'. As an able-bodied Muslim, you must perform the journey at least once in your lifetime. This annual pilgrimage declares your respect, and it carries into your name as a title as well. If I visited Mecca, Afghans would then call me Haji Abdul – and Sahib, another sign of respect, means 'Sir'. Therefore, I understood how much Karim revered his Dad, calling him only by such a formal title.

Also, putting two and two together, if Karim gave him that much respect, those two women in the courtyard must both be his father's wives. Islam allows Muslims in Afghanistan to marry up to four wives; in his turn, the husband has to support them all equally, and financially as well. However, I have heard an Afghan saying that God forgives a man for loving one wife more than another. The rule of four wives was implemented because many women became widowed during the early fighting years of war, and Afghan society didn't need them lining the streets. Men were allowed to marry multiple women to keep them out of trouble, and from having to beg for a living.

These days, an Afghan man tends to not break marriage and fornicate, but rather hoards enough money to pay a decent dowry, getting married again in order to satisfy his sexual desires and needs. This seems to me to be another thing that religion brought to mankind; as time changed and so did society, men used it mostly to serve their own needs. It's crazy but true – rich men with the dowry money could have up to four spouses and reproduce maybe twelve children with each one, creating a much stronger family clan and tribe. The kids married within the tribe as closely as second cousins, only adding further to the growing list of tribal numbers.

This left many children to be born with mutated limbs and other medical problems, from the blood and chromosomes matching too closely. But it's a cultural matter, as Afghans tend to distrust any people outside their immediate families. Looking around Afghanistan, I could see many kids with some type of physical or medical difficulty, even in Karim's small courtyard – there were a few.

Our compound happened to be situated next door to a large mosque, as I saw a blue dome right over the walls; attached to the top was another one of those prominent loudspeakers. Thinking, I used deductive reasoning to draw the conclusion that Karim's father was most likely the Mullah of this mosque. Also, chances were that he had actually built the Mosque, and it was probably even named after him – such as is customary in Afghanistan.

Shortly, one of Karim's boys brought me dinner: brown rice and lamb prepared with a thick slice of oven-baked Afghan bread. Once I finished, I was ready to possibly meet Haji Sahib. The azan or prayer call blared over the loudspeaker, and so I took the time to wash up, performing 'ablutions', the cleansing of the body with water or sand, preparing it for prayer. When Karim came back, he silently watched me carry out this simple task, respectfully not saying a word. But I thanked God as I finished up, dwelling on how Mom had taught me the proper prayers and rituals when I was younger. I looked like I'd been doing this all my life – it was performed passably. However, one thing I was missing was the prayer rug; so I rose from my knees, asking Karim for it.

"Why would you need a prayer rug, when we live directly behind the House of God?" he asked, making me realize my error. Thinking for a sec, I nervously saw I was too new in this neighborhood to be strolling into the mosque during evening prayer without people noticing me. "That was Haji Sahib who called for prayer, and he doesn't like it when we're late. So let's go, my Brother!" Grabbing up my hand as before, Karim showed me to the small door out, and we walked directly into the mosque.

I was a fully trained Marine, and we used our left foot to lead off on our strides forward – but Muslims always lead with their right foot when walking into either a house or a mosque. The right side is considered to be the 'clean side', with the left side delineated as the 'dirty side'. I had to really concentrate to remember or notice for the first time these small things, as I didn't want to throw anyone off, with people thinking I meant any signs of disrespect. My mission entailed that first and foremost I had to show everyone that I was your basic, ordinary, normal Muslim Afghan, without any detectable identifying features you could pick out of the crowd. I needed to be bland and blend in, so I could squirm through places, gathering up info as I went, getting to where the hostages were being held as soon as conceivably possible.

This mosque, at the point of time we entered it, held about twenty people. I couldn't tell if that was too many or average – it was nonetheless strikingly beautiful inside, with nice, detailed rugs and carpets, and a cement infrastructure for the walls. Clearly, Haji Sahib had invested plenty of money into this Mosque, for a reason – and I soon saw why. In one nearby corner, four Taliban men were dressed in black, conversing and whispering as I gave them my patented three-second stare. One of them instantly caught my eye, and I shifted quickly over to the front of the mosque, pretending like I hadn't seen anything amiss. Meanwhile, Karim kept one hand on my shoulder, which told everyone looking at us that I was coming in with him. They'd then all treat me as if I was his brother, or another relative of some close kind.

Without looking at me, fortunately, the Taliban men all rose, moving up to the front. Next, everyone got down on the floor after a brief period of standing, kneeling the proper way in a carefully unified manner; everything was synchronized. Haji Sahib stood in front of us, now as Haji Mullah Sahib, gaining this title from being a clergyman who led us in the ritual prayer, or 'salat'. Once the prayer was over, I sat on my haunches, not getting up any too fast, thanking God and hoping my wife and son were both doing okay, wishing fervently that God would watch over them in my absence.

Wiping my sweaty face with one sleeve at the end of the ceremony, I headed straight toward the door, with Karim following me close at hand. The second I reached the door, donning my pair of flip-flops, one of the four Taliban men called out Karim's name, loudly and with an air of extreme authority. Turning back toward the mosque without a flinch, Karim hurried up, as if he was in a rush to see what the man had to say. I figured they were only local thugs, and that Karim was scared of them like they were bullies at a middle school, ready to pounce on and devour any weak students.

Feeling my fists ball up involuntarily, I suddenly realized they might be the very men I'd been hunting for, the ones I longed most deeply to kill. Peering around one corner of the Mosque's large front door, trying to be sly, I saw the Taliban bad guys were now seated, looking at Karim, with one pointing his finger at my dear friend. Three seconds didn't pass by until they all stared at me, including Karim. I'd been *caught!* Looking askance as fast as I could, I walked a short distance away from the mosque, heading in the general direction of our compound.

In a few moments, Karim came out, pretending nothing had happened. My miserable heart dropped; I didn't know if this meant something terrible was about to occur, if word had gotten out about me, or if I had to get ready for a fire fight. But I didn't even have a concealed weapon on me! I decided to glue myself to Karim, and we simply sauntered back into the compound. But it was time to take advantage of this moment. Grabbing Karim by the shoulders, I begged him for what was going on.

"Everything is fine, my Brother," Karim drawled in his most reassuring voice.

I didn't believe him for an instant, asking him, "Why were they pointing the finger at you, and then they stared at me...who *are* they, Karim?"

Scanning my worried face, he decided it was his turn to probe me. "What is it that you do again...Abdul?"

Frowning, I responded, "I told you already, my Brother; I am a builder." But the Taliban were obviously thinking something else by now. Reading my mind, Karim boldly stated, "They thought you were acting scared, that you might be an informant." To handle this, Karim had led them to believe that I thought one of the Taliban gang looked like a relative of mine, and that's why I was staring at them. "I'm not sure I had them fooled...anyway, it's not a problem anymore," he softly said. The threat had gone over to him, because he was vouching for me, saying I was just this 'nobody' who was only here to look for work and building projects.

This had been a near miss, one the Taliban didn't follow up on, though their security involved closely analyzing their surroundings and people. We'd made our being suspicious seem like an absurd notion, as I'd played my cards right, and Karim's soft heart had backed me up concerning his promises to those men. We were both out of immediate danger, at least for now. But during this time, Chuck left me six missed calls and three text messages, begging me to call him back several times.

Telling Karim that I'd meet his father in a little bit, as I needed a nap, I left him to go to my quarters, locking the door behind me. The cell phone's reception sucked dog eggs, and Chuck was the type who wanted to talk a lot, but I couldn't – the kids kept running up to my door, screaming at me, asking for more gum and, now, some American candy. It may've been a mistake to give them gum, but I'd bought it locally at an Afghan store, at least. Anyway, I managed to text Chuck, letting him know the game had begun, and that I'd be moving in for the intelligence about the hostages starting bright and early tomorrow. He wasn't worried about it, but took the grid points from my phone, texting me that I was in 'bad territory'.

Coughing, I asked him to tell me something I didn't fucking *know* – he kicked back with some further timelines, and important things I needed to know about the hostages, agreeing that we'd talk later on. I turned my cell phone off, taking out the SIM card memory chip and stashing the phone in my secret compartment, where I now kept my money. Lying down on the room's musty old cot, I dozed off into a daydream, thinking about Shama. I could text Chuck with no problems, letting him know I was alive and things were okay, but I couldn't do the same thing with my own wife.

I knew Shama; she was worried sick, but I couldn't calm her nerves. I was presently on a vital mission, and operational security was something I didn't play around with, knowing it could compromise me and my comrades severely. Poor Shama would have to tough it out, like she'd done countless times before.

Sitting down at a small, tippy wooden table, I wrote down everything I'd seen on the way to the village and within the compound, describing in detail the goons we'd encountered at the mosque. Not having been officially trained in this, I had no idea of their levels or ranking structure, but knew they were typical Afghan bad guys. This was at least a lead of some kind, and it might eventually take me to where the hostages were suffering imprisonment.

Ready for a good, long nap, I startled awake when Haji Mullah Sahib tapped on the door – his voice sounding like a heavy-toned version of Karim's. I instantly knew it was his father, when he cried out questioningly, "Abdul?"

Deftly opening the door, I bowed way over in deep respect, grabbing his hand and kissing it repeatedly, crying, "May God bring you in peace, Haji *Mullah* Sahib!"

Smiling, the man gave me a blessing swipe over my head, saying, "Karim told me you made it here, and I wanted to thank you for your help with our vehicle, my Son." Then he detailed how much money I'd saved them, by helping him quit the crooked mechanic who'd been cheating them.

This Mullah was a giant man, preposterously so, with a Santa Clause white-laced beard bushing out in all directions. His hands, well-manicured by his wives, spanned large enough to belong to an NFL player, and his full, round belly sustained the Santa image I was getting. The hair on his beard crept up high to his cheeks, maybe half an inch away from his bottom eyelids. He was indeed a grizzly, hairy man, about as tall as Chuck, and I could tell he'd earned a lot of respect merely through his overall image. But I could swear he did look *exactly* like Kris Kringle – in Man Jammies.

Well, he was huge, wealthy, and held a big enough title to make him a person of vast influence and prestige out in the boonies of Afghanistan. Surely he was the very person to assist me in gathering some needed info about the hostages. Karim was second in line for this, seeming to be the last son the Mullah had, probably the weakest one too on the whole. Passive and not aggressive, Karim owned a warm, loving heart, and that sort of thing doesn't cut it in Afghanistan – he was staying safely within his immediate family, not splitting off from the tribe like his older brothers had.

Karim's father was his main refuge and security. I didn't know much about things, but from what I did know, this Mullah was my only current method 'in'. I was careful to treat him like he was my grandfather, respecting him as a great leader with a strong, authoritative voice. Fortunately, he liked me, and I could see that from the beginning – though he grilled me with multiple questions. I simply refrained from going on at great length about my personal history. Mostly, I went into my back story about the tragic things that had happened to my family, stating that I was a loner in answer to the Mullah's questions about why I'd left my tribe behind to come here. This was the hardest question a Pashtoon could answer; but I told the Mullah that I yearned to make my own way in the world, and that I needed the money.

This was usually the excuse for a person to leave his home tribe. Haji Mullah Sahib couldn't see any problems with it, soon asking if I wanted to look into a job doing mechanical rebuilds. I told him we'd see about it in the near future, as I first had to scout for various things that'd fit into building structures. Affably, he asked what I thought of his mosque – was it built reasonably well – and I replied, "It's one of the best such mosques I have seen in your greater region, for its size especially, and whoever built it performed most exceptional work." Telling the Mullah that I also had experience with contracts, I mentioned that I usually supervised a group of laborers while they did most of the jobs themselves.

He said, "I like it when someone knows more about how to supervise, instead of doing the petty jobs...although, performing small jobs is good at first, because everyone must gain in experience."

Deciding to switch topics before I revealed my total lack of knowledge about building structures, maybe too suddenly for my own good, I brazenly stated: "I was working on a project near this area last year, and one of my nephews was taken by the Taliban as a hostage…because he'd studied the language of English at school. They thought he was working for the American forces. My poor nephew actually only learned English for me, so he could earn money interpreting my contracts to anyone who uses that language in this region."

The Mullah, scratching his beard fitfully, blurted out, "Well, my Son, there have been a lot of things of that nature happening recently. Some people were taken away just a couple of weeks ago to a neighboring district." Bingo – *score!* There it was, via the good ol' baiting 'em in with simple conversation trick, leading to a huge piece of info.

Without thinking, I replied, "Oh, yeah, I heard about those foreigners, right!"

The Mullah, taken aback, stammered, "I don't know, but I'm sorry to hear about your nephew, knowing that he is probably dead by now." Turning away to look at his watch, he continued, "Listen, my Son, it's been great talking with you. Please go get your rest, and it was also a pleasure to eventually be introduced to you." That put a brilliant capper on my day; maybe I hadn't made the old man suspicious. I went to bed with a clean, purified soul, no longer bothered with visions of being blown up for now.

At the butt crack of dawn, Karim woke me up, wondering why I'd missed morning prayers. You see, Muslims have to pray five times per day, no excuses except for a few concerning women when they are menstruating or people when they're sick. I had no answer for Karim, feeling stupid, like I stood out. I actually did know the rules; in Afghanistan, people prayed before sunrise, and it was mandatory. It wasn't a case of whether you felt like it, so I had nothing. I was slipping my cover, doing stupid shit, missing out on matters of an important religious nature! As I apologized to Karim, though, he simply laughed it off, saying, "We're all human, my Brother, and you were clearly tired from our long journey." I was *so* relieved! Agreeing heartily, I mumbled that I was a heavy sleeper, missing my alarm from home to wake me up.

Karim, wanting to proceed from there, asked me if I'd like to go to his store with him, to sit around and maybe find some business people – seeking my possible employment. I knew he was bored at work, needing friendly company, but I also realized that it was definitely time to seek out and locate those hostages. So I told him I'd come up there in a little while, getting a ride from his father or something. After he left, I jumped on the horn and called Chuck, advising him of the fantastic intelligence I'd collected yesterday; he was ecstatic, ordering me to keep on pushing things.

Staying in the same clothes, not needing to wash up again, I headed out into the village to see what I could find. A group of older kids were on their way to do farming tasks, while the younger children loitered around, playing with no cares. Strangely enough, the adults seemed to be doing exactly the same thing; maybe they were killing time before the next set of prayers. I had to move quickly, as another prayer call would come around the early afternoon – giving me very little time to work on finding new leads and information. Glancing around, I located a small station where a farmer sold fruit from his pushcart, talking to him while he went on at great length about his land and how he had nasty disputes with his neighbors frequently.

"Your pomegranates are *amazing,*" I breathlessly told him, guiding him by the nose as best I could. "And your grapes are superior to *any* that I've seen!" This simple farmer smiled, showing me one rotting tooth in his whole mouth, from lack of proper oral hygiene; there were very few doctors and dentists outside the big cities of Afghanistan, and although the U.S. has poured money into the country, I doubt it's much better nowadays. At any rate, this man had great spirits, and seemed talkative; I asked him who he thought was creating problems for him, telling him maybe I could help.

Pointing East to the district lines, he said that's where the local bad guys hung out, taxing him for various things with no real right to do so. "I make nothing as it is, and have to pay them money so they can do their dirty work," he spat out. Asking if he knew these guys' head elder, saying I could pretend to be his nephew and go there to represent him, he said he didn't actually want to make any trouble: "Young man, you're too kind, but it's impossible to reason with these people."

Deciding to jump right into the deep end, not wanting to waste another moment, I asked him point blank, "Sir, is that the same group of men who took those hostages recently?"

Startled, the old farmer gawked at me weirdly, like you shouldn't talk about matters such as that one in public. "You...are a brave soul, and I see you need more things than just to help me out," he murmured. I came back with, "Sir, my real nephew is out there somewhere, probably taken as a hostage. I need to find that place, so please don't go and tell anyone else that I asked you about this."

Patting my arm fondly, he said simply, "I would *never* say anything; why, it would probably cause my *death,* dear Son! You're playing with your life...look through that mountain pass, over there."

This seemed an odd thing to say. But he was pointing his dry, ashy, hardened finger toward a valley between two mountains. "The first hill hides a village of very few people, right behind it. They're called the Black Wolves, and their elder is named Bacha. Once there, you may find all the answers that you seek."

That fast, that easy, it was done. I'd gotten all the info I thought I needed in just two days; less than that, really. If I had tried to work this job in uniform or use some other American asset, bringing in this info would've taken several months. Coming out here as an honorable Afghan man proved that the locals had all the intelligence we ever needed, as usual. It was filtered somewhat by the time it finally came to us, but collecting it by myself honed it into pure knowledge, which was important. Thinking through the names and titles in my file, which I'd memorized, I had the group commander's name from the old farmer; it matched the one on the file. *Bingo bonanza!* Bacha, the bad guys' leader, had a name that meant 'king' – how ironic was that?

Like in a chess game, I was now set to checkmate their king, even to kill him if needed.

Hiding my absolute joy, I bought an armful of fruit to take back to the compound, shook that wonderful farmer's eager hand to pass him a wad of Afghan currency, and headed back, preparing to make it all happen. I would have to move fast, as the route through the mountains required a driver or a taxi motorbike. Back 'home', I grabbed up my phone, passing the new intelligence on to Chuck – who was blown out of his mind, not believing how the rumors and info on their side was all wrong. He grilled me deeply about exactly what was said during my conversation with the farmer. I told him the next step was for me to head out with my GPS device, to get a grid locked onto me so that they could pinpoint my location. Briefing him in minutes, I hid the small GPS in a deep pants pocket, which billowed enough to successfully hide it.

I also told Chuck that I'd have to leave in the early afternoon. But he yelled that he needed more time, to brief all his guys and also Rogue. Retorting curtly that I didn't have time for such bullshit, I yelled: "Just make that shit *happen!*" Finally, I gave Chuck the brief for emergency response, in case some guys thought I was squirrely. He was overwhelmed back in the States, and didn't know where to start; he raced off to Rogue's office to brief him. Before he left, I told him that was the last time I'd talk to him that day, because carrying the phone on me wasn't an option. He agreed, knowing the only other way was to wait for my signal 'blips' to appear on his screen.

I was doing everything I could to maintain a calm poise and posture, but my heart pumped machinelike, with me thinking this was probably my 'Judgment Day'. Feeling crazy, I opened an inner dialogue with myself, dampening my spirits to make me less stressed. "This is do or die time, Farid! Now or never, you have to step up to the plate and hit a home run. The entire country is waiting for your answers."

Pacing back and forth, I concealed the GPS some more, thinking of cover stories and lines in conversation that I'd have to pursue. I was and am the type who has no patience when approaching the accomplishment of a task. Swooping out of the compound like a thinly disguised desert Arab, I entered an alleyway, stopping a teenager on a motorbike – pulling out 1,000 Afghani, in other words, twenty bucks, screaming at the boy to give me a ride. Jumping on the bike's back, I hugged him as we zoomed into that mountain valley off in the distance, with a bright red, orange, and yellow sun sitting placidly on top of it. Our spattering dust kicked up from an obvious car trail, as we drifted through the widely open desert fields.

This would surely mean either my success or my death – nothing else.

Chapter Thirteen
Captured by Goons

As the sun faded behind those two purple, spread-eagled mountains, I realized we'd better get there pretty soon; even though we moved fast, we were still a long way off from my destination, wherever it might be. The bike kicked up clots of dirt, skidding on small rocks and pebbles, sending them flying to either side as I tightly hugged the waist of the kid sitting in front of me, another one with no worries or cares. Unable to speak over the noise of the motorcycle, I busily enjoyed what might be my very last ride on this planet. Finally, I tried to say something, with the only thing coming out of my mouth being, "Are there...any IEDs...on this path?"

I heard back only a muffled, "No," but that was all I needed.

Entering the mountain range's valley, I could just make out a small village near the edge of what locals called 'the skirt' of one mountain. Throngs of 'Koches', small nomadic tribes, camped around there – usually gone in two days. They'd pitch their rustic tents, hobbling their camels, dogs, and sheep, and tie down their supplies and equipment, which they hauled to God knows where on their journeys. But the village zoomed into sight in split seconds, as I deduced that there was no other available place but this one for the hostages to be located. Now I only had to wonder which group of Taliban would be there when we squealed on in. I'd figured that letting them know I came to the village to resolve a debt I owed one of the villagers wasn't enough; I would also tell them I sought my nephew, to see if he was being held hostage at their location.

Screeching, suddenly pulling over to one side, the bike stopped. That kid summarily ordered me away, saying, "You're on your own now, my Brother," not even waiting for me to get completely off before he spun around, kicking up a huge cloud of smoke and dirt, and speeding home. Watching him, I saw his clothes flutter gently in the afternoon winds as he hauled ass safely back down the road.

Turning around to face the music, I heard dogs barking merrily somewhere in the near distance. I was completely alone in this forbidden land, and had to stew for several minutes over what was going to become my plan for the rescue. Looking every which way, I saw a lack of the normal traffic flow of people; no kids raced around like chickens with their heads cut off, as was their usual. Clearly, I was in for a night of drama, an episode of chaos that could easily end with my death. But I'd faced the same prospects for many long years, so this was nothing altogether new for me.

Reaching into my shoe, I pulled out the insole that covered the flat GPS system – I'd decided my pants pocket wasn't sufficient to hide it – and turned it on. This was the only means for anyone on my side in the real world to know exactly where I was. Slipping the GPS back under my insole, I began to walk past the lines of mud huts forming that small, temporary shelter of a local village. The walls of the huts were a lot taller than I'd expected; meanwhile, the noises of the Koches echoed from the back of the village, adults yelling at their animals to get them to return to the main campsite. Once there, the herds would graze the tall grasses and rest for the day.

In the way of weaponry, I had one little knife I'd brought in with me, my only means of security if something went the wrong way. I had taped it near my crotch, wearing tight American underwear to ensure that my only blade wouldn't fall out, regardless of how strenuously I moved. Passing each house, I saw it was empty, peering inside the ones without doors. My curiosity remained unsatisfied – this was apparently an Afghan ghost town. But obviously there was no better place at hand to secrete the hostages. It was just a matter of time before I found out where they were; it would then become a question of precisely how to approach things.

Chuck, certainly, was wired up on a screen in the States, monitoring every breadcrumb of the trail I was dropping for him. One thing I didn't want to do was start calling out for anyone, as I didn't have any names in the village other than the Taliban boss's. But wait, I could holler for my supposed nephew! So I started going loudly, "Jawid! *Jawid*! Where *are* you?" There was no answer, and the valley echoed hollowly with my lengthy sighs – but I decided to push on.

Seeing the Koches' lamps hanging lit up near their tents, glowing off far in the distance, made me think there might be somebody further on. Wandering with care, I gazed into the last flickering rays of the sun ducking below the horizon. It'd get dark real fast – I needed to make contact before nightfall, when it would be difficult to gauge friend from foe. Cautiously approaching the first tent I encountered, I leapt back, startled as a pretty girl came out, scaring me a good one as she spotted me and then spurted directly again into her tent. "There's a *weird guy* outside!" was shouted in their local dialect, and soon, a grown man burst forth from the flapping cloth, staring at me with vast outsider hatred from a short distance.

I cried out in true supplicant fashion: "Asalam Alaikum," a highly formal Muslim greeting, one you reserved for special people – waving my hand in what I hoped was a totally friendly style. Growling, the man crouched in front of his tent, probably thinking I was trying to spy on his beautiful daughter. But I openly declared my greeting again, meekly approaching him.

He swiftly put his hand up, saying, "Hold it!"

This stopped me dead in my tracks, as my heart reentered my mouth – I slowly spat it out with, "I am only looking for my beloved nephew, Sir."

The man, who appeared to be a somewhat older gentleman, maybe the girl's grandfather, said not one word but gave me a look I'd seen dozens of times before from the bad guys. If I'd had a gun, I would've seriously considered training it on him. Suspicion radiated like a glowworm from his scowling face. I felt threatened to the point of no return, so not saying another word, I walked away. This felt highly awkward, and I kept thinking I'd fucked everything up somehow. I looked over my shoulder a few times, to see if anyone was following me, but the two people I'd seen had vanished summarily back into their tent.

Time wasn't anywhere near on my side, yet, I could easily spend the night under the stars on the warm, rocky ground – though it would slowly turn into a freezing, arid landscape with no clouds above to retain what was left of the day's heat. But hearing more voices somewhere, I pushed East, away from the mountainside, to try my luck on the other tents. Finally, I reached a couple of kids playing marbles in front of their tent, who'd drawn a circle in the dirt for their perimeter. Walking over like I owned the entire mountain, I got down on one sweaty knee. Neither of them cared; they were talking trash to each other, completely absorbed in their game.

After a long moment, one of them looked up at me, frowning dismally. I smiled, saying lightly, as if I belonged there, "Hi, guys, who's winning?" Laughing, they both stopped playing for a minute, only to resume their trash talk. Soon their mother appeared from the tent, having heard a strange man's voice. But she wasn't wearing a flowing, all-encompassing burqa; obviously, she was too old to care if anyone saw her without one. Like the man earlier, she may've been the kids' grandmother, not the mother. She glibly spoke to me freely, surprising me outright – I shifted my head down in submission as we first made eye contact.

"Is there a problem, young man?" she breathed, an elderly sigh soft as lamb's wool in the gathering skeins of twilight.

"No, ma'am, I'm merely looking for my nephew, Jawid." Gazing at me with deep concern, as any mother or grandmother would, she must have thought I'd lost a youngster in this harsh environment.

Thinking to herself, she swiftly replied, "I haven't heard of any Jawid around these parts. What do you mean, you're looking for him?" Caught, I really didn't know what to say, but this was the only method I had currently of finding any new leads. So I recited my fiction story about how he'd gotten nabbed by the Taliban, and that he might be a hostage somewhere in this vicinity, as the old farmer had told me.

Taking a much deeper sigh than before, the lady told the boys to go inside the tent; as they entered it, I stood up, keeping my head bowed in a show of respect. I already knew she was a widow, because too much time had passed and no protective male figure had summarily emerged to take over our conversation. Whispering, the woman nervously told me that I had a lot of courage to come this way, settling into unknown territory. I nodded my sweating, itchy head, thanking her for knowing what this meant to me.

That look from the older gentleman had a sound reason behind it, more than just being for an intruder; I read in between the lines of this older lady's words, understanding now that her group was a bunch of Taliban sympathizers. They'd shown every sign I knew of this, while on the other hand, this woman probably only 'rolled with the pack' to make sure her kids were fed, making their lives easier the best way she knew how. But even though she had children, I could tell her heart was somewhere else – I would've bet a zillion bucks that the Taliban had killed her husband, leaving her with all the responsibilities of a 'grass widow'. Due to her kids, they'd left her somewhat alone; otherwise, they would've raped her repeatedly, used her as their whore, or married her off to a low-life vermin scum from their ranks. As a nomad, she simply occupied space, floating ably with the wind as was her tribe's wont.

With one last sigh, she told me to look up and stop being so formal; in fact, she practically ordered me to revere her as a mother, not a stranger. When I finally saw her soft, caring face, there were scars lining it everywhere. This took me completely aback; I didn't know what to say, staring, breaking eye contact and making it again. Without any alarm, she shifted her eyes, stating, "Look over yonder...do you see the edge of the mountain, where the great rock formation sticks out?"

Breathless with fear and wonder, I said, "Yes, ma'am, I most certainly do. What of it?" In that formation, she said, where the hill basically began, was a small platform leading into the mountain's insides. In rank disbelief, I was duly fascinated; I'd thought I was great at analyzing the area and my surroundings, but I'd *totally* missed this! It turned out to be exactly what and where I was looking for. This showed me starkly how foreign I still was to this country, even after the many years I'd bandied myself about here, researching things.

Pointing at many distant holes in the ground under the platform, she told me there were bunker caves leading into the mountain's 'stomach', as she put it. The whole thing was a gigantic jail cell, where the local Taliban kept their hostages. She didn't need to tell me these details; I simply put two and two together. Those scoundrels were smart little devils when it came to sneaky tactics. I'd never have thought that someplace that precise could be built by them underground, leading into a mountain and containing enough space within to hold their captives. *Brilliant!*

Well, there it was. I needed to go upward and enter the mountain's stomach now, hoping that I could give the Taliban a major case of heartburn. Thanking the scar-faced woman, I began to carefully tread my way over to the platform. At first it appeared to be close, but distances involving large objects like mountains are quite deceptive, so it turned out to be a lengthy hike. I was sweating bullets ten minutes into my walk, thinking constantly about the patrols I'd gone on where we passed similar mountain edges, not realizing that hostage holding cells could be incredibly close by. Considering our non-local American 'dullness', I bet those sneaky ol' Taliban dudes watched us as we passed by, laughing at how stupid we Americans were for not spotting their simple but callously elegant tricks.

As the mountain inched closer, the platform became much more visible. It was leveled, just like she'd said, and I was able to reach its top after about thirty more minutes. Lighting up a cig, I sought to calm my nerves for what might lay ahead. But peering over the edge of the platform, I spied two Taliban goons sitting on the floor, near an opening in the boulders – barely enough space for a human to pass through it. Spotting me quickly, they leapt up, and unsurprisingly, each man cradled an AK-47 fully automatic assault rifle – pointing two barrels of death straight at me.

There we were, with me thinking: here's where everything ends. When trying to kill rat bastards like the duo standing directly below, this was almost one of the moments I forever searched for in vain. Most of my Marines, no, *all* of them would've died to be there, having their rifles armed and being that close – face to face with the cowardly enemy. The Taliban were the ones who always ran away, or hid behind their women and children. They were mice, not men when it came to formal combat. But now I was in a similar position, being armed only with a knife the size of a can opener.

Having nothing to say, I thrust my hands skyward as my cig burnt out its last tobacco leaf, falling from my red-rimmed mouth. It burned my index finger, making me yell out the word 'Fuck!' So one of the Taliban screamed, "You must be out of your *God-damn* mind!" and he rushed me, his AK-47 pointing at my face. He pulled me down sidelong to their level, the floor of the platform, as we skittered among dry rocks and stones on the small cliff side. "Shut your God-damn *mouth*! What are you doing here, and you better start *talking fast*!" the other man thundered.

Getting ready for a major panic attack, I couldn't think straight, staring at the man pointing his rifle at me for several seconds. Turning the rifle around butt-first, he smashed my face, while I felt it crack me open like in the day with my brother Sal, knowing as I did back then that my nose was instantly broken. I hit the ground hard, going into a groggy daze, blaming myself for my gross stupidity and American ignorance, believing I'd made the biggest mistake of my life – coming here unarmed.

Suddenly, a radio bleated static in one of the men's pockets, crackling his call sign: "Spider, come in, Spider." The man kicked me over onto my back, and I could feel the blood rushing into one ear as I attempted vainly to look up, one of my eyes shutting from being bruised, filling up with white blood cells. Only vaguely conscious, I again heard, "Spider, come in." That brute pulled his radio out, responding, "Boss, we got an intruder…possibly an *informant.*"

If Chuck was still watching my breadcrumbs trail, he probably had noticed by now that I'd moved to a semi-enclosed location, hidden somewhere unknown, and he might be viewing that as a 'red flag'. But I didn't know what the hell he was actually doing; for all I knew, he was banging 'Rotten Crotch Susie' in the office's coffee room. It could've gotten boring, monitoring my whereabouts, you know. Maybe he was smarter than that, though, thinking of the things playing out for me, because of how late it was and how actively the GPS was moving. I could only hope this to myself, as one of the goons – with a dismembered hand – reached down to pick me up.

His nasty paws had tampered with one too many IEDs, and now he had only two fingers left on one hand. Also, there were scars on his arms that resembled Shama's nephew Mo's battle wounds, a true identifier of shrapnel sizzling deeply into his raw, protesting flesh. Anyway, he cruelly dragged me into a hole where some space opened up between the rocks, all the while stating on his radio: "Boss, we're en route."

The other goon followed closely, turning around quickly to snarl, "Stay *here* and watch the opening, *stupid!*"

I saw now that I was there alone, only me and this guy who'd shattered my nose crouching triumphantly over me while the other goon went in to report me. Bleeding profusely, I wondered how I'd let that *cocksucker* get away with this shit! Turning over and groaning a fake moan, I rocketed Kung-Fu style to my feet, standing up firmly enough to grab his collar in milliseconds – slamming my forearm and elbow directly into his nose. You see, I'm the type who doesn't wait for vengeance. He dropped down fast, with me cursing at him, spitting on him with righteous rage, calling him an infidel – while what was left of his nose gushed twin scarlet geysers. He'd passed out, from both the pain and his own cowardly fright.

Smiling, I neatly picked up his rifle and radio; but when I looked at the cave, there were other rifles aimed at my chest and head. Out of all those damn Taliban goons, it had to be the three stooges from the mosque, when I was with Karim. I should've *fucking known!* Those guys had been on to me – the reason they'd practically eye-fucked me back there was that they were the ones holding the hostages. Their role was to bring in anyone they thought was giving out information about them, and to kidnap any people for which they could demand a hefty ransom.

An older man – what *was* this, Senior Citizen's Day? – ordered me to drop the weapon or 'see the light of God's judgment in the next world'. Yeah, I was done; that was it. All the progress I'd made, the work I'd put in, was immediately flushed through the tubes with a loud sucking sound. I was a dead horsepucky. Looking down regretfully at the idiot I'd taken vengeance against, I decided I should've killed him a very long time ago, as he looked pretty much familiar to me. Maybe he weighed about a hundred pounds, soaking wet. How could I suffer a little bitch like him getting me captured? I'd calmly let him break my nose, because I hadn't wanted to spoil a plan that didn't even have a real end point yet. I was so fucking *stupid;* why didn't I take his weapon when he'd first gotten close, killing them both and possibly getting away?

Well, it didn't matter anymore; it was all a moot point. Standing there with an angry look on my mug, I trembled more with rage than fear as one of the three goons sauntered up to me slowly, taking the weapon and ordering me to turn around. The older goon cried out, "Search him, and bring him inside *fast!*" Any fears I'd experienced were over – all I noticed now was hatred and spite for the years of crap I'd taken from everyone, not just the Taliban. I'd learned long ago that being nice to people was a weakness, which proved to be true repeatedly in my life. Society attempted to make me believe that humans aren't animals; we can always reason with each other. But survival of the fittest was how I lived my life, not via 'have a nice day'! My ways were wrong to everyone else; I had to accept other people's norms, and not act savagely. Fuck, that's why I was so *soft,* and got myself *captured*!

Fuck everybody – they'd never seen any real life shit, nothing outside of the 'Mayberry' vanilla-white streets they lived on. Here I was, trapped in Afghanistan as an Afghan-American, trying my best to help folks I didn't know, ending up getting captured, put in the position of the very people I was trying to rescue! Spitting at my feet, the Taliban frisked me, and weirdly, they kept touching me all over, those depraved sickos – any minute, they were gonna find my hidden knife. But no, they didn't really pat down my groin area, *yay!* Not saying a word, the man searching me forced my hands into the air, in order to complete his pat-down search. I gave him my meanest hate stare, but he simply stated, *"Don't* make me repeat myself!"

The idiot I'd gotten back at finally woke up from dreamland, rising slowly as his 'friends' chuckled. "You weren't expecting a broken nose, huh?" asked one of them; obviously, they didn't experience the camaraderie we Marines did, where we were eternal friends and companions for life. Taking this as a cue, I looked at the other broken-nosed man, breathing heavily, "Okay, retard, that's what you get...does it feel good?" Staring at me with rage, he spat, "I will *deal* with you...you'll see what happens to *you*!"

My hatred overrode any other emotions, transforming me back into the hateful killer I was born and bred to become. I'd accepted my death long ago, letting my ego flow wildly and freely, drunk with nausea, bloodlust, and pain. As the goon I'd 'gotten' waltzed off into the cave, the other Taliban told me to take off my shoes. That's the last of me, I reasoned, as they'd now find my GPS. No more excuses or claiming I had a nephew to rescue; the device was a dead giveaway. I hesitated, but there was no way around this, so I took off my flip-flops, savagely kicking them over to my captors. Fortunately for me, the GPS didn't fly out into sight.

Grasping me by the shirt, as another goon picked up my shoes, we all entered the small cave, a cold, moldering stretch of oily rock that continuously slanted downward, eventually opening up to a massive, moss-lined cavern. I was dazed, thinking this wasn't humanly possible; but I'd heard a lot about cave living structures in Afghanistan. This wasn't man-made though, looking like some Indiana Jones style of crap. Maybe it was as old as walls from the 1300s, with prisoners chained up to stakes and tortured Muslim-style – which could be pretty rugged, I understood.

This was crazy – for a moment, I dreamed that Moses was locking me up for being irreverent, with the Ten Commandments about to be read one at a time to me over that minaret loudspeaker. Where the *fuck* were we? What the hell *was* this place, and why did it smell of fecal matter and *dead bodies?*

Looking over my shoulder, I could barely see – there were only two candles lit for the entire joint. By the flickering candlelight, I saw that the dark grey walls hadn't escaped the 'moon dust' that filtered freely into every crack and crevasse of Afghanistan...and there were blood marks and streaks running down the walls. Where was this Taliban's 'religion', which was supposed to be so pure and noble, when they couldn't manage to bury their decomposing dead within the twenty-four-hour religious timeline? Obvious corpses lay prone on the cavern floor, as disrespected and disdained as anyone could be. I'm gonna join them soon, I scowled; dead as a doorknob...probably *decapitated* too!

Meanwhile, broken pieces of bricks were scattered around. I stepped on one, thinking at first that it was shards of glass. I bet those poor victims had only eaten old, stale, dried-out bread, given just enough to stay alive – so those goons could collect their ransom money. The idiot that dragged me inside took me over to a wall, tying my hands and feet tightly with a rope and connecting it to a metal stake hammered into the ground. Growling like I meant it, I thought this was a weak way of locking someone up; but it was the least of my worries, so far anyway.

My eyes started closing up from my broken nose. But I saw two people chained to the wall straight across from me, who looked nothing like our captors. Both wore ripped, filthy clothing, and their heads hung so low I couldn't see their faces. Wow, their dirty blond hair proved they were foreign; my work *hadn't* gone to shit, not yet! I'd single-handedly made it to a pair of detained hostages, and I felt a well-deserved warmth creep over my body as I saw that I'd nearly accomplished the mission at my end. The GPS would eventually lead a team over to us, as long as Chuck and Rogue had grids locking onto my shoes that worked inside a huge mountain.

Realistically, though, I knew the last 'hit' they got was outside the cave, right before I went in, because no satellite signal could pierce through that much solid rock and scree material. But anybody who arrived out there would find the cave's entryway; if they weren't captured, they might even get here super soon!

My poor head pounded from my aching nose, and I didn't know what my life or death was gonna entail. We Marines had gone through courses of hostage situations, how you're supposed to remain calm, etc. Maybe it was fatigue kicking in, or my cold heart for everyone and anything, but at that moment, I was calmer than I'd ever been before in my life. Like those Afghan kids, I didn't have a worry in the world; but the one thing making me think twice was the GPS system. Since it hadn't fallen out of my shoes, I was planning on sticking to that story about my kidnapped nephew. But if they'd found the GPS, I was totally over with – I wasn't really worried about it, just concerned for Shama's and Zmaray's future lives and safety.

That sneaky rat bastard they called Spider ducked into the detention area, hovering over me like a bleakly angelical demon. Not able to stand him, I yelled out, "I can't see you, but I can *smell* you, you *fucking rat!*" I shouldn't have done that. He stomped on my chest multiple times, cursing me, my mother, and my wife, claiming that he had sex with them repeatedly. Guffawing loudly, though it hurt, I spat at him, knowing that in Islam, it's the biggest sign of disrespect you can give a man. His answer was to kick me extremely hard, and I only sneered, laughing, "You *skinny fuck,* I could've killed you in a *heartbeat!* You should be kissing my feet, not *kicking* me, for sparing your life. I stole your weapon, broke your nose *with my bare hands!*"

Leaning over, breathing his moist, sticky, obnoxious breath into my gaping face, he shut me up with one punch to my horrendously pain-wracked nose. Agony, vast and unconscionable, shot straight to my head, passing me out until next morning. When I awoke, I was shocked to be alive. But voices nearby were screaming, coming and going, while the cold, hard ground thrived with grasshoppers, crickets, and other insects crawling itchily through my pants. They'd made me wake up multiple times during the night – I was being *eaten alive!* I traveled into and out of thought, for long stretches believing fervently that all I was going through was only a dream.

Breaking dawn early, the cave heated up quick; it was just a shaded enclosure with scarcely any light beaming in. I knew if I had a mirror that I wasn't pretty. My face must've looked like someone's gym punching bag. Both my eyes were stickily, permanently sealed shut. I couldn't see, but could hear stuff in a muffled sense, wanting to make contact with those two American-looking hostages. At least able to think straight, I reasoned that I was lost from the grid for about fifteen hours, and someone on our side was bound to send an emergency mission our way, sooner or later.

Straining to listen for helicopters, I thanked God that in spite of my braggadocio I still breathed through my poor nose, albeit in a whistling manner.

Off to one side, whispers of Pushto filtered through the mucky air. I couldn't make out the conversation fully – every time one of the goon Taliban guards came in, everyone went silent, letting me know the guard had walked by. One of those shits kept coming up to me, cursing me and throwing water in my face, seemingly every couple of hours. One of them spoke to another one, saying that this guy is definitely not from here, look at his body – he's built too oddly. I figured this was due to my working out, as my muscle tone made me appear highly structured in their eyes.

They figured I was some kind of special soldier or fighter, and they passed the word around that I'd whipped Spider's ass a good one. They were duly impressed, so maybe that's why I was still alive. But hours crawled along as my eyelids slowly pulled puffily open, with me hoping to witness a team of American warriors racing through the mossy rocks, massacring the Taliban right in front of me. I knew by now that nobody had found out about my shoes, or I'd be dead for betraying their location and being an obvious and ripped, beefy, well-off American.

But when I was finally able to gaze out into the open floor, there was only the burned-out remains of a fire, keeping the cave warm at night, and my shirt and shoes stuck out of it, mostly burnt to ashes. This meant a lost signal, for God knows how many hours, days, or whatever. I reflected on this: what was Chuck up to? Did he require special permission to rescue me? Was I *unimportant,* given up on as MIA and not worth following? What *was* the deal here, *hey?*

As more hours crept past, and I was starving, I yelled at whoever was there to get me some food. In return a guard strolled over, informing me that if I kept on whining I'd receive another punch in the nose. Not needing more pain, I wised up, growing nice and mewing, "All I want, my Brother, is a bite to eat." I'm human, I can't live unless I get my meals. In my training, I'd learned that when being held captive, food is a total necessity. The Taliban knows this, as few rights are given either by or to them, and that was something they couldn't argue about. In minutes, I got a decent piece of bread to eat. And the guard who brought it untied me, stating that if I did something stupid, I was gonna get shot in the head, like those other idiots lying in the corner.

Not wanting to die for a change, or bring any more attention to my flattened nose, I came to my senses, realizing it was time to play 'the game' once more. I'd have to, or Shama would be a widow, and Zmaray would have no Daddy to upchuck on. So, I silently swallowed my bread, straining inside to figure out what to do next. Bread was good with me. It's all carbohydrates, and I needed fuel if I ever got any more chances to fight back, escape, or bring help to this location and save the remaining hostages.

What about my one and only weapon? Squeezing my legs, I sensed the knife I'd taped near my groin – amazingly enough, it was still there! None of the goons had actually appeared to like searching me sexually, so my fears were unfounded. I now had to come up with a way to get out of there, and do it fast, because God only knew what Chuck and Rogue were actually doing about my capture. I had thought that plans would be firmly in place for such a risky mission, as the likelihood of my getting captured was extremely high in this case. But nobody had taken the time to brief me on exactly what to do when captured, really. Well, it was a time-sensitive mission, and that's why I'd gone ahead and immediately jumped into the deep end of the piranha pond.

Mostly, right now I needed to find out if those two foreign hostages were among the ones on my list. I waited, calculating carefully when the guard was making his rounds, striving to hear what their radio call names were and exactly what was being said between them. The first opportunity I got, I looked over at the two hostages, hissing a soft "*Pssssssst*! Look over here, speaking *English*!" The two hostages' heads bounced up, like I was suddenly their only hope and savior. One of them, the male one, made eye contact with me – sincerely baffled as to what was going on.

I whispered, "Listen, I have a plan! I'm here to get us rescued, but I'm gonna need your help, okay? Do you speak English?"

Staring at me with the expression of a surprised cat, the man replied, "Yah, ein bissen." Holy cow; they weren't American, they were *Germans*! He had said, "Yes, a little." Straining hard to recall my Deutsch from decades ago, I tried my best to communicate. But he told me he could understand me a little bit as I messed up and mangled my German. Meanwhile, the female hostage gazed at me lovingly, like she was already free – a Special Operations Soldier had clearly come to save their schnitzel day!

Not wanting to disappoint her, I told them both to keep quiet, and then, a few of what I'd thought were dead bodies stirred. It turned out that they were the local Afghan hostages, as they began to talk in local dialect, begging me to tell them what was going on. They were skinny and in a very bad way, which is why I'd originally thought they were corpses. One of their older gentlemen proclaimed in a near-death croaking voice, "Listen young man, don't try something foolish…I don't want to end up dead, over there with the rest of those people." He was referring to a pile of actual corpses nearby; the ones the guards had shot in their heads. But I told him breathlessly not to worry, that everything was going to be all right…his response was for me to stop trying to be a hero, as most of us would be released once our families paid some nice lump sums of money for our ransoms.

Frowning, trying to make him understand, I told him that wasn't likely to happen – we'd likelier end up dead, no matter how much money was given to those callous, war-hardened Taliban goons. I'd seen this type of situation before, and they always take the money and end up killing their hostages. Whispering from the other side of the room, the Germans peered over at me as I asked them how long they'd been there. After they gave me the pertinent facts, it appeared that everything lined up with the remarks, notes, and information stored in my manila file. These two were the right ones, and I needed to at least get them out of here, and everyone else too if possible.

"How many Taliban are in this cave, altogether?" I asked.

They thought for a minute. "We saw a couple new guys last week, but roughly four men take care of everything from the front of the cave to the inside."

I decided that wasn't too many, as long as I could wrap my hands around one of those AK-47s. The whole day after that was spent planning, plotting, and watching the Taliban's every move. Their boss eventually showed up, in order to brutally question me about who I was and why I had appeared with such a show of forcefulness.

I repeatedly answered with, "My nephew Jawid, that's all I want, and that's why I came in here," sticking like glue to my cover story. He wasn't buying it, screaming: "Who do you work for, the *Commandos?*" Those were the Afghan Army Special Forces. From my general demeanor, he'd decided that I was a soldier with them. While we bantered, the two Germans stared – the Taliban leader kept kicking me in my chest, leaving it raw, bleeding, and bruised from his interrogation-style tactics. He didn't believe my story for one minute, finally stomping over to the German lady, yanking her up by the hair caveman-style, showing me her screeching, fear-streaked face.

"You came for these *infidels!* Did you come here to find this *whore* and her *pimp?*" he declared, trying to get a rise out of me.

Knowing this, I sighed, "Fuck them, you can keep the infidels...just give me back my nephew."

Breathing hard, the Taliban boss came back with, "I have yet to know this *nephew* of yours, but trust me, I will find him *too*...and he will be here next to you, sooner or later...*if he exists at all!*"

I remained still and quiet, trying to look distressed at the very idea. But I'd successfully diverted him from thinking that the hostages were my actual mission. The boss left as fast as he came in, yelling at the guard to not feed me anything for the night. I didn't care, as this'd give me time to get at my knife blade. Their goons, like our troops, were ordered to stay awake all night. But unlike us, they tended to pass out once they figured we were all asleep. Their laziness and lack of motivation would prove out, costing them severely. I needed to break free fast as I could, heading home and calling Chuck from my cell phone. They were playing 'hold ass' for too long. I couldn't wait forever − losing my one window of opportunity.

Like I thought, the laziness of the guard prevailed. Telling him I needed to take a leak late that night, I woke him up, with his groaning the bitter entrails of lazy grief. Telling me to shut the hell up, he slapped me hard upside my head. But I kept begging and begging him to take me to the edge of the cave and let me urinate, so he finally untied me, shoving his rifle into my back and ordering me to hurry up.

Wandering over to the edge of the rocks, I relieved myself with my back turned to him, keeping him from hearing the tape unseal from the knife. My hands were still tied, which would make things much more interesting. I coughed a lot as a cover sound, but he wasn't paying any real attention to me. It shows you how sloppy the Taliban can get. What more could I expect? This dude was probably a simple farmer last week, getting paid to watch over the hostages as of days ago. But I didn't care; it was good enough for him to die on that clammy, moss-covered night.

He let me finish up, and then I asked if he could help me with the string elastic for my trousers, as my hands were roped together. Staring at me with clear disgust, he spat out, "You must've lost your damn mind...*hurry* and get the hell *done*!" Turning back to walk, the knife hidden in my hand, I let my string go − halfway back, my trousers drooped in front of everyone.

The guard saw my naked rear end as he stood behind me, blurting out, "Have you no shame, you *pig*?" This was all part of my elaborate Bare Ass Plan, to get his attention diverted away from my knife.

He drew close to me, and that was my opportunity. Wheeling in a circle, butt-naked as a carefree Afghan kid, I forced the five-inch retractable blade straight into his left ribcage, feeling it drive into the bottom of his lung. He let out one little 'peep' as my formal training as a Marine kicked in, with me twisting the blade furiously, ripping it out of his body with a most sickening sucking sound. This is a surefire way to kill someone, as it ensures that they will bleed to death mercilessly.

I watched casually as his eyes rolled up to his skull, neatly catching him on his way down. His blood drenched my naked fore and hindquarters, as I let him slide slowly, cutting my rope to free my hands. Gently, I pulled up my bloody trousers, noticing the whole room was still asleep – except for the Germans, whose rheumy eyes popped open wide in shock. They'd seen something deemed a man die in front of them, although I wouldn't have called him a man myself – more like a casualty of war.

Chapter Fourteen
Switching Sides

After letting the guard slide lethargically down my body, feeling equally lethargic, I watched the pair of German hostages. They were almost gloating, carefree now, thinking this meant that they were completely saved. I didn't mind them and their needs, though; I had too many other matters racing through my mind. Who would be next in line, for example, to explain himself to Almighty God?

Picking up the AK-47, grateful to cradle a real weapon at last, and also the radio the guard had stowed in his pants pocket, I tore off his bloody shirt and donned it. Hopefully in the dark, I could pass for a few important moments as one of the enemy. Glaring down at the guard's lifeless body, I cold-bloodedly scanned what the blade had done to his insides. Its serrated edge had caused severe, necessarily fatal damage, but that of course was the entire point and nothing else.

Death was merely death once more for me; as I've pretty much already said; whether you die choking on a small piece of candy or from a horrific, gut-wrenching knife wound, the end result leaves behind a soulless chunk of mortal flesh, one that used to belong to a living human being. All this time, the Germans were too tired to be frantic or scared in any way – they were probably spy operatives, used to the sight of death, fully aware that it was inevitable under such circumstances.

The most important thing now was that the guard's buddy would materialize soon enough, especially if he didn't see his partner reporting at the front of the cave. So, I slunk over and waited near the entrance, putting the AK-47 down for a second in order to calculate the next kill's silently creeping approach. With due certainty, the other goon walked right in, looking around for a minute, wondering where his friend had disappeared to – whispering his name aloud. Gloating, I waited while he finally spied his buddy, on the ground spread-eagled over a mounting puddle of blood. As he stood riveted, I simply crept up behind him, yanking his long Afghan hair back, stabbing him hard and fast twice on the side of his scrawny neck.

The serrated edge didn't slow down, spreading his neck and arteries open like melted butter. He gasped loudly, experiencing extreme pain as I lightly turned him about, dropping him to his protesting knees. Holding his loud mouth shut, I stabbed the other side of his neck, a final means to kill him off and silence him faster. Out cold now, he was dead in seconds, from bleeding red fountains out swiftly. Two down; the other two were most likely sound asleep and would make incredibly easy kills.

In the pitch black darkness of the chilly cave, I used my experience in unlit areas to my advantage – humans can adapt well to the dark, seeing lighter and darker contrasts as our eyes assimilate them. And having no flip-flops on helped a lot, although I had to think to myself that I was doing things that I wasn't supposed to be doing. Unofficially, I had just killed two people in an aggressive manner, defying local laws. But then, I had to arrive at the conclusion that neither of them were really people, only Taliban scumbags who regularly hurt innocent others for their own lousy benefit.

I was almost a trained operative, or something along those lines; people back in the States who didn't have any training could kill others with ease, so the situation that God had recently put me into was probably good, and for an excellent reason. Sitting quietly down, I let my blood pressure and breathing calm me, turning the radio dial down so as not to blow my cover. The next item on my agenda was to place both rifles where they couldn't be readily reached, just in case something went wrong. The easiest thing to do presented itself; I simply walked over to the

Germans, untying them and handing each of them an AK-47, ordering them not to move until I returned.

The last two goons, as I suspected, were out cold for the night. Their breathing, slow-paced and even, let me know this; their weapons sat right next to them. This didn't render them out of reach, not just yet. I leaned over, sweating badly, having to peer into their ugly faces – one dude from Haji Sahib's mosque was closer to me, laying on his stomach to sleep with a small rag under his face, probably his patu. I gently but quickly forced his face into the patu by grabbing a thick chunk of hair from behind, breaking free with my bloodlust, not caring about anything. His softened, muffled screams sounded almost like sexual moans in the dark as I furiously slammed my blade into his back and neck regions, going for an easy, noiseless kill.

Releasing his limp body, I glanced over at his buddy, the last goon to kill. He was also the idiot who'd broken my nose, so he needed my extra-special loving care. Aggressively, I screamed in his face, not needing to worry about sound levels anymore, and spat right into his surprised and open mouth. Then I stabbed him, while choking him simultaneously, just to prolong my enjoyment of the moment. Mostly, I wanted him to know exactly who was murdering him, letting him realize what an inefficient, inept little monster he was. In this world, buddy, other monsters wait to kill you.

Everything being over in under five minutes, I'd wasted all four of them. Emotions rushing through my head, I fell to the ground, the 'high' from my blood lust crashing in and on me. Coming back to reality, I noticed I was soaked in blood, and began crying, not even really knowing why. What and who was I…I was simply not myself. All the time it was happening, I deeply enjoyed it; this is exactly what leads a man to do these awful things, simply for the rush and the adrenaline. The only difference between a ruthless killer and a more moral individual was that the latter feels the aftereffects of another person's death, as I was managing to do. Locked into an emotional rollercoaster, tumbling up and then downhill, I recovered in no less than three minutes from whatever the hell had hit me in that dark, dank, stinky cave.

Luckily, this was all occurring at night; in Afghanistan, traffic stops during the nighttime, whether foot traffic of people or car traffic – signals and transmissions included. Anything important could wait until early dusk the next morning. That meant I had to abscond with one of these goons' motorcycles or whatever transportation they used, heading back to the village to grab my bag's cell phone. I'd let Chuck and Rogue know about my 'win' so that they could determine what to do next. It was probably the middle of the night, I reasoned; we only had a few brief hours left.

Not wanting to compromise anything, I journeyed back into the open part of the cave, where I made all the local hostages wake the hell up. The Afghans were wide-eyed already – they'd heard my witless scream of triumph, after I slew the asshole who broke my nose. Speaking first to the German couple, I told them to watch over everyone, not moving an inch from their present location. It was by far the safest possible place during the nighttime. They agreed, knowing that traveling through these parts in the dark wasn't safe, also considering how their golden hair made them stand out. I further told them not to release any of the Afghan detainees, because it might result in more problems for them. They should wait for the other forces to come help them, I said, and they both nodded their blond heads – with me adding that if worst came to worst, I'd be back before dusk to set everyone free, leading them all to safety.

Carrying out one of the radios, I left one behind, asking the Germans to not change any frequencies on it or fiddle with it in any way. They could, however, use it as a last resort to contact me, if I didn't come back soon enough. Well, that was it. I hopped onto a motorcycle I found not far from the cave entrance, revving its engine to top speed, careening down the skirt of the mountain. The entire tribe of Koches had summarily vanished, moving on again as was their style. They'd disappeared without a trace of who they were and where they went. This was normal; it's why the

Taliban stayed near them, because nobody would ever expect the bad guys to be located in their vicinity.

Thoughts and mental pictures of the gruesome murders I'd so freely committed ran like rivers of blood through my skull, but I reassured myself that it was profoundly a case of either them or me; their deaths enabled over half a dozen people to go on living. I kept telling myself that God wanted this, intending it to happen exactly that way. Maybe when those four goons felt my blade drive into their necks, they realized how they were going to see their maker, with all of their sins rushing forward in time as they became instantly frightened to die. True believers and those free of sin don't mind going into the Hereafter, for it means a swift ticket to absolute Paradise.

Lost in my thoughts, I looked back at the mountain range growing smaller in the distance, zooming ever closer to Karim's village. I rehearsed what Karim or Haji Sahib were likeliest to say, because I'd pretty much abandoned my house, not going to prayers and vanishing without a word to them. But all of a sudden, I heard a horrible sound in the distance, unable to believe my ears – I thought it was surely a trick! That sound had haunted me, not letting me sleep at night, as I'd heard it repeatedly for many long years. Those double propellers penetrating the air, showing the force of the machine, sounded like a massive diesel engine ripping gorily into the sky...I pulled the bike over, squinting my eyes against the mounting light of the early sun.

There they were! Those CH-47 Chinook helicopters always flew together in pairs, used for their reliability and speed. I couldn't believe they were our choppers as they soared over the mountains, circling them, and then beginning their planned circular descent. Chuck had obviously sent in a basic rescue team of heavy-hitting soldiers at long last, ones with unexcelled military training. They were heading for the last spot they'd seen my GPS pinging at; I couldn't see them land, but they must've gone to the very area I'd just burst out and down the road from.

Sitting there idly on the motorcycle, I didn't dare drive back, as it was too far away now. Fifteen minutes later, the birds soared up into the sky, returning to base. How *stupid* could I get; that was my ride *back home!* I was supposed to have gotten on those 'copters, along with the other hostages. Feeling abandoned and like a prime fool, I couldn't figure out whether the miss was my own fault or that of the agency. I'd been abandoned, lost in a terror zone with a broken nose, most of the threats still around. But when I saw the birds head in the direction of the airfield, I knew that the hostages had probably been found and saved. What the hell was I gonna do *now?*

The feeling I had was similar to if I'd walked into my home, seeing my wife cheating on me in front of my eyes. I'd been betrayed, and didn't really know what to do next; my body felt so weak, and I was going quietly crazy. Kindness and military training, what little I had of either, kicked in; I had to go home and try to call Chuck and Rogue, in case more Taliban were entering the area. Revving the bike again, teary-eyed, I made my dismal way home to Karim's compound.

Getting to the village, I was extremely paranoid, having two black eyes from my visibly flattened nose, thinking that everyone had heard the news about the 'mountain raid' by now, with the hostages being found. Covering my face with my own patu, I stopped at the small door into my room's area, barely getting the key into the lock with my hands continuously shaking. I 'owned' a dead man's motorcycle, and needed to get the thing inside before someone saw me. Finally, I walked into an eerily quiet and people-free compound. This was weird – where were all those little kids, running around like there was no tomorrow? Paranoid and nervous, I twitched at this scary movie scene; anything I heard made me jump six feet straight up.

Going to my dwelling's door, I noticed the lock was broken, like someone had hit it repeatedly with a rock – from the dusty buildup on it. I slowly opened the door; it screeched, covering over me calling out Karim's name.

There was no answer, and as the door let the sunlight into my dwelling, I saw that my main bag was gone. All of my personal belongings and everything else, including the cell phone, was hidden away in that special bag. My heart sank; I didn't know what the fuck to think. Overwhelmed, I fell on the floor once again, not knowing if this was due to trauma mixed with excess stress, or just me knowing how bad of a bind I was in.

Gathering my winded wits together, jumping to my feet, I kicked the door off its hinges, realizing that Karim was the type of person who tended to be suspicious, probably needing to find out all about what I was doing. That meant he'd found my money and everything else – my cover was indeed blown. Walking into the courtyard, I called out loudly for Haji Sahib, but no one responded. My head pounded with a thousand ideas, thinking the Taliban may have gotten on the radio while I was held captive, and then they came directly to the house. Maybe Karim and some local Taliban fled with my money and other stuff, possibly to sell it.

I was done; I had nothing, not even a lead. All I knew after several minutes wasted of strolling around the compound was that I had to leave immediately, or risk being either killed or captured again. I leapt back onto the bike, riding out of the compound, not even knowing where I was headed. My main idea was to vacate that area, because what was done was done, and I couldn't ever return. Chances were that I was a target now, so I rode out, leaving behind anything I had there.

I'd also left behind four dead goons and eight freed hostages; the good at least was outdoing the bad. I rode swiftly through the bigger, paved streets, not knowing enough about the smaller ones to understand what blocks or IED threats might occur on them. When I finally reached downtown, I tried to find Karim's store; but the shops in the city tended to look too much like each other. This burg was huge, and I didn't know it well enough to make out where I was at the time. The thing to do was to try to make it to the airfield, and see if the people there would accept me.

My only problem was a total lack of documentation. People in that area spoke English, so it wasn't to my advantage to know it to prove my identity. The soldiers would probably not believe me, or even comprehend what I was talking about if I told them my weird, unprovable story. Everything was on a Top Secret basis. And I didn't suppose that the Afghan National Army would let me through their preliminary checkpoints, or anywhere near the airfield. This was not to mention how suspicious I looked, with my broken nose and busted face, and my blood-soaked Taliban attire. Nonetheless, I had to try, for my own sake at least.

Once at the airfield, it all played out as I'd thought. If I'd been on those soldiers' side, I wouldn't have let a strange-looking person like me onto an American Forces base either. There was no reason for me to even try anymore; I had to face facts. I'd been accidentally abandoned, left behind only to rot. I'd put in my greatest efforts and will to finding the hostages, and was getting screwed at the end. Mostly, I hoped the German couple would say something to the Americans that rescued them; but I figured that had been screwed up too, with me leaving the scene before help came. I also knew the bad guys well enough to see them jumping all over the scene where the helicopters had gone, probably making sure to go get their deceased friends' bodies. So there was no point to returning there, to hope for a second rescue attempt for me.

I had no options left. What *was* I gonna do, where was I gonna *go?* Keeping my motorcycle, my only friend, within arms' reach at all times, I ended up sleeping outside for a couple nights, with my eyes slowly improving and the swelling settling down for my nose. But I had to beg for a bite to eat from passersby, receiving meager handouts from the locals strolling past me. So there I was, a bum in my native country, smelling worse than a pile of donkey crap. I hadn't taken a shower, brushed my teeth, or had a real meal in more than four days. Miserable, I hated my life – stuck, with no one looking for me to save me from this hell hole of an existence.

Afghanistan is a place where everybody is out for himself alone. Survival of the fittest is the mentality, and I had lived by that creed too; but now I was thoroughly screwed. The fucking agency, Chuck and Rogue, were drinking champagne, celebrating their win, while I was suffering, rotting, and dying. Each minute that crawled by, I felt more contempt and hatred for them, lying in the dirt under a tree and contemplating my navel, hour after unmitigated hour. I had done all the hard work, had put my freaking ass on the line, and for what? Shama was right; she had an idiot for a husband, one who didn't listen enough to his wife. I'd lost everything I had in the last twenty-four hours; I had to do *something,* and do it fast!

The only thing coming to mind was to head for the neighboring province of Helmand, going to my old Marine base there to seek help. Vigorously plowing through the bike's saddle compartments, I found a stash of cash the goons had kept for themselves. God was into helping me one last time, giving me some money to assist me on my needed journey. It wasn't much, but in Afghanistan you can make a lot out of nearly nothing sometimes. First buying food and drink, I also filled up the tank, asking a couple of people which road went west, lighting out on my bike as fast as its three speeds and halting, chugging motor would take me.

My ride was loaded down with thoughts, and I had more stale, irate feelings toward Chuck than I did toward Rogue. Chuck had been a Marine, and you never, *ever* leave your Marine behind! That was our creed, but I knew they wouldn't come back for another mission, or so I thought. And my mind also boggled from reflecting on Karim and his family. Did they get slaughtered for housing me? Maybe Karim found my bags and money, deciding it created a great opportunity for him to take off; but what about the wealthy, non-needy Mullah Haji Sahib? He had no reason to run from the Taliban, so why would he rob me? The only conclusion I could reach while riding the long, dusty, winding road was the old man may have taken the blame for me, probably being killed or taken away as a hostage himself for assisting me.

Yeah, it must've been that yellow-footed Karim who got scared, taking my bag and popping smoke before the Taliban got to him. Suddenly, I remembered the radio I still had on me, the one I stole from the goons to possibly signal the hostages. So I pulled my precious bike over to the side of the road; the tires screeched complainingly as I swept the radio out with one smooth motion, thinking: those low-life *Germans!* Why didn't they radio or signal me like I'd said, if something was happening? Seemingly, they'd never showed the Special Ops team that I was the one who'd saved them and killed their Taliban captors. Enraged, I harshly turned on the radio, trying to catch any signals; nothing came over but scattered static.

Turning it back off, I shoved it deeply into my pocket, now feeling only embarrassment. There I was, stuck, riding merrily away, with no one in the whole world knowing who I was and where I was really going. I was only a loner, one who couldn't break my own inner dialogue in my head. Thinking I was going crazy, I knew that I didn't have any actual plans. I just needed to get to a place where I might find refuge. The neighboring borderline was coming up fast, and it held a lot of checkpoints and police – one thing I couldn't trust was the cops of Afghanistan. They'd sell you out for anything; not all of them were bad, but it was enough for me to steer clear of them in general. Corruption was rife throughout their government, not assistance.

So there I was, entering a province I hadn't seen since my days in the Marines, when we simply ran through it inside those little Humvee trucks, destroying the enemy right and left. Six years later, I was on a similar front, as awful as the day I'd left it behind. The poppy farms glowed as freshly as ever, and the canals supplying the water to those fields were just as filled with light green water flowing through them. As I've said, much of the world's supply of heroine comes from this place, making it not the best or brightest region of the world. Meanwhile, back in the good ol' USA, Chuck and Rogue were probably more worried about national security than they were about me personally. By now, they'd visited Shama at our apartment, interrogating her about my whereabouts and me – where the fuck *was* I?

They'd surely ask her if I'd made any type of contact with her in the last couple of days, approximately a week ago or so. Shama's interrogation, as I found out later, didn't go very far at first – because she fainted once she realized that I was missing, and the agency didn't even know my whereabouts. This was a clear sign that I was long lost. Those agency bastards didn't come at her in a kind or caring way, after I'd done all their dirty work for them; they just drilled her with unstoppable questions about my behavior, to pick up on any signs if I was turning stakes. Maybe I was a *traitor!*

They also got debriefed from the Special Ops team about the four dead Taliban goons, four AK-47 rifles, and three radios found on the scene. They went over the blood, noting that the Taliban were killed from behind with major stab wounds, not having enough time for more thorough forensics; but it was enough for Chuck and Rogue to see that I'd gone right ahead and taken matters into my own hands. Often, a mission doesn't play out exactly as intended; it just kind of becomes improvised as things occur. Chuck and Rogue probably thought I'd been trying to play hero, maybe even wanting more bloodshed themselves, but for security reasons they couldn't just let me go that way without some kind of penalty.

I thought it might have to do with some of the Top Secret gear I was carrying with me, and the identification documents they'd supplied me with, too. This time was one of those when you become just an 'asset', and the gear and my reputation were the only reasons for them to even contact poor Shama. They weren't coming home with an apology for having lost me; they only laid a hammer on her head, finally leaving without giving her any insight about me, solely for security reasons. Security reasons *my ass!*

Shama ended up calling all my friends right after they left, while Chuck and Rogue already had her phone tapped, to get any conversations traced.

First, Shama called Jimmy's wife July. As Jimmy was my best friend and Shama wanted to meet with her, finding out as soon as possible if maybe I contacted Jimmy or her somehow. Shama then called Melvin, Steve, Jose, Adam, and Big Dee from the gym, waiting on a coffee date with July later on. Even my cousins Tuna and Habib were notified that something had gone horribly wrong this time. All my contacts were on our phone, and Shama wasted no time in meeting with them each one by one, getting no info from them as it was the first time they'd heard that anything had happened to me. Her main intent now was merely to let them know, so if I did contact someone, they would get over to Shama with it as soon as possible.

My friends all loved Shama, and while they tried to be casual about this horrendous situation, they feared my type of work, having no idea what its bigger picture was actually all about. They'd heard plenty about my deployments and trips to Afghanistan, but had no real idea of what I was doing over there. Shama told them not to tell anyone else about this situation, and they all vowed to respect that. Naturally, Chuck and Rogue traced every call she made, taking their own turn to check on things.

They nabbed Jimmy at work, pulling him out of the hospital by showing off their badges, telling his boss that he was needed by the U.S. government but was not 'in any trouble'. Then Melvin, Big Dee, Jose, and Adam were taken off their jobs, all in a four-hour span of time. They were brought to the agency's holding booths, unknowing of what had taken place, each and every one of them locked into terror – due to their long-time friend disappearing in Afghanistan. Their group was interrogated all at once, so that none of them could alter their stories; each one was told to swear in for their statements. They were drilled with extremely elaborate questions about my jaded past, and what kind of character I'd presented to them. Going down a whole list prepared by the agency, my friends all had nothing but good things to say about me, of course.

Going especially after Big Dee and Jimmy, Chuck and Rogue were speedy in making small threats, attempting to eke out any smidgen of info about me. My cousins were next, and their interviews were even longer, as the agency wanted to compile a family lineage, to see if I'd contacted any distant relatives. They thought perhaps that a second or third cousin might play a role in these matters. But everyone had absolutely nothing new to give them, so they were released many long hours later, worn out after being questioned repeatedly – ready to just head home and cry over me.

However, Jimmy and Big Dee asked to stay in contact with Chuck and Rogue, in order to offer any further help that they could. Furthermore, Jimmy wanted to fly out to Afghanistan; but the agency denied that quick, only interrogating him further for his efforts and for the fact that he'd recently converted to Islam. Hispanics usually didn't do this, so it was highly suspicious to them. And Big Dee being a prior Marine, they dove fervently into him too, thinking he knew something simply because he was so avid to help them find me. But little did Chuck and Rogue know about my friends – they'd never say or do anything to hurt me, being part of a small, eclectic handful of people close to me, the ones who always had my back. I don't get what the agency's real intent was, or what kind of pattern they were looking for to judge me by, but all my friends were finally dismissed, now totally fearful for their own families and lives.

July wanted Jimmy to not intervene, keeping with his regular ways and work schedules. Shama thanked everyone, and they all pledged to be there for her, with Mo also finding out about things and coming over to support her. Shama felt deep trauma, and if anyone could help with trauma, it was Mo – after he survived that blast, and as a very positive, motivated person. Those days were the hardest for Shama, as she stared at my carbon-copy baby boy, little Zmaray, who was growing bigger by the day; his mother, breaking down frequently, kept to herself and just cried alone.

As her life was suddenly a complete mystery, there was nothing for her to do but wait, hoping that her husband was going to reappear someday from the hidden depths of hell; she didn't know that I'd killed four men for the sake of others' lives. But even if she did, she wouldn't have looked at me any differently. Shama was not one to judge me, and I wish I'd been there with her, wiping away her tears and rocking her to sleep in my loving arms, like we'd done so many times before.

I couldn't, though; I was stuck out in the middle of nowhere, with only a vague 'plan' and a new cover, looking somewhat like the Taliban. And oddly enough, I was deep in heavy thought about this very thing – eventually deciding that I wasn't gonna keep being America's little puppet! It was time to break free, to become who I really was, what I was born to be. I *wasn't* born in America – I was born in *Afghanistan!*

Why else had I constantly returned, year after aching year, to the country of my origin? I'd never achieved my best goals in America or by working for Americans, as much as I'd tried to – pushing hard as possible to be an integral part of American society – but they didn't accept me or my deepest, most honest core beliefs. I was slowly growing incredibly angry about all the things I'd done to help America, proving that I was true to the very country that had left me abandoned, desolate, and alone. No, I wasn't truly American; *I was Afghan.* That long journey to the border by motorcycle made me realize that I was stuck hunting for my own people, my own distant heritage. I was slowly redefining my roots, turning my back on everything I was supposed to be.

Back in the day, I recalled my mother telling me, "Farid, think about how you were always the black sheep in our family. You joined the U.S. Marines, and they are considered to be crazy, fearless killers. Just think: if you were born in Afghanistan, you would likely have become a

Taliban killer." I wasn't a normal American, and by golly, she was right; I was a person who wanted, no, *needed* to kill, relishing the taste of death and liking to bring it to other people, albeit only the bad ones.

The war had turned me into something wild that craved a kill. The feeling of killing another man is undeniably the hottest rush you can get, greater than anything coming from any drugs or even sex; the power surge is *awesome!* You're in charge of one of God's creation, and it's a lot like giving birth, the taking of a life. You are the one being who can send that other soul to their maker for final judgment.

On that long bike ride, my feelings for America were changing into something I couldn't deal with anymore. That fast, I saw why I was a jack-of-all-trades, master of none, needing to make an imprint in the concrete of this life, and to have a legacy to leave for my wife and son. Who was to judge me about right and wrong? Did anyone judge the agency, the people who'd left me behind? Was there anyone to judge the Germans, saved by an Afghan, who couldn't even tell me about the helicopters coming to collect them? Germans killed Jewish people and many others by the millions, and were simply the most racist people that I knew. Why did I go in to save them, when nobody in particular but my family and friends cared about me?

Did the Taliban, *brown men like me,* know that so many white people were two-faced? Like me, was it *possible* that they also were being torn in two? Hey, maybe I was wrong before; what if the Taliban were really the good guys, and everyone else in the world, like they thought, were the bad guys? I mean, these dudes were at least all warriors of a similar kind, giving their full attention to God. How is that a bad thing? Why did I deny my own culture and faith, for these unholy American devils who would always leave me behind, deserting me in a heartbeat?

The point behind the Taliban, as I understood it, was to wreak hell on the heathens in their country, bringing in Islamic law full force. What if their attitudes toward women, girls, and going to school were something I could *change?*

What if they only needed new leadership, a person like me who could willingly assist them in doing whatever they really wanted to do – showing the whole world that they had terrific, honorable intentions? I could be a big-time leader in my own country, saving and preserving the reputation of what the title 'Talban' actually meant. Those men are students of Islam after all, and they would take proper care of the mosques, ensuring that the clergymen received ample food and were kept *safe* from the infidel outsiders who didn't believe in their version of Almighty God!

Maybe the *real* Taliban, which I'd never actually met, only contained a few 'bad apples' who could be fixed. After all, they were Afghans, and it wasn't the Taliban who flew those planes into the Twin Towers in New York City. It was the Arabs, who always had their slimy hands elbow-deep in terror. The Taliban weren't *really* marked terrorists; not one Afghan was on that flight list, and not one Taliban had ever been publicized as a major terrorist, either. Osama bin Laden was a Saudi, and so were all of his goons. Mullah Mohammed Omar, on the other hand, was a warrior who helped fight the Russian invasion, saving two girls who were being raped in a compound near Kandahar. He was part of my legacy, a real hero – the spiritual leader of the *Taliban!*

My time as an American, which was unreal to begin with, was finally completely over as I rode through the lingering miles of Taliban poppy farms. I didn't feel any fear now, not anymore. My beard was filthy with slime, and my clothes were equally dirty, albeit the blood had turned them black. I stopped multiple times to be a proper Muslim and pray, pointing my direction of prayer toward Mecca, feeling a continuous epiphany about who I was, what I needed to do in this life. I deeply repented the killing of my four brothers, in Islam and in arms, wishing fervently to make up for their deaths.

Sitting there on my folded up patu, kneeling in devout prayer, I saw the bloated sun nestling like a red-breasted bird on the horizon, hot as ever. I've heard that when a red sun sets, and the sky turns scarlet, where the redness overcasts is an area of many sins and wrongdoings; God is showing his creation the color of their sins. This new province of Helmand was rank with utmost sin; but I was done sinning against my own people and my new, far more understandable and precious faith.

Swearing to become a student of Islam, I fully accepted my true destiny. I brought God down into my heart, and Almighty God showed me the one true light during that bike ride, because I believed that when a man has nothing going for him and he is at his lowest point, only the richness of God could fulfill his spirits again. When you're down, the only way left is straight up; so it was my time now and forever to *rise!*

Chapter Fifteen
Life in the Taliban

Each passing moment, it sunk in deeper that 'my' so-called country had betrayed, back-stabbed, and denied me, leaving me to rot alone in the deserts of Afghanistan. This was the worst mistake the USA could make, especially the agency. Maybe they knew I had no future anymore with them, and that I'd learned too much about their intelligence – the only way to set America straight would be to go back *home,* to where I originated, no longer denying my Afghan heritage, roots, and ethnic history.

Really, I couldn't tell for one second if I was going insane, or if I was just letting my hatred ooze through my warrior's soul, ingrained purely enough for me to realize that the agency had decided two Germans for a half-American, ex-Marine was worth the trade, choosing them without worrying about me at all. Last time I'd checked, we'd been shooting them from five hundred meters out, in the last world war. Now these infidels, these 'real Americans', had deserted me for some low-life Germans.

Who the *hell* did the agency think they were? My friends paced provocatively through my feverish mind as I raced from one village to the next, watching the villagers watch me, seeing in front of them a man with a new mission in life. I didn't know where I was going, heading deeply into the province, thinking that no one could ever know exactly where I went. Hot after a new life, you could say I actually desired my old life back, the one that I'd never had the chance to attain before.

I was good with weapons; for the simple folks out here, any small craft or trade I built up over the years would appear superior to them, due to their lack of formal education. Emotions, though, built up explosively within me – I didn't know if it was God or the Devil persuading me to go on a binge of deaths, of raw killings. Someone had to die for the wrongs done me, and it was time for America to feel my worst possible wrath, the full fury of a dispossessed Marine who loved to kill.

Reflecting on Big Dee, how he would say he was 'used and abused' by the Marine Corps until his knee went bad and they pushed him out of there the first moment they got the chance, I saw how his hard work was set aside just because he couldn't run three miles in a timely manner anymore. Big Dee, built like a Greek god, provoked the jealousy of older, fatter officers, who went by the guidelines and honorably discharged him. That embodied the face of America, which I'd begun to truly hate.

My brother Sal now entered my thoughts, recalling the time we hunted Boon, and Sal told me, "If we plan ahead, we can get him." This was my time, a time to plan ahead and get my enemies – the agency and America. I'd been strung out, working so hard to catch the bad guys that I didn't realize who the bad guys really were! I made myself believe that the Taliban was always evil, when in reality, they helped out a lot against the instability of the rural areas of Afghanistan. The whole country was lawless after the Russians broke things in two, while the Taliban restored some order again. I hadn't admitted it before, but they were a powerful force for *good,* not evil!

When you sit somewhere across a fence, it's easier to see the flaws on the other side. I saw how the agency and its people were corrupt, wanting only to benefit themselves for the sake of career advancement. Chuck and Rogue had only used me, making themselves to look better in the eyes of their command. I was their idiot, being too weak and brittle, living with my lowest emotions because it was my norm.

"Hey, *hey* there!" yelled one of the villagers. I brought my bike to a slow stop, as he snapped me out of my daydreams. I yearned to know what this man, now my countryman, had to say. "Are you Nasir?" he implored me.

"No, my Brother, my name is Abdul," I responded, keeping to my cover story, looking him up and down, finally beaming a broad grin at him.

Smiling back, he blurted, "I'm sorry; where are my manners? Asalam Alaikum!"

I swiftly replied, "Walaikum Salam, my Brother." We shook hands eagerly, and I asked him for his name. He said that it was Basir.

"Pleased to meet you, Basir, but I am not Nasir, I'm afraid."

Smiling again, he asked me, "How far are you taking this road?"

This told me there was no Nasir; the gentleman only wanted a ride. Asking him to hop on, I said that I'd take him anywhere his heart desired, as long as he showed me the way there. Thanking me profusely, he jumped aboard. It wasn't like in America; here, anyone would scoop up a hitchhiker for a ride. Cruising out slowly from the village, I let Basir guide me out to a bigger road, one which we could ride down much faster. He told me not to take the smaller roads, due to the IEDs in that area.

The same old formalities presented for me, such as where I was from, my tribe's name, and my family. I answered everything in its turn, staying with my cover like before, and Basir was evidently pleased. I asked him the same things out of respect, wanting to know more about who he was. Amazed that I didn't recognize him immediately, he pulled silence for a while. Finally, I leaned back, turning toward him and asking, "What do you do in Helmand Province, my Brother?"

Chuckling lightly, Basir plainly stated, "I am a District Shadow Governor."

The word 'shadow' meant only one thing: he was *Taliban*! If my life wasn't confusing enough already…what

211

was I to do about *this*? I paused briefly, saying, "Wow, that must be nice – Sir," trying to sound like I was giving him due respect. He asked what I did, so I dropped my cover story, telling him I was a Taliban warrior who came over to Helmand to fight in the Jihad.

"Really?" he chortled. "I need a couple of good men for my son's group; I've been looking for new, trained young men."

I should tell you that Basir was older than me, standing at about my height, wearing clean clothes and with the same length of beard as me; but it was laced with strands of grey hair throughout. He also had plenty of war scars, having paid his dues richly in order to become the 'owner' of a whole district. Suddenly, he asked if I had a cell phone on me. I quickly replied: "No, Sir; that is *forbidden* in my law!"

"I like you, Abdul; you seem to have gone through a lot of farming as a youth, for your stature is *very* firm," he cried out, gripping my shoulders.

Laughing in the whistling winds, I returned to my cover story: "No, Sir, I am but a simple builder." I let him know I was deeply fascinated with weapons and building infrastructures, telling him I had no formal training in IEDs but could handle weapons superbly well. Pointing, he had me veer off at the next dirt road going south, apologizing for taking up my valuable time; but I interrupted him with, "I am here for the Jihad, for all I have is God and time."

"Then today, it was your destiny to meet me," he bragged, going on about how he could see into people's hearts, souls, and minds – it was all hard for me to believe, seeing how he'd needed a simple ride to wherever he was going. However, the Taliban didn't ordinarily use their own transportation, as they could be too easily spotted. And I heavily needed this dude. I was fully there for him now, and he was gonna become my new Rogue. I would aim smartly for the top of whatever pile he lorded it over, deciphering and plotting all my new plans, what I'd do to let 'my people' give me another chance after having killed four Afghan natives cold-bloodedly for a lost cause.

Bumping into Basir created a new cause for me; it was the same as getting in good with a major Don in the Mafia, and becoming a 'made man'. I laughed inwardly, feeling like I'd picked up Al Pacino on my ride to nowhere. Basir was clearly a high-level man, not kidding me about his role in things. The route we were taking led straight into a desert path made previously by other motorbikes. We were launching deeply into foreign territory, and I was on top of my own little world. My heart didn't flutter, and my conversation with Basir was nothing but nice, well-paced, and civil.

Laughing together in tune, we bantered somewhat, with Basir mentioning some guys he had to meet soon, to give them both money and his orders. I asked if they were smugglers, and he leaned over my shoulder into the wind, looking hard and fast at the side of my extended face. "Abdul," he declared, "From now on, you're my nephew...don't let anyone tell you any different." There it was − only in Afghanistan could you create a family relationship with someone in less than ten minutes. In my 'new' country, the man you picked up on the road treated you like a king, giving you half his house and a measure of his certainty and glory too.

But Karim popped into my open mind, making me feel bad that I'd judged him as a rat bastard who only stole my stuff; the Taliban had probably caught him, letting him 'have it' somehow or other. Who knows? Anyway, Basir was probably the same type of man, who would give you everything that was his, with the exception of his wife and children. But he'd surely destroy me if I double-crossed him. I suddenly felt overwhelmingly lousy, as at that moment. I realized that I was responsible not only for the deaths of four people, but probably also another two men, maybe the two women back at Karim's compound as well. I couldn't leave it all behind me, somehow.

What did I *do* that for? Was it all for America, or for a German 'whore' and her 'pimp', whoever they really were? Regardless, it was my time now to fully make up for it, no matter what happened to me. Meanwhile, we approached a small opening in the fields, as a new district line was being crossed, a river appearing right in front of us. A bridge loomed ahead, and Basir hissed into my ear, "Make sure you don't grow nervous; this is the district which I run. The police and the Coalition Forces may ask you questions, so just remain cool, calm, and collected. Tell them you're only taking me to the medical facility for treatment."

Frowning, I replied with a firm, staunch voice, "Basir, don't worry. I got you on this, and will handle everything with ease." Slapping my shoulders as a show of confidence, he slid a wad of cash into my pants pocket, saying, "If they request a bribe, give this to them. I will take care of the funding for this ride and anything else in expenses." I was growing worried; Basir seemed pretty paranoid for a top official in the Taliban, considering his important role and rank. It's true that locally, they were considered to be an illegal group, banned by Afghanistan. But he had a kind heart as I would find, taking care of those who took care of him. He wasn't different than any older guy I'd met who just wanted to look out for the younger men.

Fitfully, we cautiously approached the district borderline, patrolled by a bunch of nasty-looking Afghan police and a group of Coalition Forces. Moving up slowly to a place where signs declared a 'Talashee Area', which meant search place, we took this as a cue to hop off the bike. A young man strutted straight up to me, looking back at his co-police partner. "These guys are suspects," he flatly stated.

His friend glared at me, saying, "Taliban, I bet." I didn't know how to take such a remark; I'd been stationed at this type of checkpoint before myself, saying the same things about strange-looking men trying to pass through. In our case, they ordered me to put my hands way up, starting to speak aggressively; I simply did as I was told and went on calmly with the procedures, being as cooperative as a razorback clam.

The men asked simple questions about where we were headed. Gazing with a worried but humble grin at Basir, I softly muttered, "My uncle here is sick, so please don't waste our time."

Sizing Basir up now, they asked, "Do you live here, Sir?"

My new friend nodded, stating, "Yes, my house is near the third village to the right." I had to smirk over this, given what the response to such a general answer would be from a cop in America. Well, they searched us and the bike carefully with a measured level of respect, ordering us to be on our way, but things were far from over. Soon after we left that control checkpoint, an American ordered us to come to an abrupt halt, a second and potentially difficult obstacle.

It was a First Lieutenant in the U.S. Army, dressed to the teeth and looking beefy, loaded down with magazine pouches and a passel of military gear. He began talking to us, going through an interpreter. This was obviously, perhaps fortunately, a random vehicle checkpoint like in the States, when they stop you to check for drinking and driving. In our case, though, it was more about getting to know the people who were passing on through. The interpreter stared at us like we were alien beings, while the Lieutenant droned on with a formal dialogue concerning security – all about how he was only there in order to help make Afghanistan a 'safer place'.

Listening avidly, I was dying to hear how his words were restated by the local national interpreter, with my usual professional curiosity. The interpreter, like most local nationals, didn't translate every single word but gave us the gist of things instead; it wasn't his fault, he simply lacked most of the needed vocabulary. This type of thing embodied what was overall wrong with the war – guys in the field or outside the wire usually got the worst linguists, even when their jobs were the hardest ones.

Sitting there straddling the bike, I thought about Basir accompanying me, and if this would slow me down some. Behind me, Basir's chest pounded, each heartbeat reverberating into my sweaty, black-streaked back. He was mortally terrified, rightfully so, as he clearly had no idea of exactly what was going on or how things were going to end up. But from prior experience, I knew the best way to finish this conversation was to listen carefully and respectfully to whatever the Lieutenant had to say, and then we probably would be allowed to continue on our journey.

Agreeing with all he spewed, I pretended to speak only a little English, making both men smile when I used the most horrible accent I could muster. Basir exclaimed in disbelief, seeing that I spoke some English; but I figured he was stuck thinking about what a valuable asset that meant I could provide for him and his men. My quick wit and way with words was certainly getting us through this sticky situation.

Ending his long speech, the Lieutenant waved us on through. Heaving a sigh of relief, Basir exclaimed into the oncoming wind, *"Wow...*that was unusual for me! I was actually *scared* for a change!"* Not sure what he might be covering up, I chuckled, telling him, "No matter what, I wasn't going to let anyone hurt you." Hesitating a moment, Basir replied, "Abdul...would you be my new bodyguard?" I responded in the affirmative as he patted me on the back, pointing his index finger down the road.

Our ride turned out to be coming to an end, as we swiftly entered a vast piece of opium farmlands. Basir told me to edge up toward the riverbed, speeding down a hidden dirt trail and bypassing another bunch of military checkpoints along the way. Pulling back onto the main road, we soon found a massive village thronging with locals; the only noticeable traffic out in these boonies was from motorcycles and pedestrians. This place seemed to belong to a really big, related tribe, with all their homes close enough together to make up such a huge, eclectic village.

As we rode by, the bike sputtering sparks in the hot winds, people greeted us with smiles and open arms, proposing to hug us if they could. Basir was a popular dude here, for sure, and this was the first time I'd seen so many folks greeting us as if we were their long-lost relatives. This village didn't look sketchy, or like something to be afraid of; I kept following Basir's directions, as he deeply impressed everyone that I was close to him and not there as any threat against them. People already regarded me like I was his bodyguard, and nobody appeared to mind my presence very much.

Getting off the bike, parking it and walking, we headed into an alleyway, coming into a compound that was literally full of Taliban guys. Anyone seated stood up as Basir walked in – immediately, they quieted down from any of their activities. I felt good; they were clearly showing me how much respect my friend warranted. I dug the whole 'bodyguard' thing, glowing with special Afghan pride! Basir had opened his heart up to me, letting me quickly become one of his most trusted men.

Glancing over the group assembled before us, one by one, Basir held their gazes for about one second before ordering them all to sit back down or return to whatever they'd been doing when we walked in. A man who appeared to be his deputy came over, greeting him with a small, formal hug, starting to brief him about the wounded personnel he'd taken out of a firefight that occurred the previous day. Basir asked where the wounded were, and his deputy stated that they were taken to the local hospital; by now they were en route to Pakistan, he said. "I'm still standing by for confirmation," he explained, turning in some mild perplexity over to me.

"Excuse my manners; Kamran, this is Abdul." The deputy was Basir's second in line of command, considered to be an executive officer. He gave me a warm welcome, loudly saying, "Abdul, let me know if you need anything. I'm here to take care of all logistical and operational tasks." I told him I really appreciated that, thanking him and shaking his hand. Then Basir turned to Kamran. "The first thing you must do is to get Abdul one of the newer AK-47s, so that he can protect me. He is my new direct bodyguard, and also my personal driver." I smiled, but my old, entrenched instincts warned me that someone else was giving me that Taliban death stare, burning my image into his wide open eyes. This other man was likely to be Basir's old direct bodyguard, a position he certainly didn't want or need to lose in the organization.

Putting his hand in a fatherly manner on my left shoulder, Basir proclaimed, "This man speaks several different tongues." Nodding his head sagely, Kamran added, "That's what you've been talking about, Sir; exactly what we've needed for some time now, a multi-linguist." Reacting to this, I realized with astonishment that the Taliban goons I'd heard from previously never talked this professionally, in such an erudite manner. I'd figured this bunch was all thugs, and we'd be speaking in gutter language or slang. But I was listening to two men in formal conversation, thinking that they sounded rather intellectual, not like killers with no motive, rhyme, or reason.

Harrumphing, Basir continued to Kamran, "Abdul speaks the language of the foreigners, while these younger idiots normally around us don't speak anything but Pushto. I'm sure he will make a fantastic asset to our organization."

Deeply impressed, Kamran responded with: "That is wonderful – maybe we can use his services for a couple of important operations ahead of us, Sir." Basir then asked him if 'that reporter' was still asking to come around. Shaking his head, Kamran stated that after yesterday's 'episode', he wanted an interview in an undisclosed location.

Gazing fondly at me, Basir asked, "Abdul, my Brother, do you think your foreign tongue is sufficient for translation purposes?" But I kept silent, calmly receiving my AK-47 from another, younger Taliban member, making like I hadn't a worry in the world. Carefully but swiftly, I ops checked my weapon, looking up to Basir with the full confidence of a former weapons specialist.

"Sir," I finally replied, "Translating to me is easier than breathing; but that is not the issue here and now." Puzzled, Basir wondered what this meant, and I was soon drawing the attention of the whole room, filled to capacity with roughly twenty-five soldiers. With a stern voice, I told Basir, "This weapon hasn't been cleaned for a very long time; as reliable as it ordinarily is, I'm sure this is exactly why you're taking so many casualties out on the fields, *Sir!"* Astonished, Kamran glanced over at Basir, thinking that perhaps I may have disrespected their field leader.

Basir only laughed aloud, screaming out, "You *see?* You *see* this *shit!* This is *exactly* what I've been *talking* about! You all have no discipline, and are *sloppy!* We are truly lucky that God has sent us such a *multi-talented warrior!* I found him for us; now all of you better get with him, to *check your weapons!* What is the purpose of going out and getting killed, when we can win the battle with better prepared guns?"

Not wanting to interrupt with any further criticism, I didn't know if these new-to-me Taliban goons were gonna be upset with me, or happy — even though my knowledge would probably help to save their lives. Once Basir was done, I asked Kamran what the whole reporter thing was about; he merely shifted his eyes at Basir, indicating something about the man they wanted to see. I didn't know what was going on, but it had something to do with peace in the area, or war negotiations in other words.

After finishing his little lecture, Basir had obviously vented enough, so the Taliban shouted as one man, "Yes, chief, *we will!"* He then told them to go make sure their weapons' stash was cleaned properly, turning to me to say, "I want you to ops check *every* weapon, giving me the names of any men who don't obey my orders." Agreeing, I watched as Basir spoke with Kamran. "Why are my boys and these newer generations not more like this young fellow of mine?" Shrugging with a kind of perplexed despair, Kamran replied, "Sir, this new youth is...totally *different* from our men."

This was nearly all the questioning they did regarding me. What boggled my mind was that I wasn't being investigated or drilled with tribal questions, not at this time anyway. Everyone just thought I was a Taliban fighter as I'd said. But I didn't know what to do when the time came around for my reading aloud the Holy Quran, while I couldn't read or write any Arabic or Pushto. This could've potentially led to some knotty problems, so I decided then and there to take charge of all the soldiers, becoming a major new leader, to see how many of them would follow me.

Starting with teaching classes on how to break down the AK-47 rifle, I learned that most of the men didn't know how to do such a simple action the right way. I had a bunch of raw recruits to teach, and so, I became a Marine Drill Instructor in the Taliban. Shortly, I told Basir that his men needed a physical fitness routine; he agreed that his boys needed to be in better shape, to move around freely in the vastly open lands. I also taught his men how to brief before they went out, making sure that their supplies were in place and intact before any and all patrols. I was teaching the Taliban my American ways, unbeknownst to them, everything that I knew about running things.

Days zipped by fast, while they fully accepted me as a new leader. I grew much closer to Basir, who showed me an awful lot about Islam. For some reason, he never questioned me about why I didn't know most things about the religion, seeing it as a way to trade our skill sets instead. He also made sure that I always had money, keeping to a line of careful respect about me when talking to me in front of his subordinates.

One night, I decided to ask him about the reporter, when we had some free time to spend together. Sighing, he declared that he was growing 'old and tired', that he'd been doing his job here for quite a long time. Pulling me aside, he explained how his whole family was killed early on in the war, through an aircraft attack. His brother had been a hardcore drug smuggler, supplying most of the province's weapons through drug money. That's what led to the death of their family – Basir ventured out one fine day, returning only to find his home a pile of concrete rubble, stinking of bodies. The one thing left was the drug money, stashed outside his house, more than enough to flee with.

But Basir said he didn't want to leave, that he'd made a promise to fight against the people who'd slaughtered his family. He didn't fully agree with his brother's dirty dealings, but saw the rest of his folks as innocent bystanders. Patting me on the shoulder in a fatherly manner, he laid his head against my neck, shedding more than a few tears that night. This and many other events were leading me to understand that these Taliban dudes, now close to me as brothers, were vastly different than the types I'd judged and seen before; those prior goons were only a handful of unimportant people.

I told Basir again that I was a local builder, that I'd learned English in Pakistan, coming back to Afghanistan to build infrastructures for Taliban sanctuaries – that being the finest way that I could help them. I'd learned about weapons, I said, because my father was part of the Mujahidin in the South part of the country, which the Russians had brutally invaded. Basir, respecting me hugely, told me I was 'one smart kid' and that I was gaining lots of heavenly credit for what I was doing. "God will see you taken care of in the Hereafter, *my Brother!"* he cried, as I turned away, embarrassed. What he didn't know was how I'd ruthlessly slain four of our Taliban kindred, and that I could just as easily be going to Islamic Hell instead.

But Basir, patting me on the back, would only happily exclaim that I had a lot of fantastic skills, telling me not to ever waste any of them. Meanwhile, I began to learn more about the journalist. He was a freelancer that traveled at his own will, and Basir had already negotiated that the Taliban wouldn't harm him, because he really sought to get our general message out. I was worried, thinking that this is exactly how a hostage situation arises; but they must've kept in contact with this journalist for some time, seeing how long it was taking to make this interview happen.

One problem Basir faced was not wanting anyone to come with him. He was planning on sending his warriors out to pick up the journalist, in a crowded area so that they would be covered by thronging people and couldn't be easily followed. This journalist had enough nerve to believe them, but I'd seen this type of thing before – the reporter was probably highly passionate about making something out of the Taliban, even if it meant the risk of his own life and limb. Journalists are definitely thrill seekers, seeing that previously most cases of hostages had consisted of reporters.

Smiling, I told Basir I would ensure that his words sounded pure as could be when I interpreted them. Of course, he had no idea that Marine Linguist had been my job for many years, but there was no reason to open up that can of worms. I'd never be able to wriggle out of it, and would have to explain everything. However, I informed him that after we pushed formal word out about his group, I was gonna get the guys together, and we could build a new ops room – to provide for a bigger, better cause in the Jihad. Basir only laughed, shouting, "One day at a time Abdul, *one day at a time!*"

The next morning, I saw Basir clutching a satellite phone in his hand as he walked up to me, saying that I needed to call the reporter and give him the instructions on what time and place we were to meet. However, I told Basir that I needed to make plans first to ensure that we didn't get caught, during the process of things. Grinning, he stated that we were going to meet this guy in a populated area near the shops in the neighboring district. Disagreeing with him, I said I had a similar plan, one containing a way to keep anyone from being able to track us down. Respecting me fervently, he readily agreed to listen to my plan, as I told him to have a seat.

My good ol' Marine ways of organization were coming to the fore. I told Basir that I would be talking quickly, and to wait for his questions until I finished. Glowing with pride as though I was his son, he waited for my brief: "We should take up to nine soldiers on the trip, breaking down two on each motorcycle and one alone. That equals five bikes and four two-man sets of people. All of them will wear black, and the call to the reporter must advise him to do exactly the same. This will bring in utter confusion, if anyone tracks where we're going from overhead.

We have to brief our guys, telling them not to take any radios, cell phones, or rifles with them. This mission can only be done with handguns, for concealment purposes. Our bikes must enter the shops area one at a time, staggering them on the way in, and then we group up and all meet with the reporter. When leaving the populated area, we must all disperse and go our separate ways, none of us taking the same route back here. Upon our arrival, everybody must stop in separate compounds that have phones set up, and the rest of us will have to meet at the compound where the reporter traveled to – this will lead to a successful pick-up, and the drop-off will go the same way, but in reverse mode."

I was making simple drawings in the dirt to illustrate my plan, and Basir's mouth had dropped open, as I could see when I brought my head back up. I asked him what he thought about things; he was amazed, struck speechless. Getting up quick, he commanded all of the boys to come to the main meeting room immediately. Then he told me to brief the plan one more time, but slowly – so that his men would completely understand it. Once in the room, he demanded their full attention to go to me, and it was riveted all the way to the end of my brief.

A man then stood up, asking for permission to speak to the chief. Thanking both Basir and me for looking out for their lives, this lower-level soldier stated that his comrades couldn't sleep last night, believing that they were going to die from the pick-up. They thought it was a surefire way to go to the Hereafter. I nodded, asking him to sit back down, and let his comrades know that I wanted to review their handguns before they headed out. The men jumped with glee to show off their new weapons training and handling, locking their chambers to the rear so that I could do an inspection and function check. After that, Basir handed me his phone, and the news reporter answered on the second ring.

"Hi, this is Kevin," said the somewhat infamous journalist. I greeted this Kevin with a news anchor style of voice, which made him swiftly ask, "Who is *this?*" I told him, "You have a meeting with us, and forthcoming are your instructions. They are to be followed to the letter." I figured he must be wondering who was speaking such professional, clear English to him, not telling him about any of our plans but just saying where he needed to be and what time he should be there. I reassured him that he'd be completely safe, but told him not to bring any electronics, and that his entire report would have to be handwritten on pad and pen. Pausing briefly, Kevin agreed, ending our conversation.

Basir and the rest of the Taliban gazed at me in amazement. Basir said, looking at me like he'd never seen me before, "Your dialect sounds just like theirs, *my Son.*" This was the first time he'd called me that, and I felt proud in a great sense; days prior, I was considered to be his little brother. Beaming broadly, I replied, "Everything is coordinated; we are now on schedule. I thank you, Sir, for your kind words, and I'm here for you and your orders." My respect for Basir couldn't be any greater.

Giving me a big bear hug, Basir and I held tightly to each other, as his long beard tickled my back. My freshly cleaned, pressed white clothes felt terrific as the entire group of nearby men closed in for a group hug ensemble. It was truly a big day for us, and I never felt more accepted during any other time in my life. This meant and fostered a unity of purpose, when that many men could openly share their respect and emotions with me for leading and helping them to perform their righteous, God-given duties. I knew I was right and sure in my ways, doing the things I was doing for them.

All thoughts of me turning traitor or doing something wrong were in the past – *forever!* I had sinned before, but now I was performing my mission in an appropriate, well-centered manner. Our goals hadn't taken place yet, and we weren't successful until later on; but I guess this group of guys had lost an awful lot of their friends, needing more of a morale booster than mere words could say. I was the one bringing their hopes in, the one to let them know that circumstances were only gonna get better. I'd become a full, privileged leader in the Taliban, and this time, I was not only moving up, but had absolutely everyone else needed on my side for now.

Chapter Sixteen
One Important Interview

My plan to pick up Kevin, the journalist, was all laid out and set, with everyone involved in the highest of spirits about this new mission. It was only left to sit down with Basir, while everyone else prepared to push out early that morning. I was ready to perform my first Holy Mission as a faithful Taliban Muslim!

Basir, meanwhile, got cleaned and preened, bathing and donning brand new white clothes for the important meeting. Combing his long, thinning salt and pepper beard, he sang to himself, some little Afghan ditty for children, I believe. He appeared much happier than usual; I was glad to see him without the long face he usually bore regarding his dead family, an insult to his pride and purpose that never went away.

Deciding I'd best clean up too, I approached a metal pipe, thrusting like a demented spear out of the ground, one with a long, metal handle for pumping clean water from deep underground. It's fascinating how things stay simple in Afghanistan, remaining at the peasant level in spite of major technological changes. Washing my dusty beard and face a few times, I tried to get a smooth, almost wet look going, although I wouldn't be very prominent in the interview, I figured. A good thing; it wasn't five minutes later in the scorching heat that my hair was bone dry. If I ever started a business out there in the boonies, it would be in the line of lotions and moisturizers! That would be a good bet, as it stayed incredibly dry throughout the day.

Thoughts of what Kevin would probably say and ask filtered slowly through my heat-baked mind, but I found that I was pretty much happy to have taken on this role. For many years, I'd been on the other side, trying to talk semi-tough to the bad guys and negotiate laws and deals with the more cooperative ones. This day would be something totally different, new, and highly unusual for me. I was used to being a translator, but saw my role in this more as a planner, with translating, taking a back seat to everything else needing to be done. But my prior experience surely would come in handy.

Basir was now praying in the outer compound, sliding his prayer beads that looked just like a rosary to me back and forth with his thumb, intoning a high-pitched sing-song chant: "In the Name of God, the All-Merciful, the Most Gracious…" Smiling, I plunked my butt down next to Basir, and he smiled right back – we liked each other an awful lot, and he definitely regarded me as his son and second-in-command.

"Son," Basir sighed, "I am so very happy to have you here with me. I truly believe it was an act of God, the bringing of our two paths together." Putting my hand in a caring manner on his devout knees, I told him that I was planning on saying something exactly like that myself to him. "Today is a big day for me, Abdul; I can finally get the story of how my family was destroyed off my chest," he sighed.

In my experience, every soldier or warrior must decompress at some point in time, and I saw that Basir had a black cloud perpetually hanging over his head. He wasn't the type to lust after killing, or even a 'bad guy' type of any kind; he merely felt obligated to avenge his dead family members, without killing any innocent people. Whenever he found village civilians charged by the Taliban with 'helping' the Afghan government, or those up on other, similar petty charges, he would only warn them to stay away from the Taliban, and just remain law-abiding citizens – such was his merciful, entirely fair outlook.

Other Taliban men I had heard of and also met would either kill such civilians, or punish them with ruthless, extreme measures. But Basir wasn't one of those horrible nut jobs, and by now, I saw that I wasn't that type, either. I was okay on whatever I was doing for him, and it brought a new light to my face every time.

"I know you're a smart young man, Abdul, so if anything ever happens to me, know this: I want you to be the one who leads our group." Although I'd been expecting something like this for quite some time, I was taken aback by his honesty. "Sir, don't speak like that! I am here for that very reason – I won't let *anything* happen to you! I am your permanent bodyguard, and would gladly *die* to save your noble life!"

At that moment, Kevin called in, saying that he was ready to enter his position; I told him that our people were entirely prepared, asking for reassurance that he'd complied with the order to wear black clothes, like our Taliban guys. He told me that he felt 'like a widower', but that he was complying with a stately black common suit. Hanging up, I briefed Basir while we waited until the motorcycles rolled in, one at a time, with everyone aboard, sporting black clothes in the hot, unforgiving weather.

We still had a little time to pass, so I went into the idea I'd previously mentioned, about the sanctuary we should eventually build. "After Kevin leaves, we will *not* really be safe anymore – compromise is too likely," I sternly admonished Basir. Shrugging, he agreed, asking how we could do what I was proposing without being caught. I told my boss that I had a great cover story – we could build a boys' school right next to our current compound. "I'm a builder, so no one will be suspicious," I said.

It amused me how delightfully Basir's eyes opened up, wide and childlike somewhat. "Abdul, you've been smart...until now." This was unexpected, and I was again taken aback. "Why?" I asked him. "How do you think that will slide over with my own boss? We are supposed to be messing up the schools, and now you're saying we should build one...have you lost your damn *mind?"* Ouch! I'd thought his initial reaction might not be a good one, but I hadn't expected outright dismissal. I replied, "Sir, wait for a sec – let me finish, and if it still sounds stupid, you can shoot me."

Laughing now, back to his usual way with me, Basir proclaimed, "My son, there is no need for shooting; but go ahead and finish with your crazy ideas." I began by explaining that if we built the school, it would be a Taliban and Holy Quran school only, not teaching any outsider, heathen, pagan, or secular subjects. "A Mullah will run things, on the subject side anyway, and we can use this as our cover. There's no way anyone will be able to hurt our people, because of the children. The kids will come to school, learning about our holy religion, mastering it as they're supposed to. It will only benefit them, and the gain for us is that no forces will find out otherwise and raid us. The room will be built and set up for school, meetings, and communications, nothing else. And only hand weapons will be allowed in; nothing like explosives or drugs."

Letting me finish, Basir tilted his head to one side, a sign that he was deeply perplexed but considering something. While he said nothing, I felt like a little kid again, waiting for an answer back from a suspicious, worried adult. "Abdul," he breathed, "I have to say, you really make me think; I have to learn how to understand the way you think of these types of ideas. How would we fund the infrastructure?"

Remembering my childhood, when my mother said I needed to pay homage, or Zakat, to my older family members, I asked Basir: "Sir, when is the last time we told the villagers of our massive, widespread village that they had to pay us our dues? When is the last time their kids had any type of formal schooling? The prosperous families here have plenty of money, Sir; let's do exactly what the other Taliban groups do, but while making sure there's something of value for both our sides. Let's make an honest, closed room for conducting our business and plans. I *know* I can make it work!"

Telling Basir that today's interview would constitute a special test, to see if my planning was really worthwhile, if we could come out of things successfully, I saw his face look thunder-struck once again. He was stuck, not able to do anything else but agree with me that the only major thing he was waiting on right now was the interview and Kevin finally showing up.

"Do you understand how long ago this meeting was supposed to happen, my Son? It has been nine full months, a pregnancy's length of time that we were arranging to meet; now it is near to happening, I don't want something to go wrong." Our timeline was drawing closer, so I asked to excuse myself and went outside to check if anything seemed out of the norm. Speedily, I passed through the village – telling some clustering local kids to join up with me. I'd bought some candy for an easy bribe, deciding that I was gonna create a packed feeding frenzy of children gathering around, to create confusion when the motorcycles came by.

Fifteen minutes later, the first set of guys roared in, going to their various portions of the compound. Everything was working perfectly, timed beautifully about eight minutes apart for each bike; the third set had Kevin perched quizzically on the back of a cycle, peering at me as though he thought this was some kind of crazy dream. Each cyclist had been given an alleyway route, ending up there with Basir in less than thirty minutes, all beaming proudly, confident enough to not hide their faces.

Disembarking his bike, Kevin walked right by me and the children, not knowing yet who I was as I played with the kids, eyeing him to see if he'd attended to my instructions. He wasn't stupid, and had done what he was told only because he really needed this story, wanting to gain the credit to advance his career. He was about to make the grade, interviewing a major Taliban leader for the first time. Kevin's main goal, like mine previously, was to make it out alive and in one piece – however, he was probably prepared to sacrifice everything he had for the sake of the story.

I followed him into the inner compound shortly, and he was already greeting everyone with an ill-pronounced "Asalam Alaikum!" He kept saying it loudly, over and over, with some of our people greeting him in return; others just gave him a hate-ridden death stare. He was an outsider, an infidel, and many of our men would rather have seen him dead than give him a disclosing interview with our beloved leader. But they were all waiting on me to come in, with the lower-level dudes forming up like tittering schoolgirls at the prom. The entire group sat down immediately, waiting to hear from Basir, the journalist, and my own linguistic capabilities.

Gazing at them with coolly professional disdain, I exclaimed in Pushto, "Ready guys? It is going to be *fun!*" This brought forth laughter, with our men seemingly giddy, grateful to have come home from a mission they'd earlier envisioned as a death trap. Kevin and Basir still stood up, as I walked over to Kevin – with his greeting me in Pushto, or maybe Pashto in his case. I answered back in Pushto, then went straight to English. Kevin, dressed fully in black, sported an awkward-looking scarf on top of his sweaty American head; he must've thought it meant something to wear it.

I told him to relax and doff his cover, as we were inside closed doors. Gazing at me in a profoundly weird way, he apparently knew that 'cover' was a term used for headgear in the military, especially in the Marines. He thanked me in English, and when he scooped off his black scarf, why, there it was – a shaved head, all the way to the temple, a 'high and tight' like the Marines used! His bangs hung out a little bit, but the razor buzz on the back of his head proclaimed him a 'Marine' all the way. Now I was *really* taken aback; I didn't know what to do, seeing that Kevin was equally intimidated, so I ordered him to sit down after I introduced Basir.

Glaring backward at my pack of assembled wolves, I asked the group, "Has he been searched thoroughly?" They answered with a rousing "Yes, *Sir!*" all at once, like my bunch of recruits from the House of Pain at Parris Island. Kevin, who must've had some Marine involvement, didn't need to speak Pushto to see who his Drill Instructor was under these circumstances. But Basir calmly segued into his greeting, while Kevin noticeably was nervous, desperate to hear everything he had to say.

Staying with my own thoughts, I gave Basir ample time to vent and speak his mind. He was normally a reasonable man, but I saw him flaring up, while Kevin just about shit himself every time if my translation wasn't as precise, accurate, and fast as he was hoping for. The journalist, however, let Basir finish, swiftly going into his prepared line of questions. They didn't pertain to anything Basir had spoken about, concerning the death of his family; I let things go for a little while, steadily growing upset that Kevin's intentions and motives were so wildly different from Basir's.

Abruptly halting the conversation, I let Basir know that the reporter was talking to him as if he was planning on publishing his story, but didn't care to hear about anything pertaining to his folks. Then, shifting my eyes back to Kevin, I said, "Listen, you hot-shot mother *piece of shit,* this man just poured his entire heart out to you, about the family members he lost – and you're asking *irrelevant questions!* If it isn't about a little *white* girl, then why should *you* give a fuck, right? Let me guess; you probably had some fucking combat camera job in the military, and now you got this."

The whole room stared on in shock as I chewed Kevin up and spit him out, with his having no idea what was happening: "You thought you'd come see some fucking Haji Taliban, and make it out alive, while you could lie about your own fucking war tales, huh, Kevin? *You know what you are?* A media whore...you only want to make a story for yourself, not the people of Afghanistan or America. I'm sure you're planning to broadcast us all as heathens and savages, *am I right?*" Glaring at me with outright hatred, Kevin suddenly calmed down. "No, Sir, I have no intention of doing such a horrible thing," he mumbled in measured, drawn-out English words.

Calming down, I realized I was trying to verbally destroy this long-awaited journalist and possibly the needed interview as well, due mostly to Kevin's popular image. His pretty-boy Marine cut and his feeble ways with our culture had coaxed me into going insane. Even Basir looked at me like I'd gotten out of hand; but he and our men trusted me so much, I could've declared: *"Hang* this idiot!" and he would've been instantly strung up ten feet. Kevin began apologizing numerous times, but I stopped him from completely embarrassing himself, telling him to proceed with his questions – prepared in advance though they were.

Tugging gently at my sleeve, Basir asked if I was okay – I told him that the journalist had said something stupid, so I had to put this infidel into his place. Basir then patted my knee, breathing softly, "Good job Abdul. He looks exactly like those guys that regularly kill us, anyway." Breathing heavily, I let them proceed with their conversation, translating everything as needed. Kevin grew obviously wary, shifting his topics back to things he hadn't prepared for in order to make me happy, apparently.

Our meeting took some time, but I remained deeply engaged, although eventually both men were only making small talk about the rugs in the room and the chai tea that we tended to drink at the compound. Standing up, I ordered our black-suited men to rise, telling them in Pushto to use the same cycles they'd come in on, taking different routes in reverse as previously instructed. I also ordered an immediate gun ops check. Kevin's heart pounded like a cheetah's after a hunting chase, as he heard my men draw their weapons, pulling the sliders to the rear to set rounds in their chambers.

Turning to Kevin, I noticed that he looked deathly pale, drenched in cold sweat, thinking this was his moment to die. I simply drew his attention over to me, telling him to say his goodbyes to Basir. "Listen, *Jar Head,"* I growled, sure that he knew what that term meant in the Marines, "Your intentions were good, but I'll tell you one thing: if you ever return here, I will personally drive a spear through your fucking head and stake it out in the village; are you picking up on what I'm laying down?" Nodding his head silently, Kevin mumbled, "Check, good to go, Sir."

"I promised to secure you back to your path, but if anything fishy occurs along the way, I've told my men to kill you on the spot," I spat at the intimidated reporter. *"No, Sir,"* he trembled. "We're good…all I needed was my story, and I've got it written down as procedural, like you asked. I have no intentions to compromise your compound or your men." Shaking Kevin's hand before he left, I whispered a few last words into his timorous ear: "We're truly a wolf pack mixed with night owls; *don't you forget that!"* Frowning humbly to himself, Kevin waltzed off with his group of our men, and they were swiftly gone.

Basir, breathing hard after having bared his soul to the journalist, came over to me, stating: "That was *intense!* What did you say to him at the very end, Abdul?" I sighed, "Sir, I only told him that if it wasn't for your merciful self, I would've had his body skinned with a rusty blade I keep out in the barn." Laughing his fool head off at this rustic statement, Basir cried out, "You were the brains of this operation, but I hardly thought you were such a cold-hearted killer, too! We must make you something bigger in the Taliban, as you pay for your time here, Abdul."

I then mentioned to him that I had a couple of Afghanis, the local currency, if he'd let me use his satellite phone to make a quick call. Guffawing loudly, Basir crowed, "I pay *all* your expenses, my Son; remember, go into that other small room, my phone hangs there in my jacket pocket." Up 'til now, no one other than Basir was allowed to enter that room, and he was giving me this new chance – I was *awed!* We were definitely growing on each other, and I had no further doubts about how my conscience was totally, fully free, unencumbered by guilt anymore.

But I had to do something: I needed to call my good ol' friend Jimmy, letting him know I was doing alright, asking him to tell Shama that she didn't have to worry about me. It was more than high time to do that. I'd written a letter to Jimmy, sending it to him as soon as I got the chance. I'd been waiting for the heat to die down from the agency, hoping I could get around them finding anything out. My life was no longer in America, and I'd give the details of my current situation to Shama later on if possible. Missing her and our son, I thought constantly about them, hoping someday to send for them to come to Afghanistan with me. Going outside, I called Jimmy from the open fields, once everyone else had left for whatever duties were on their plates.

Jimmy didn't answer at first, so I punched the numbers for Big Dee, who seemed to be still asleep or heading out to work. I waited, trying to gather my words together, and soon I got hold of Jimmy, giving him about three sentences before I hung up. Jimmy was bright enough to dig that I had something coming to him, and I knew he'd keep it to himself and not go running to the agency with it. I erased both numbers from the call logs, telling Basir that I only took a couple of minutes to call out, but that it hadn't worked and I hadn't managed to get hold of anyone.

What I did that day was to open up a new can of worms for Jimmy and Big Dee, forgetting somewhat that Chuck and Rogue were probably still breathing down their throats. Problem was, the agency never really goes away; they're on the clock when everyone else is taking a vacation. I had figured they couldn't track my calls, or find out where I was on their radar. Yet as I found out later, they responded immediately, going straight for my two friends again at their jobs.

Jimmy, meanwhile, notified Shama that I was alive by texting her. Big Dee was dragged forcibly out of his workplace; being as massive as he was, he got more than a little stressed out – the agency men calmed him down by tasering him, those *schmucks!* Jimmy played matters differently; the moment he saw guys in suits walking up, he punched one of them out cold. This was of course considered to be a federal offense, so he took off running.

Really, he had no reason to run, seeing the worst would come anyway, but the agency needed him alive for the info he possessed. He could play on his luck, somewhat, getting away for about ten minutes, dodging cars and running behind alley walls. But their alternate team lurked nearby, nabbing him as he fell down swinging.

The agency's response was to stuff my friends back into those booths again, and this time, they weren't asking their questions nicely. Jimmy had a black eye and a bloody nose before he so much as sat down, praying in Arabic − the interrogators laughed at him, yelling in demeaning, racist voices, "Aren't you supposed to be a *Chicano,* Sherlock Holmes?" Jimmy's sole response was a withering *"Fuck you, pigs!"*

"Listen, tough guy, we're not pigs; we can fuck up your whole life now, because you've been working with a terrorist," was their considerate reply. The agents then laid out pictures of me on a desk, saying that I was working with a known terrorist cell, helping to aid the killing of Afghan and American forces in Afghanistan, as a major Taliban member. Looking down all the way to the ground, Jimmy's heart sunk into his ankles as he saw the picture of my face with a long, bushy beard, and me sitting next to a skinny old Taliban dude. Kevin, unbeknownst to us, had entered our room with a spy camera located within the second button on his black dress-up shirt. Should've known, from his Marine attitude! He took plenty of pics of me during that meeting, sending them out through his chain of command.

Poor Jimmy had no idea about any of this, swearing that he at least wasn't involved. But they slapped him around, lumping up his face a good one, continuously asking him about the conversation we had between us. They didn't understand what it meant when I told Jimmy, "Ahh, you're weak these days...you need to go to the gym and work out." It was my method of using humor to mask telling him to go there for the pickup of my letter to him...that's all. But Jimmy thought that if I'd gone that far, I might actually have turned stakes on America. Being patriotic, he never had any wrong ideas himself concerning the USA; but he was often harassed by the police in our area, because he looked pretty much like a Hispanic gangster.

Considering his wife, Jimmy had to care about his daughter too, so he let the agents know what my message likely meant. In answer to his faithfulness, they kept him locked up for quite a while, until they got everything they needed. Meanwhile, Big Dee had nothing for them, but they weren't gonna let him go that easily. And Kevin, the Marine-poser journalist, had already made huge headlines en route back to the States, simply because he worked for the giant media corporations. He wasn't about to let his First Amendment rights be taken away by the agency; it remained for him to spiel out his heroic tale, letting the world 'in on' our important interview.

Poor ol' Basir wasn't even his major subject anymore. I'd been overly prominent, while blissfully unaware – word was in America that I'd become a bipolar Jeckle and Hyde counterpart. Of course, social media on the Internet lined up for any info on me, spreading it faster than a plague; the interview's best photos went viral. My pictures started hitting all the news tabloids, and Kevin grew into the most anticipated person to hit the States in years. The story of espionage and my treachery smacked into the mainstream media with full force, clogging things up for weeks.

During this entire time, I had no clues about anything, not getting any word about what my poor friends were going through. Jimmy may have chosen the path of American righteousness, but he was still a big target for being a Muslim; in today's society, it's hard to remain a true believer, as people associate it with terrorism. Other things that happen around the world, like when a woman is raped, a child is killed for no reason, or a school is mowed down by youths with automatic weapons, are considered just to be common, ordinary crimes. They bring terror to our families, but because only Christians are involved, these aren't considered to be terror-type acts. But the moment a Muslim does something stupid, it's broadcasted everywhere, with the media fueling everyone's fire, making the hatred of Islam and Muslims blossom profoundly.

Various regional cults in the States would be classified as terror cells in other parts of the world; in America, it's Muslims that get pegged instead. Big Dee was also called on by the agency, and he could've helped them more than anyone else because he comprehended the Marine mindset – but he was a Christian, so they had no reason to believe he had further info for them. Shows you how the system really works! Society in America only concentrates on one group of people; they forget about their surroundings, falling asleep to the other impending threats around them.

It's like when I heard my higher ranking enlisted service members say, "There's a scope on your rifle for a reason. But if you become dependent on it, and your other eye shuts for too long, the enemy you can see from a distance might have a friend right behind you, and you'll never see it coming." America was closing its eyes to other kinds of enemies, so I meant to make an example of how weak those people stood as a dominant nation.

I was plotting to get rapidly through potential explosion site checkpoints, as the clerks and employees slept during their shifts. Too many of them were lazy, not caring about their positions, always whining about their hours and salaries. These were the weakest links, and I reflected on how many times I'd passed through security points and important buildings in the States, without anyone questioning me. I just made like I knew where I was going, showing no fear – if you're a guy in America and carry a clipboard, people think you're important and know what you're doing. I wasn't deeply worried, but my inner dialogue and brain were speeding along at a million miles an hour, preparing to prove that my former country wasn't the place people thought it was. They could call me a traitor, but I was making my plans, and they'd soon be set in concrete. I could've saved lives and no one would particularly care, but the minute I did something wrong, I was considered to be a terrorist, put on the enemies' list for infinity. America is not a kind country; it's a nation full of malevolence, lusting to take advantage of any opportunity to see someone suffer, in full Technicolor and on YouTube.

At any rate, my greatest focus was to get my name and Taliban rank known throughout Afghanistan, and secondly, to get that ops room built in our war compound. That space was going to lead to a big, important meeting for me to present myself on the shadow side of utmost rule. I wanted my Muslim brothers to feel every ounce of my vast pride and extreme hatred, egging them on to go for the big kill. I had a plan boiling, ready to whistle and scream like a tea kettle exploding on the stove.

After the interview, Basir called out to the villagers, introducing my ideas about the boys' school, with his deputy, Kamran, and their logistics group working to win over the villagers' hearts and minds. I didn't show up in things yet, placidly biding my time as Basir came back into the main room, saying, "Abdul, your plan is working. Many villagers say they will chip in and help with the labor." Kamran, now third man down in our Taliban, gave me a loving, manly bear hug. "Brother, I hope this *works out!*" he exclaimed, not jealous in any way and a true Muslim in the best of senses.

Happy as a morning lark and excited to the point where I had to sit them both down, I told our other men to leave the room – I had to talk about important business matters with our leaders. "Brothers, I have some news, and I will need your help. I have a plan to bring the infidels to their *knees!*" Throwing me a look of concern, Basir calmly asked, "Abdul, my Son, are you going to do something out of the norm? We are not very large as a Taliban unit goes, and most of these guys want to live to see their families for the next couple of years." Chuckling, I told Basir, "I need nothing but a bigger unity of our widespread people…you must call on many others from the different provinces. Reach out to your contacts, promoting a large meeting so that we can get together for a massive attack. It will happen on American soil, and here, on Afghanistan's soil also, totally against the oncoming infidels."

Frowning, doubtful, Basir sighed: "Abdul, do you know how long it would take to get those types of guys over here? Do you *realize* what you're saying?" I saw that I must convince Basir that although the room build would take some time, I needed to get the undivided attention of the biggest, worst group leaders possible. I didn't need guys who were petty, or who couldn't conduct a real attack. I needed guys more like myself, with plenty of confirmed kills: the bloodthirsty type. That would be the only way to make things happen; colossal, horrible things in the name of terror and revenge.

"What about your *family?*" I firmly reminded Basir. "Are you not here for that main reason?" I had to jump into his head, getting him to realize that he hated the infidels every bit as much as I did. He'd lost everyone near and dear to him; I didn't want him to risk his life, letting him know that all he needed to do was to coordinate the most hideous, most murderous guys from every province, arranging for them to arrive at our compound in exactly one month. If the whole village agreed to the school, helping us build the ops room, then we were already successful and could meet any necessary timelines. Basir was hugely intrigued by my passion to lead a massive full assault, but he wanted to be briefed on the plan for it right then and there. I could only reply with, "Sir, that's something I cannot do, because it requires more thought…you know that I only brief when I've done all my homework first."

At this, he chuckled amiably, saying, "I know you well enough; just worry about the school and our new room for now. Until then, I will do whatever is on my part." Fortunately, I had deep faith in my brother Basir, feeling that he'd execute each requirement, emphasizing once more that he had to bring in only killers who would push our meeting forward. I *didn't* need a room full of pansies! Basir, acting reasonably as usual, stated that he fully understood, and not to worry; he'd do whatever he could to help me – if I was that serious, he would be just as serious too.

The only thing left was to bring in the villagers, and I let Kamran take control of this aspect of my mission. Incredibly happy that I didn't overstep his boundaries, he took his job and this opportunity with Basir as something special and important. The supplies were brought in about a week later, and Kamran ordered the villagers to pour and work on the basic foundation, while we waited for further materials to come in. Our busy little bees swung forcefully with their shovels and wheelbarrows, running back and forth, hour after hour. I kept inside most of the time, watching casually and drinking cold chai tea, while thinking about how I'd brief about the massive attack.

In the time I spent there, I'd learned about how terrorism was mainly an attempt to create massive panic and confusion. During an attack, many people run toward the attack site, trying to help the injured after an explosion or whatever else was happening. My plan, in a simple sense, would be to create a couple explosions, having them appear separately in different areas. That in itself would create the most confusion, and instill the most lingering and malicious fears. This plan had no flaws, because America was lying to itself, saying that they never forget – they really forget things very quickly. But I would ensure that my actions led solely to totally unforgettable events.

There was nothing but death and destruction on my mind, mixing and coming together with my personal thoughts of revenge. I wasn't gonna let Chuck or Rogue get away with what they'd done to me; I wasn't gonna let America take away my hard-earned blood, sweat, and tears I'd put in for them, as they spat on me, leaving me behind to rot. I would surely show everyone that if I left a legacy, it was going to mean something unforgettable, something long-lasting and permanent. If fear itself ever had a meaning, then I was going to *make sure* my name would be connected to it!

I held no remorse in my Muslim heart, desiring only to let the world know what I really was and whom I really supported. I would give America precisely what it deserved, no more and no less. It wouldn't be easy or simple, but I had to take on this new challenge. The planet would see that if it ever went against Islam or Muslims again for no good reason, it would feel our nasty bite. I dwelled on my day of being electrocuted, realizing once again that God kept a special destiny for me, and here it was. It was now or never, and I would fulfill it before it was too late.

Chuck and the agency were probably searching for me, knowing somewhat about the things I'd been doing, but who were they to judge me? I'd sunken into the belly of the beast too deeply to emerge alive and clean – my folks back home might hate me, or think that I'd given away my secrets to what they considered to be the enemy. Anyway, I needed to gather up the contacts for my plan, and Basir was taking care of that matter from our side. But mostly, I needed those major people in the bigger cities. The only thing really left for me to do was to get on some type of Internet capability, granting me access to a social site to get word out to other potential followers.

Kamran had become my 'go-to' guy, and he could score those types of things from the city nearby. So I educated him about procuring a small satellite and booster cables, enabling us to access the Internet on a reliable speed. The router box had to be encrypted, and we had to ensure that no one other than our friends and colleagues could find us or tap into our system. Kamran, praise God, knew a computer savvy Taliban agent, swearing to pay him handsomely to assist us with our holy mission. Time sped by as I got word out after a couple of weeks – while I was all over the news in America. They knew I was Taliban, and Basir wanted to speak to me about this issue.

It was possibly the worst thing that could've happened. I thought for sure now that the others would go against me, seeking my death and dismemberment. But Basir wasn't angry; he actually supported the issue, saying that I had twice the courage to come out and do these things only in order to support the Jihad. I was shocked that our people were taking the news about me so kindly, not being upset about me lying about my past as an American spy. It turned out that the Taliban embraced propaganda, loving that I had made such an effort and gone so far to support them. It was a clear sign of them winning in their eyes, and they also saw that I had a lot to offer them.

Smiling, Basir spoke about how the guys who hadn't responded initially were literally pouring in, once they knew more about me. *Tons* of more Taliban dudes craved involvement with our meeting and my overall plans! We got messages every day about people giving us praise, wanting to fund our cause. I didn't know how to take things, but Basir told me that I was a high-ranking person, and things occurred that simply sometimes when it was God's will. I couldn't sleep, dwelling on how far I'd come and how much thousands of people either loved or hated me. There was no turning back; all I had on my part was God and enough of the divine spirit to make the Taliban's interests move fully forward – now was my chance to truly *shine!*

Chapter Seventeen
The Last Explosion

I was locked into the mounting thrill of each new moment; shattering, life-altering circumstances had molded me into exactly who I was, changing me from an American spy into a Taliban warrior. This transition went smoothly, much easier than my earlier transformation into a Marine – and unlike back then, I was now the master of my own spectacular fate. I went over everything I needed to say those last few nights before the big meeting, getting about as much sleep as an expectant father. Reciting the Holy Quran, an English version kindly supplied by Basir, I turned my inner sight deeply into the fathomless depths of my embittered, transitional soul.

Flocking, colorful memories flooded in, those of the past leading to how my life was turning out to the present day. There would surely never be another story that could come anywhere close to mine; I was being slowly torn in two – my thoughts, actions, and inner dialogue flowing first in one direction, then cascading into the other. My plan for attacking America was set in stone, engraved six inches deep, and I wouldn't let the ravenous membership of the shadow provincial and district governors of the Taliban down. Why, this would be like a State of the Union address for them!

How significant, how important of a person had I become? Running through my mind was the term "In Sha Allah," meaning "With God's Will." I'd heard this term multiple times, in both the States and Afghanistan. What I was able to do came solely through the will of God, but I was predestined to win; there was no more defining moment of my life than the one I had right in front of me.

Yet somehow, Shama and Zmaray floated around as lost spooks in my mind, as I wondered what was happening in America – were they stuck, pestered repeatedly by the media and the agency? Finding out a few things through my Taliban comrades, I heard that they went on a couple of interviews, in order to let the world know that I wasn't the man the authorities claimed. I'm sure this netted my lovely wife plenty of hate mail, death threats, and other things that would drive a normal person insane. Not my Shama; she thrust her head up high, throughout outright insanity.

Wondering next about my close friends, how they were affected by my actions, again, I got some desired info through my Taliban contacts. It was all dreadful, but at least my friends were managing and in good health. On the other hand, the agency was practically keeling over dead, from how they'd messed up in the spotlight they sought so desperately to avoid, having to waste resources and money on me. Hell, I couldn't care *less* by then! None of those people would stand next to me on Judgment Day, when I went to meet my Maker. None of them would've vouched for me, or were able to help me in any way; who cared about *them?*

At the end of my frequent flights of fancy, it bounced back to how I'd started out: it was always between only God and me. My finest moment of truth would be that I lived for a righteous cause, which was either totally right or totally wrong. I truly believed in either case that God was the most merciful and the most gracious of all universal beings. At the end of the day, my wife and baby weren't going to be there with me; but I really didn't want them exposed to the violence. My friends would also be absent, but I profoundly felt the gifts that God was giving me. I remembered sitting on the floor on that construction site with my cousin Habib, going through utter shock from having been electrocuted – deciding that my life was special, different, not like anyone else's.

God had been giving me signs and signals all my life, and I didn't want to ever deny them. I'd started out with fear and ignorance leading me by the nose, coming to Afghanistan the first couple of times, not knowing what my actual mission was to become. It was during these experiences that I came to understand the 'oneness' I anticipated with God; it threw my other life messages out the window. They simply didn't matter anymore, as God's divine power makes you into a better person, one becoming direct family with the Divine, in ways that others cannot fathom. Now I was finally at peace, not searching or running around like a headless chicken, trying to comprehend what I needed to be or do in the world.

In some ways, I was returning to my older methods of diving into my inner dialogue, which told me to live as if I was already dead. I'd said this to myself many times before, but thought that it was only due to my desire to take the fear away, whenever I faced something terrifying in my life. I even sensed my father's essence as I sat outside in the compound, perched like a rooster on a tool shed's roof, thinking maybe he wanted me to do something for him; but I'd surely find out more about this in the Hereafter.

Mostly, though, I was contemplating the things I would do to make the Americans bleed for their recklessness and wrongdoings – not just those done to me, but for the sake of the whole world they'd cheated of happiness, life, and freedom. Too many people in Afghanistan and elsewhere had suffered from the activities of those in the agency and other American groups – they would *pay,* and I would see to that!

The plan was briefed over and over in my head, and I called smaller local commanders into our new, still rough ops room, to find me more contacts in the States and abroad, such as in the United Kingdom and Canada. I found some folks online who responded to me, plus orgs and sites where they held heartfelt conversations about Jihad and the menace of the infidels. I made occasional stops to check out the ongoing building of our new meeting room, surveying it randomly for any problems. But Kamran was doing an outstanding job. I asked him questions about the building parts needing to be involved in the infrastructure, because I needed the communications portion of the room to be solid, without any inherent flaws. Ever helpful, Kamran always told me he was proud of me, equally fascinated by the things he himself was accomplishing. He spoke to me with the deepest respect, like I used to see him talking with Basir.

All the people of our surrounding village and within the Taliban compound were near and dear to me, helping me with anything I asked for or needed. I was gonna show the bigger guys, the Taliban leaders en route, how to build IEDs that couldn't possibly be traced or found easily when buried. Ordering new explosive materials occurred in tandem with ordering a young teenager to gather up school supplies, as I was planning to promote the boys' school a day in advance, wanting the whole district to understand about this new enterprise, so that no one would become suspicious about strange guys suddenly entering our village. This cover was perfect, and I briefed those 'in the know' over the phone as Basir mainly watched me, overseeing things as I performed most of his tasks. I had pretty much taken over our local Taliban; it was just that simple.

Telling him the operations he normally dealt with had to be put on pause for the big event, I stated that all his men were required by me, to put the effort into the ops room and my plans. Basir was exceedingly happy – he was clearly tired, exhausted in fact, from the hard work he'd been putting in for years. He caught up on lots of sleep, and I was content that I could assist him during these times of emotional stress. It was nearly impossible to coordinate such a large event, so I brought in the local kids, telling them they each had to get a guest room ready at their parents' house. My cover story was that the incoming visitors were teachers, attending to speak at our new school. This somewhat reminded me of a seminar, how much it took to stage a realistic event and care for the many overnight guests. Word about me and my plans traveled far and wide throughout

Afghanistan, miraculously with nothing leaking out to the authorities – as I said, God was definitely on my side. All these Taliban people wanted to know who I was, but nobody had a way to properly thank me for everything that I was arranging.

One day, I found a highly motivated teenager, doing every task I ordered for him. His righteous name was Kaleel, and he freely and faithfully offered up his time to me. Hushing my voice, I told him I had a grand task for him, but that he must keep things secret, and that if he told anyone I would take his life. He agreed, showing his basic submission; so I ordered him to go buy me some nice, ruled paper and a pen from the market out in the square, and also an envelope. "It needs to look official; nothing cheap," I sternly whispered, handing Kaleel a crumpled wad of money. However, before he left, I grabbed him harshly by the throat, pulling him close. "If you make this happen, I will *make* you into something *really big!*" I breathed this into his rapt, believing face. Releasing him gently, I gave him several soft slaps on the cheek.

Kaleel was wise enough, beyond his years, to know that I was only testing his fear threshold and that I was dead serious about these matters. He was a brave little soldier, and I'd chosen him for that reason alone to fulfill my important task. Other people seemed to all know me by then; they would show no passiveness in my presence, talking about how I hated a man who showed signs of weakness or insecurity. I had turned something that wasn't their norm into one, and there was a great difference in each of their confidence levels from my ruthlessness.

The great day was fast approaching, and I'd never been more ready for something in my life than the speech I was going to give. I've always had a way with speeches, especially back in my community college course days. I dominated those classes – I loved it, as it made my blood pump and gave me an energy surge, from those crowds avidly listening to me. My speech was well planned, laid out point by point, but I needed it on paper, and that's what I sent Kaleel out the door for. I'd played it around in my head thousands of times, reflecting on everything I would have to say, as a good speaker should always do. I'd only have one chance to speak my hearts' worth. The most important thing was to stay in character, never varying from my new path as a Taliban leader and devout terrorist; I mustn't waver, I daily told myself.

Two nights before the meeting, a shitload of Taliban guys rolled into town, having been ordered to not come through the main routes, and to stagger themselves. I'd given orders to set up IEDs on all of those private routes, and no one could come through them safely except for our personnel. I had men dispersed, lining up individually on these paths, to give the big Taliban leaders safe passage – sending orders that I wasn't to be seen until the meeting, and that the villagers be set up for the Taliban guys filtering in now, hour after heated, dusty hour. Still, afraid somewhat of being seen as unimportant, I wasn't gonna actually show my face and make myself feel that way, needing more time for my own personal issues and for my speech.

I told Basir to coordinate the unrelated school opening event, leading it for the villagers and their thronging male children. Accepting the money the Taliban brought in to fund our cause, we spent some of it on supplies and other things the school needed, having clergymen and the Mullah sign agreements and schedules for the school start and end dates, etc. It was a glorious event, one which I didn't attend – not being my business, the school was primarily a cover for something far more important.

The two main structures could be seen from where I sat on the roof of that tool shed; I lazily drifted, drinking chai tea and plunging into deep thought. I observed that the two buildings appeared very similar, yet, were a lot sounder than most other such structures for miles away. I'd made sure that a high wall separated them, and that they stood a good distance apart. Well, that was it; time was up for my celebration! I was to become the dude famous for crippling America, or at least as the man who gave it one extreme series of massive headaches. It was too much to expect that my explosive actions would break or kill the country, but if I could leave some permanent damage, people would always remember my name. It was payback time, and my Taliban brothers were ready to hear their orders and execute them in a surprisingly short time span; nothing was going to be left to chance.

Meanwhile, Kaleel returned with my designated stationary supplies. I wrote down an awful lot of information, creating enough paperwork to stuff the envelope, whipping it out quickly with a lustful, light-hearted gusto. When I was done, I called Kaleel back over, sending him out once more with the envelope, ready to be mailed once it had the needed postage. I'd given him enough for that, making him swear to God that even if he died, my message would still reach its destination. I ordered him to go into the city and send it overnight, the fastest way possible. He didn't ask me once who it was for, knowing it was something important to me, and that I wasn't about to tell him anything whatsoever regarding it.

The call for prayer, frequent as ever, came once again; I cleansed myself with clean water, droning my last prayers before the meeting. Bringing Basir inside, I asked him to remain in the small side room in the other building, quite far away from the ops room, and simply wait for me to finish my speech. Sensing something odd, he was puzzled; I gave him a hard, manly bear hug, telling him he'd done enough to assist God in this world. It was time for him to rest and relax, as he was over with doing all this Taliban stuff. Protesting, Basir said he wanted to hear my speech, so I told him I was gonna brief him on everything when I finished. He settled down at my soothing words, and I knew he'd do exactly as I asked.

Then I ordered the local kids to round up their hosted Taliban dudes in the early eventide, having them come one at a time to the brand new meeting room. I was wearing beautiful, sparkling white, loosely fitting, baggy Muslim clothes, and a bright white head wrap, the color of which demonstrated my ritual purity. I combed my long, frizzy beard way out until it was silky smooth, grooming every inch of my hair and body to its utmost perfection. In one hour, I was ready – this was indeed 'it'!

My life passed by me almost drunkenly, as I recalled moments of important events happening within a short time span. Feeling like I was swimming, not walking, I made my way slowly inside, with my enraptured audience already seated and babbling amongst themselves. Gazing fondly out the windows to the right, I saw the beautiful landscape and kids playing in the distance. I'd ordered them to keep very, very far away from the new ops room, and they made a wonderful foreground for the purple mountains stretching off in the far distance, virginally untouched by our righteous doings.

As I entered the room, I said, "Assalamu Alaikum Wa Rahmatullahi Wa Barakatuh," meaning: "Peace be unto you, and so may the mercy of God and His blessings." This is the full version of the main Islamic greeting. Turning to the left, looking out those glassy windows, I viewed lengthy desert paths...a river flowed greenly with people washing up, at peace and achingly far away. Clearing my throat, suppressing a small sob, I repeated the saying one more time for those who hadn't heard me. This is how a Muslim finishes the ritual prayers. It represents the angels nestling on our shoulders, giving them a formal greeting or goodbye.

I was finally inside the massive ops room, as everyone fell instantly silent, standing up in deep respect for me. They popped out of their seats one at a time, resembling salt shakers with turbans. Many of these men were much older than me, being the ancient, established Taliban leadership, and deeply entrenched. I gave the Muslim greeting a third time, receiving the reply in a completely unified manner, somehow ending up in front of the microphone. This was in spite of the fact my head was swimming in salt water dripping from my forehead; I thought I was about to faint. As nervous as I should've been, this was beautiful, and quite natural to me. I was ready to lead the entire Taliban in my religious, Jihad-fervent devotion.

Coughing once more to clear my throat, I began my speech with rigor and passion. Most of these folks had heard about a man who came from the South of Afghanistan, spending his life growing up in America. They'd also heard about him fighting against the Afghan Taliban and the Jihad. Then this man, bent under the divine will of God, had an epiphany, touched by faith to help his true friends in arms.

"Today, my brothers, I ask you to sit down if you have not yet killed a man with your own hands. I am looking only for men who can handle the pressure of killing many others for a just cause – as in the story Muhammad told in the Quran about Allah, the All-Merciful. God or Allah reached out to suddenly kill a man, which deeply impressed Muhammad; this impresses me also. I need only those who can freely kill to commit to our glorious new cause."

A handful of men sat down, those who were younger, probably receiving their ranks via no particular rhyme or reason. I then stated that in the side room of the other building was a man named Basir, who'd guide the seated men on what needed to be done to further the Jihad, asking those younger folks to now leave the room. "You will be granted full credit and success for your honesty," I proclaimed. "This is not a way to discriminate or go against you, my brothers; it is merely a method I use to guarantee our success. I'm sure you've heard a lot about my exploits, and I want all of you to hear the latest on our Jihad plans. So please, the men who have never killed, file out of the room; however, the men who have killed ten or more times, please move directly to the front of the room. I want to set our rank structure right now, as I base it on how many souls you have purposefully sent to the Hereafter. These kills may have been done personally, or through orders you gave to subordinates; either one is just fine."

The biggest, baddest dudes in the Taliban puffed up with wayward pride, hustling forward swiftly, knowing full well that they had paid their required dues. The rest of them understood, letting those major killer gentlemen move forward. I next advised them that this was also being done to pick the most experienced for my main plot against the infidels. "They are the enemy, and they will be our targets," I said in the little Arabic that I knew, with everyone putting up their hands as if they held a holy book in them. It's what Muslims do when someone is preaching, as if they are reciting the Quran.

Glancing up at the ceiling, all I could see was light. It was time to put my biggest ever plan into operation; the worst Taliban were sitting down in front of the stage, merely a few feet away from me. The thick vest I wore under my clothes, olive-toned to match my skin color, should it be accidentally spotted, was made of cheap Pakistani wool – sturdy enough to force ammonium nitrate and ball bearings into it. This vest acted as a High Material Explosive container, once charged with a detonator. The HME is made from a fertilizer that is also used, quite practically, as an active agent to make poppy plants grow stronger and faster. My vest was evenly packed on both sides, letting it stay camouflaged. It held a single hand remote that triggered the detonator, placed amidst the highly explosive material, so easy and cheap to order.

I was lucky that Muslim clothes on men flow around their chests; it made concealment ever so much easier. And, oh yes, the walls contained multiple small packets of C4 explosives and more HME packed tightly around them. These packets were tucked in neatly by me as the structure was being built, at night, when I came in to inspect the ongoing building structure. The packets were daisy chained through a link of small fuse wire running through them all, unnoticed completely by the builders – I told them that it was part of the sound system's circular electrical wiring, telling the electricians that it was part of the building's newly designed infrastructure. The main and biggest packet was right behind me, closest to the podium during my speech. Tugging at the detonator cord, I exploded instantly, and so did the entire room; milliseconds later, my suicide bomber 'grand plan' was completed, over much faster than things had started.

* * *

Life, as I knew it, was done, and I was headed to the Hereafter. Did I die as a martyr, a suicide bomber, a hero, or a terrorist? My whole life had passed before my eyes, as I acted randomly and unknowingly in a way, like many others before me. I killed every single major element in the Taliban in that room, with the fury of one single blast. A blazing fireball torched skyward, black columns of smoke swelling out fifty feet high, as a slightly dazed Basir stumbled from the other building's side room, gape-mouthed, watching the orange flames turn into grayly fetid cloying smoke.

After that infamous day, everybody on the planet would know me for that one hard kill. The reality is, I have been fooling with you; there is no way I would *ever* have turned on my country or my beliefs! I was only the bait, bringing every single Taliban murderer into one room to perish along with me. I killed them the same way the enemy killed us, with no mercy, no better than they were. We needed to die, but I took full responsibility for sending the Taliban back to God. My heart held no mercy, for I'd become the best, most *dishonest* spy of all time!

I didn't care about anyone else, as my bloodthirst for the bad guys drove me insane…I only thought of those innocent little girls, their throats cut ear to ear, every single day of my life. My war wounds festered, far from healed; I chose my path in each likelihood because of them. I knew profoundly that I wasn't gonna make it back to my life in the States. I'd ventured into life after the hostage situation while thinking that death was absolutely right around the corner, so why not go out in style – killing the major bad guys, the worst ones that could be reached by death?

Along the road, I had to make everyone believe that I was a turncoat, a Benedict Arnold Taliban terrorist. Sorry, I needed to let everybody down to make one single, sickening, heart-rending point, as stereotypical words flared up about me on the major American news channels. My sole concern was my son and wife, what they thought of me. If they were true American patriots, which I knew Shama was, then they'd only be proud of Zmaray's' Dad. They'd both eventually see me as a man dying in combat, giving the world his ultimate sacrifice as a true Marine *should* do!

Suiciding to take every bad guy in Afghanistan along with me was the only way to show the terrorists how it felt for us – giving them a taste of their own medicine. Like a bully who one day is bullied, they'd realize it wasn't fun to be on the receiving end. They maintained the worst intentions and motives, but *I* wasn't gonna let America down, not after what my parents went through! My father did everything possible to get us to safety, and the USA showed me what *freedom* was, what it truly meant to be brave, proud, and free. I had lived in the greatest country on the face of the planet.

I could only recall my life, every soul-shaping thing that ever occurred, in that letter already en route to the President of the United States. I will never know what eventually happened to Basir, or those younger Taliban kids who walked out of the room. I will never know if the school was ever attended, if the building was rebuilt, or if the local boys and girls finally got a chance to tackle their studies in peace and freedom. I just left completely behind what I wanted to happen, leaving a hard footprint in the crumbled concrete pylons of a once beautiful new building. My judge after that was God. Whether I was right or wrong, God would decide that, and it would be up to Him where my soul would spend infinity – not the agency or America.

* * *

Looking over the lengthy message, some of which read as if immediately after the young Marine had died, the President frowned. How had that young man managed to stuff so much information into a single folded-up packet?

The journey to the Oval Office of his bulky envelope constituted an act of Divine Providence, just as the Marine had mentioned in his letter to the President...

"If this letter has reached your hands, and as God remains my eternal witness, then by now, I am much less of a threat to you and America. I want to let you know, Sir, as Commander in Chief, that you were never meant to be disrespected by me, nor did I mean to disrespect our loyal nation. I was born a second time in the House of Pain, transforming me into one of the world's elite, a U.S. Marine. I wanted to make a name for myself in this world, and I had to take measures to ensure this would happen by taking fate into my own hands.

"First, I needed to make everyone in the States and elsewhere in the world believe that I'd become a Taliban terrorist. I had to present a literal wolf in sheep's clothing, in order to best fool the enemy – I'm a firm believer that you have to crack some eggs to make an omelet, as Chairman Mao once said. If you think about the important things that I left behind to sacrifice myself for my country, then you should understand that I'm really no different from the courageous Marines who jumped on grenades to save their fellow Devil Dogs. I did what I did because there was no other way.

"Mr. President, I sincerely hope you will ensure taking care of my family, not letting them think they had any part in this. I don't want them to ever be judged, or to feel bad or guilt-ridden about what I did. This final act of mine was a true tale of what I learned in boot camp and the services, like the other members: Death before Dishonor. I had to die before I surrendered my soul to terrorism and espionage, as I could feel myself slipping in those directions, gradually over time.

"If you're in fact, reading this letter, I am dead, and so is the entire group leadership of the worst of Afghanistan's Taliban. I have crippled their forces; here is the grid location if you want to survey the area for validity:

41RQQ54323. I wrote this letter to prove to you, Mr. President, about why we Marines have this saying: Once a Marine, always a Marine. I've inherited the tradition of the finest, proudest, fewest men available who can do almost anything with the highest level of services training.

"Almost 7,000 troops, mostly Marines, died in the Battle of Iwo Jima. The Medal of Honor was awarded to more Marines there than in any other battle. The Marines knew well before they landed on that island that they were about to die, but they still went full speed ahead with it. I only took on this proud history as a Marine, bringing it to an entirely different war. Once you're transformed, the end result is that you're the type of person who can't wait to sacrifice your mind, body, and soul for God, Country, and Corps. And I've waited all my life to do something exactly like this.

"I will never regret what I have done, and I hope that a man of your vast prestige can help to clarify the reasoning and logic behind my actions. I talked to that reporter on purpose so that word would leak out about me, again, on purpose. I wanted to wake America up, because I saw how complacent our country had become. My plans were never set on our nation, to hurt or kill anyone there. My plans were to let everyone know that the world contains many bad people, and that they will go to great lengths and take huge measures to injure us. I devised my most special plan knowing that there'd be repercussions; but by now, everyone is 'on the ready' again, Mr. President!

"Everybody should be prepared in these times of great heartache and deep pain, as blood is shed repeatedly for the sake of an unfair revenge, in a war that seems, both, unstoppable and eternal. I'm happy to say that I did what I could to save more people in Afghanistan through my actions, possibly doing something to aid our troops still having a role in the war there. We are all born to die anyway, but what we do in this life makes us who we are, and shapes exactly how we will be remembered. I didn't ever want to be seen as a traitor; I earned and kept a title through my blood, sweat, and tears, and that title was U.S.

Marine. The definition of that can be felt worldwide, as we have set our boots on many seas and grounds, having fought countless wars and battles.

"We Marines earned everything we have during our time in, and later on as we get out. That's why it's called a transformation. I respect all the branches of service, giving the troops my utmost respect for their sacrifices for our proud nation...for united we stand and divided we fall. I can only say to you, Mr. President, that I was most definitively torn in two at all times, with my mind not being able to return to its normal fitness for either active duty or a normal life. I've witnessed unspeakable murders and seen far too many dead bodies, as I know many before me have. We all try hard to come back from that, but my situation was a bit different, where I soaked it in like a sponge because of how personal things got from it being a war in my native country. As an Afghan-American, the deaths of my own people hit home every day; I couldn't take it without finding a way to seek my revenge against the Taliban.

"However, every American citizen will surely feel my story hit their souls, seeing that I had no other options in this life. I was more than ready to meet my Maker, and needed to let my country know who and what I really was, opposed to who and what they thought I had become. In this world, I didn't want to leave behind a legacy that brought me shame; I wanted to leave one of pride and honor for my family, friends, and fellow service personnel. I'm terribly sorry for going against orders, or making the world think wrong of me, if only briefly, but I had to do it for the greater good.

"For as I've said before, Semper Fi, Mr. President!

* * *

That finished my letter, all about how I was torn in two. I'd hoped it would prove to the President of the United States that I wasn't the person he and everyone else thought I was, including my family and friends. Suicide is profoundly the worst sin known in the Muslim faith, featuring similarly in several other faiths I've read about. But it was a tactic used by Muslim terrorists many times before, such as on 9/11 for example. It's always considered to be a taboo thing, but I thought up to the very last day I lived that if I stayed true to my beliefs, God might go ahead and forgive my soul for it.

I had nothing but my faith at the end, and as always, I kept my feelings bottled up inside me, with my inner dialogue racing like a speeding car. I realized that it was no way for me to live – locking away my deepest and darkest secrets. It was either an ego problem, or stemmed from what the government called 'operational security'. Similar to Dan, who took his life through a pill bottle, I understood far too well what Post-Traumatic Stress Disorder actually meant. It was a mental scar, one which couldn't be healed due to the way we're forced to 'hush up' about security measures, and the harsh Marine mentality that wouldn't ever leave me also figured in.

I knew there were people and offices to help those in need, but was never the type to use them or to think that anyone would understand. I felt too embarrassed, believing that only 'pansies' needed any help like that. Regardless, I left tons of good things behind, but finishing off that many bad guys outweighed important things like my family and reputation. There was, however, no realistic way to explain why I did it; I can only plea Post-Traumatic Stress Disorder, and a deep-seated need for revenge.

Many people would say that my actions were as selfish as those of any other suicide bomber, while others might thank me for sacrificing myself to make life better for the rest of us. I have yet to really understand, here in the Hereafter, what I did…but it all came directly from my heart and gut instincts. I also believe that God was the main priority for me, helping me understand the motives of the religiously inclined bad guys and why they acted as they did. Sometimes, how they saw things was remarkably similar to my own perceptions. Although, it never made sense to me why they killed innocent people, hounding and torturing them. This was my one justification I took with me to my Maker; I would do the same, even in America, if someone went after the innocent people there. It was just who I was, how I was raised.

My time on Earth led me to believe that we will always be animals, even though the scientists say we have a bigger, more complex brain, full of much more reasoning capacities. The emotions we go through, on the other hand, make us just as savage as the rest of the animals in the wilderness. We've killed each other since our beginnings, and terrorism has been going on for the longest time…so our technology and environment around us may change, but it doesn't make us less of an animal. Our behavior and our ways will remain the same, and time will simply keep on moving forward.

Sooner or later, I will be forgotten, and someone else will make a bigger footprint in the world, regarding how he or she perceives things and how they should be. Until that happens, I can only think about what my legacy will be for my family and friends. I just hope they don't hate me, and that they speak of me in a respectful manner.

As for the President, he didn't know exactly how to take my letter. Stuffing it back into the bulging envelope, he sent it out for verification purposes, thinking the whole thing might be merely a ploy, yet another Taliban lie. So he ordered a unit over to our big village, making sure that a special forensics team tagged along. They took plenty of pictures and videos, collecting the last of the remains – my DNA was found in multiple areas of the ops room's rubble. There were leftover body parts, and they were each confirmed with the President in fairly swift order.

Our Commander in Chief soon reached Shama; she traveled to the White House with some dudes who picked her up in a Humvee. Scared as never before, she had the President respectfully showing her my letter, briefing her about the entire situation. They were holding a major press conference, and he wanted her to say a few words about me. Shama broke down, her sweet, sensitive heart pouring out its frustrations in honeyed strings; not because I died, but because I'd given my whole soul to my country, dying with respect, due diligence, and honor.

The agency having been after me, she remembered how Chuck and Rogue had threatened my life numerous times. She'd figured I was a dead man walking, secretly glad I didn't die somehow by their guns. Shama was going through total agony; but if she hadn't been a strong woman to begin with, I never would've given her a second glance, the first time I met her. Agreeing with the President, she strolled with her head held high into the press conference, to calm our nervous country down.

It was the perfect time for the President to go into something resembling my words about our complacency, how the nation was overly asleep. Taking time out from his own speech, he decided to read my entire letter, word for word, to the listening nation, giving incredible respect to my family, my friends, the world, the Marine Corps, and all our service personnel. Shama was visibly heartbroken throughout, and a lot of Americans cried along with her as her voice cracked, saying the best, truest, proudest things she could come up with about me. At times, she held Zmaray in her loving arms, hugging and kissing him as he avidly watched the funny, sad-faced people around him, peering questioningly into the cameras. What *were* all those bright lights?

Silently sobbing and praying, America heard Shama utter these words:

"Farid was bred from a self-described wolf pack mixed with night owls. A Marine in uniform is ready to die for his country at the drop of a dime, and he always reassured me of that. As a wife and a person who served our nation, I don't want anyone to judge my husband; rather, please see him as deeply, emotionally, mentally overwhelmed..." Shama trailed off as the President and the First Lady consoled her.

Finally, she simply said: "When a man is torn in two...he isn't sane to the rest of us."

CPSIA information can be obtained
at www.ICGtesting.com
Printed in the USA
LVHW020732180220
647297LV00015B/287

9 781641 826389